LIMBO LODGE

Her hands were behind her. She had kept them there, gripping the doorpost, distrusting their steadiness. The wooden jamb moved slightly as her fingers drove against it. She gave it a push sideways, her heart suddenly leaping; a section of it came away. With a swift, resolute tug she had a three-foot joist in her hands, rotten at one end. Ignoring the cloud of ant-infested dust that fell on her ankles, she held her weapon coolly, watching until the deadly skirmish on the floor came within reach; then she beat down with all her strength, striking for the snake's head . . .

Joan Aiken

Limbo Lodge

This book is in affectionate remembrance of
Jean LeRoy

*

LIMBO LODGE
A RED FOX BOOK 9780099456674

First published in Great Britain by Jonathan Cape
an imprint of Random House Childrens Publishers UK

Jonathan Cape edition published 1999
This Red Fox edition published 2004

14

Copyright © Joan Aiken Enterprises Ltd 1999

The right of Joan Aiken to be identified as the author of this work
has been asserted in accordance with the Copyright, Designs
and Patents Act 1988.

Red Fox Books are published by Random House Childrens Publishers UK,
61–63 Uxbridge Road, London W5 5SA,
a division of The Random House Group Ltd

Addresses for companies within the Random House Group Limited can be
found at: www.randomhouse.co.uk/offices.htm

THE RANDOM HOUSE GROUP Limited Reg. No. 954009
www.randomhousechildrens.co.uk

A CIP catalogue record for this book is available from the British Library.

Pen Random House is committed to a sustainable future for
our . This book is le from
Forest Stewardship Council® certified paper

Pri S.p.A.

Chapter One

THE OLD SHIP *SIWARA* SMELT STRONGLY OF dead shark, rancid oil, and rotten breadfruit. She crawled over the bright blue sea at rather less than two knots, creaking and groaning. She had after all, as Captain Sanderson told Dido Twite, already travelled about three-quarters of a million miles in her long, hard-working life, since first setting sail from the Port of London.

"I reckon it's about time she retired then," growled Dido. "Don't I wish I was back on the *Thrush.* Why are all the cockroaches jumping overboard, Cap? Not that I'm sorry to see 'em go, mind you!" The cockroaches on the ship *Siwara* were three-and-a-half to four inches long, and their preferred diet was human feet. When you went to bed at night if you did not anoint your toes and soles with dark green celandine oil, you would wake to find a few toes missing in the morning; the cockroaches would do the job faster than a monkey peels a banana. Because there were more roaches below decks than up above, Dido, Mr Multiple, and Doctor Talisman had taken to sleeping on the foredeck, despite Captain Sanderson's disapproval.

"So why *are* all the roaches jumping overboard?" Dido repeated, surveying the black procession that sped past her feet and out through the drainholes in the bulwarks. They made a soft scratching noise, like somebody secretly slipping small candies out of a paper bag.

"Why? Because we reach Aratu tomorrow."

"But why should that make the roaches jump overboard? Aratu ain't a bad island, is it? How come the roaches is so set agin it?"

"Because of the snakes. 'Aratu' means 'Island of Pearl

1

Snakes' in the Dilendi language. The pearl snakes are those little fellows, black with pearl-coloured heads, about half the length of your arm. Deadly enough. A bite from one can do for you in a brace of shakes. But their favourite food is cockroaches – you won't find many roaches in Aratu, the snakes have eaten them all. Soon as the ship docks you'll see half-a-dozen pearl-snakes come aboard like beaters. But most of the roaches won't have waited."

"I can't abide snakes," said Dido.

"Better take some kandu nuts in your pocket, then, if you go ashore. Chew one of those, it lowers the chance of dying from snakebite. But my advice would be, don't go ashore more than you can help."

"*Somebody's* gotta go ashore," Dido said crossly, "to hunt for this pesky Lord Herodsfoot we've chased after all the way from Easter Island. Is Aratu a big island, Cap Sanderson?"

"About twenty miles long, ten miles wide. The main town and port, Regina, where we are headed, is at the north tip. At the south end is a big mountain, Mount Fura, and a small fishing-harbour, Manati. In between, nothing but rainforest and spice plantations."

"What kind of spice?"

"Nutmeg, clove, white pepper, musk, aloes, dandabark, mace, vanilla, cassia-bark. And djeela-powder – very expensive. I think it should not be hard to locate Lord Herodsfoot – if he is on the island."

"Don't I jist hope he is," sighed Dido. Three months ago, Dido had been on the point of setting sail for London from the port of Tenby, in New Cumbria, on board his majesty's warship the *Thrush* when an urgent message had arrived from England, by naval pinnace, ordering Captain Hughes to make all possible speed round Cape Horn, into the Pacific Ocean, in order to pick up Lord Herodsfoot, roving ambassador to King James III of England. Lord

Herodsfoot, the message said, had been sent abroad on a mission to scour the globe for new and interesting games (or old, and possibly even more interesting games) to rouse the attention and restore the health of His Majesty King James, who lay ill and wretched in London with a mysterious malady that no doctor seemed able to identify, let alone cure.

The bulletin received at Tenby said that Lord Herodsfoot was last heard of on his way up the Pacific Ocean to Easter Island in search of a special kind of chess game which was rumoured to be found there. But when the *Thrush* arrived at that lonely and faraway spot, Captain Hughes learned to his annoyance that they had just missed the wandering nobleman by a week; he had boarded a passing schooner bound for the Loyalty Islands, in quest of a game called Friends and Strangers. And when they arrived at the Loyalty Islands they discovered that Herodsfoot had just left them, planning to sail past New Guinea and the north tip of Australia, to the Molucca Sea, on the trail of a game called Fish, Prawn, King Crab. And he was then planning to go to China, in quest of roses and greyhounds. Lord Herodsfoot, it seemed, was a great natural historian and a man of many scientific interests.

"Oh, *scrape* it," sighed Dido, when this news was broken to them. "At the rate we're going, by the time we catch up with his plaguey lordship, he'll have travelled all the way back to London. It's like a game of Grandmother's Footsteps, so it is, keeping after the feller."

There were to be plenty more annoyances and hindrances. The China Tea Wars were just now in their final and fiercest phase. A dozen Chinese warlords were battling with each other on land and by sea. The war was more complicated because the lords kept changing sides, and among this confusion it was the difficult task of King

3

James's ships to escort and protect British merchant vessels plying in and out of Chinese trading ports if the ports were being besieged or sacked by the Chinese warring armies.

The frigate *Thrush* had therefore been called to escort a group of tea and spice clippers until they were safely beyond Chinese waters, which took several more very active weeks. Then word came that Lord Herodsfoot had been seen in the Kalpurnian Sea, heading for the southernmost Kalpurnian Islands; *Thrush* had quickly changed course and gone in urgent pursuit of the footloose nobleman. At Amboina they were told that he was only a few days ahead, bound for Aratu; but here another difficulty arose. To reach Aratu, it was necessary to sail through a narrow, shallow, and winding channel, zigzagged by coral reefs; no British ship of war dare venture there.

"That's why Aratu is such a hidden, remote place," the British Resident at Amboina told Captain Hughes. "Very few foreigners ever get to it."

Captain Hughes scowled. He did not approve of islands that could not be reached by British warships.

"Who does it belong to?"

"The Angrians took it, four hundred years ago, conquered the Dilendi, who lived there, settled, and established spice plantations. But fifty years ago there was a big uprising, the Dilendi rose up and pushed the Angrians out again. Now the Dilendi have their own king. (Dilendi means Forest People, in their language.) There's a trading ship going there tomorrow, the *Siwara*; ought to be back here within the week. You could send a message on that."

"I suppose I shall have to."

In fact Captain Hughes was not sorry to be obliged to dock at Amboina for a few days, since the *Thrush* had sustained some damage during her escort duties and Captain Hughes had himself received a head wound. He

4

began to write a note addressed to Lord Herodsfoot, and then sat scratching his head with the quill pen, wondering which of his crew would make the most suitable messenger to send on the *Siwara*.

"Windwards's a capable, intelligent fellow . . . but then I want him here, to superintend the repairs. I can't spare Fossil, for the same reason; it had better be young Multiple – but is he sensible and steady enough, on his own? What a plaguey nuisance this is, to be sure!"

The choice was further complicated by the behaviour of the supercargo, Miss Dido Twite, who, when she heard that there was to be a trip to the island of Aratu on the smaller ship, the *Siwara*, begged to be allowed to go along.

"Besides, I know a friend of the old gager, Lord Herodsfoot," she pointed out. "Might be useful, that, if he's a bit toffee-nosed or awkward—"

"A friend? How can *you* know any friend of Lord Herodsfoot, child?" snapped Captain Hughes.

"It was Mr Holystone. Your last steward who – who left the ship at Tenby. He'd been at college with Lord Herodsfoot. In Spain."

"Oh. Well. Humph. I see." Captain Hughes reflected a while longer, then had Second Lieutenant Multiple summoned to his cabin.

"Mr Multiple, I have decided to send you with young Miss Twite on the *Siwara* to the island of Aratu, in hopes that you will be able to make contact with Lord Herodsfoot there, and bring him back with you in a few days."

Mr Multiple, a cheerful, fresh-faced young man, only recently promoted from the rank of midshipman, and still very conscious of his second-lieutentant's uniform, saluted and grinned shyly.

"Aye, aye, sir! Very happy to oblige." He and young Miss Twite exchanged friendly nods. "Only thing is, sir, I think I ought to mention, I ain't so handy at those confounded foreign lingoes – Portugoose and Angrianese and so on – can't make shift to get my tongue round 'em, somehow."

"Oh," said Captain Hughes, a trifle nonplussed. "I – er – I don't suppose *you* can speak those languages, Miss Twite?"

"Yes I can," she replied unexpectedly. "When I used to clean the table silver for Mr Holystone, on the passage down from Bermuda to Tenby, he used to teach me a bit of Spanish and Portugoosy. And Angrian. On account of he'd been to college in those lands. He said you never know when another language may come in handy; and the more you know, the more you can pick up."

"What about Dilendi?"

"Well, I do know jist a few sentences," Dido confessed, "jist to say 'Where is the Public Library?' and 'I wish to rent a palanquin' and 'Do you play fan-tan?' – things like that."

"Who in the *world* taught you those?"

"Mo-pu."

Mo-pu was the captain's cook, who had been taken on at Easter Island (the former cook, Mr Brandywinde, having died from drinking five gallons of neat grog in quick succession).

Captain Hughes snapped: "It is not at all proper that you, a young female passenger on this vessel, should fraternise with my cook. I do *not* approve."

Dido sighed, but kept quiet. "However," the Captain went on, "in the circumstances it has apparently had some advantages. You had best teach those phrases to Mr Multiple before you dock at the port of Regina. Thank you. You may leave the cabin now."

They did so, not daring to dig each other in the ribs with joy until they were safely on deck.

"It'll be like a holiday, Mr Mully. Shore leave!"

6

"Of course," he pointed out, "we may come across Lord Herodsfoot the very first minute we set foot on shore."

"Ay, that's so."

But after they had spent a few days on the *Siwara*, and had learned about the cockroaches and pearl-snakes and creatures called sting-monkeys, Dido and Mr Multiple grew less enthusiastic about their excursion to the island of Aratu, and began to hope that they might find Lord Herodsfoot as quickly as possible and return to the comforts of H.M.S. *Thrush*.

They did, however, make great friends with another passenger on the *Siwara* from whom they learned a great deal more about the island. Their new friend was the youthful Dr Talisman van Linde, a slight, dark young fellow who came aboard the same day they did, at Amboina. At first they had taken him for the ship's doctor, when one of the sailors, throwing breadfruit peelings overboard, got bitten by a shark, and Doctor Talisman swiftly and capably bound up the wound, dressing it first with hot tar.

But when they fell into talk they found that, like themselves, the young doctor had shipped aboard for the purpose of visiting Aratu, which he had apparently always wished to see.

"*Why*, in mussy's name?" asked Dido. "It don't seem to have much, except pearl-snakes and sting-monkeys and a pesky lot of spices."

"You see, I was born on the island," said Doctor Talisman. "I've always wanted to come back and see the place."

"Oh, well, that's different then," said Mr Multiple.

"How old was you when you left?" asked Dido.

"Five. I don't remember anything – except wonderful sweet, sweet scents everywhere."

"Different from this ship then. Your ma and pa take you away?"

"No. I fell from a cliff into the sea – but I happened to land on the deck of a passing ship." .

"Fancy! Why didn't they put you ashore at the next port?"

"Ah, well, you see," explained Dr Talisman, "there's a volcano under the sea, Mount Ximboë, about a hundred miles south of Aratu. It erupts, every couple of months, under the sea, and that sends a huge wall of water rushing north past the island. It is called the Ximboë bore."

"Croopus," said Dido, impressed. "What a lot you know, Doc Tally."

"So that any ships that get caught in the bore are mostly obliged to race past the island without stopping. And the ship I was picked up by – a Dutch trader – I fell into a pile of nets on deck, I wasn't hurt at all – there was no way of their heaving to, they got carried on a couple of hundred miles. Then a man who was a passenger on the ship, a Dutch travelling scientist, he took a fancy to me and adopted me. He thought that by that time my parents must have given me up and be sure that I was dead."

"So you never got back at all?"

"Never."

"Why?"

"Well, the man who adopted me – Count van Linde – happened to be a great believer in luck."

"Luck?"

"As well as a scientist he was a gambler. He paid for his scientific trips by his gambling wins. And on the first island where the ship put in, after picking me up, he bought a basket of oysters from a fisherman and found in one of them a black pearl as big as a cherry. It was worth a fortune and paid for the whole voyage. So the Count decided that I brought him luck. That was why he adopted me and called me Talisman."

"What does that mean?" asked Dido, who had never come across the word.

"A talisman is a thing – like a stone or charm – that you carry about to bring you good fortune or protect you from harm. It is all connected with stars and astral signs."

"Well I never! So you stayed with the Count?"

"I did, yes, till I grew up. He used to spend his winters in Europe, going to towns where there were casinos – gaming houses where they played with cards or dice – and he always won. His luck was amazing."

"So he was rich?"

"Oh, very rich. He only had to bet on a number – or a horse – and it was sure to win. Every autumn we used to go to a town in Hanover called Bad Szomberg where there were hot springs, healing waters, and a grand gaming house. In one month there he would win enough money to keep us comfortably for a year."

"Cor!"

"When he had made enough for his travels he would set off again, and then he sent me to school, and to college, and medical school, because I wanted to be a doctor. But I went on many of his trips as well."

"Where is he now?" asked Mr Multiple.

"He is dead," said the doctor sadly. "When we went to Szomberg last winter, he walked out by the waterfall late at night – there is a huge hot waterfall behind the casino – and he was found next morning, stabbed through the heart. They never found out who did it."

"So his luck ran out," said Dido thoughtfully.

"Perhaps. Or perhaps not. For the very next day I heard that the bank where he kept his winnings had crashed, and the money was gone."

"Well I'll be bothered! So what did you do then?"

"Oh, I can always earn my living as a doctor. I have finished my studies. Perhaps I will go to London later on."

"Ah, London's a fine town," agreed Dido. "Ain't it, Mr Mully? That's where I come from, and shan't I be glad to get back, jist! – So what in tarnation are you doing out here at the back of nowhere in the Kalpurnian Sea?"

Talisman said: "I thought that, before starting to work as a doctor, I'd come back to Aratu and see if I could find my real parents. There can't have been *so* many children, twenty years ago, who fell off a cliff into the sea. Aratu is quite a small island."

"That's so. We reckon to find old Lord Herodsfoot easy enough. I guess your ma and pa 'ud be main pleased to know you ain't drownded, but safe and well."

She thought of her own story – shipwrecked off a Scottish island, picked up by a Nantucket whaler, carried across half the oceans of the world without any chance to inform her family that she was still alive – how astonished they would be when she finally arrived home! But pleased? Dido shrugged and turned her attention to the doctor, who was going on:

"One reason why I was so keen to visit Aratu was that my adopted father the Count made a friend on some of our gambling visits to Bad Szomberg – a man who came from Aratu. This man used to tell me about the place, and taught me a bit of the language. His stories made me curious to come back. It's a strange place. Angrians still live in the town – the people who came from Europe so long ago. They are very stern and gloomy. Women aren't allowed in the streets of Regina – not until their hair is white. Not unless their faces are veiled or wrapped in leaves."

"Great fish! Whyever not?"

"I am not sure. There is a king – called King John."

"Did this man – your friend – what was his name?"

"Roy – Manoel Roy."

"Did he know who your parents might be?"

10

Mr Multiple put this question. He had sat silent through most of Doctor Talisman's story, watching and listening with great attention.

"No, he said he had never heard of a small child being lost in such a way. But he has been away from Aratu many times. Like my foster father, he loved to gamble. But he did not enjoy such good luck as the Count. He mostly lost." Doctor Talisman glanced along the deck and said, "Here comes Captain Sanderson. I must remind him to take his quinine."

The doctor, who had been sitting cross-legged, rose in one swift, smooth movement and strolled to meet the Captain; picking a casual, easy path among all the coils of rope and belaying-pins, canvas buckets, fishing nets, and pots of tar and other obstacles that littered the deck.

"Dido," said Mr Multiple in a low voice when the doctor was out of earshot, "did it ever strike you that there's something rum about the doc?"

"Rum?" said Dido. "Why yes. If you mean what I think—"

Her words were interrupted by a sudden yell of warning from the rigging. One of the men was aloft just above them on the yardarm trimming the sail – and at this moment he dropped something that winked in the sun as it fell, then landed with a crack exactly on the crown of Multiple's head. His skull was protected, to some extent, by his hat, but even so the blow could be clearly heard, and Multiple toppled as if he had been shot, and lay motionless on the deck.

"Murder!" exclaimed Dido. "Doc Talisman! Come quick! Mr Mully's copped a fourpenny one – he's out cold. *Quick*, come and help him!"

The doctor came running back, with Captain Sanderson close behind. The sailor who had been up above in the rigging now scrambled down, blubbering out words of apology.

11

"Misery, misery me! a hundred thousand sorrows! That such a mishap should mishappen!"

"Oh, be quiet, you silly lubberkin!" snapped Captain Sanderson. "What good does that do, yelling out woe, woe? What was that thing ye dropped on the poor lad?"

"Was my *wedhoe.*"

The sailor began searching distractedly round the deck, finally found what he was looking for and pounced on it with a cry of relief and joy. "Aha! my wedhoe!"

"What is that thing? Let's see it?" said the doctor, who had been cautiously investigating the wound on Mr Multiple's head. "Saints save us, that's heavy! What is it made of, copper?"

"How would I tell?" said the sailor, a tiny wizened man named Pepe. "It is my wedhoe. Keep me safe from harm."

"Didn't keep poor Mr Multiple safe from harm," snapped the doctor, frowning over the trickle of blood that ran from the unconscious lieutenant's injured head. "Captain Sanderson, this wound is serious. The man's skull may be cracked. His brain may be injured. He needs urgent medical attention – more than I can provide, here on this ship. Or he may very well die."

"Och, mercy on us! Ye don't say so?"

"But I do say so. There may be damage to the brain. Is there a hospital on Aratu?"

"Ay," said the Captain doubtfully. "There is one. But I wouldna be guessing that the level of medical skill is unco high in that place – 'tis only a wee island after all. Should we not put back to Amboina?"

"Five days' sailing? No, the boy could die before we got there. There may be internal bleeding also."

"Och, havers!" said the Captain disgustedly. "And he was faring up to be a right decent sensible young fellow. What in the world will I ever tell Captain Hughes when we get back to Amboina? Ye think he can be saved?"

12

"With luck."

Luck, thought Dido sadly, looking after her friend as, under Doctor Talisman's orders, two sailors carried Multiple off to his hammock. I reckon you're the best chance of that for him, Doctor Lucky Talisman.

"What time do we get to Aratu, Cap?" she asked Sanderson.

"Around dawn, Miss Twite. I have given orders to cram on all sail, as the winds are light."

Dido slept badly that night, curled up against a coil of rope on the foredeck. Her dreams were full of outsize pearl-snakes and sting-monkeys; also the same dream, over and over, of searching for her friend Mr Multiple in a house that belonged to her but had been occupied by other people, cruel people; the house was in a distant corner of some city, and the streets were dark and silent, and she had lost the front door key; and then when she did get into the house she knew that it was full of enemies, though she could not see them or hear them; she tiptoed up the narrow crooked stairs to the room where Mr Multiple might be sleeping, but he was not there, and she did not dare call his name aloud for fear the wrong people might hear and come after her . . .

From this horrible dream it was a relief to wake up, sweating and shivering, to see the sea, like a black mother-of-pearl floor ahead of the ship, a belt of luminous green light on the port horizon where the sun would presently shoot up, dark blue outlines of islands all around, and one in particular, straight ahead, shaped like the head of a thistle, solid-packed with trees. Even at this distance the sound of singing and drums could be heard. And a scent, almost solid in the air, of pepper, clove, and nutmeg came wafting on the warm wind.

"Aratu," said Dr Talisman, nodding at the silhouette.

"Aren't you excited to be going back there, Doc? Must be right spooky if you haven't been to the island since you was five years old! Will this chap you know be there, d'you reckon?"

"Manoel Roy? I suppose he might be – if he is not playing dice at some casino in Europe."

Now the island seemed to leap forward at them as the dawn wind caught the sails and the sun came dazzling out of the ocean's eastern rim. White wedges of sea broke snarling against two black claws of promontory on either side of the ship, slashing waves rolled out of the dark to cream up against slate-coloured rocks. A lighthouse slipped past them. The sound of drums grew louder and louder.

"It looks like kind of an unchancy place," Dido said, shivering. "Where's the town?"

"Straight ahead – at the far end of the harbour. There are no beaches. The island is all rock, rising straight out of the water."

What had been a pale speck at the waterline now resolved itself into houses like tiny white dice climbing above each other up a steep hill with some feathery vegetation among them; as the *Siwara* drew closer little black figures could be seen, darting to and fro on the dockside.

"The houses ain't really white, though, they're *blue*," said Dido, puzzled, as the ship slid near and nearer to the quay. "Blue and shiny. How's that, Doc?"

"Oh, now I remember. I remember so well! That was because of the Angrian settlers who came and lived on the island for several hundred years. They like their houses covered with blue-and-white tiles."

"Why?"

"Because they look handsome, I suppose. And tiles keep out the rain."

"The town ain't very big, is it? Lucky there's a hospital. Did your friend Manoel tell you about that?"

14

"Yes, he did, when he heard that I was training to be a doctor. He tried to persuade me to come back to Aratu and be a doctor there, because most of the medicine is done by witches called kanikke. The Dilendi women are witches, and the men are guides, he said."

"Guides?"

"Halmahi people. They sing the history of the island every day. And look after the sacred stones. There was a drunken old Angrian doctor called O Medico, Manoel said, but he wasn't much use."

"What a lot you know about the place," said Dido, impressed. "What about those witches, though?"

"Old shawl ladies. They have a lot of power. They make the rules. I expect the hospital is run by old shawl ladies."

"Blimey," said Dido, "I jist hope they take good care of Mr Mully. I wouldn't fancy being looked after by a pack of witches. I can see why your pal thought it would be a good thing for the island if you came back and set up as a doctor here. So the witches wouldn't be able to boss everybody."

"I suppose that might have been his plan," said Doctor Talisman thoughtfully. "I hadn't thought of that."

"And what was the thing that the sailor Pepe dropped on poor Mully's head?"

"His wedhoe. It's a luck charm. All the Angrian men on the island have them."

"Why, do they need luck more than women do?"

"Oh, the women have their own luck charms, but they wear them round their necks on a grass string."

"Like yours, on your silver chain?"

"Oh, no, mine is quite different." The doctor stroked a fine medallion, like a fivepenny piece, on a thin chain. "It has my family name on it, so – if my parents are still alive – it should be possible to find them."

"What is the name?"

"Kirlingshaw."

"Why," said Dido, astonished, "I had an Aunt Tinty Kirlingshaw. Tough old gal she was. Came from the Fen country."

"Hi, hi, ho!" shouted a sailor in the bow, and sent a coil of rope whistling across the narrowing gap of water on to the dock, where a man was waiting to receive it.

They had reached Regina, the port of Aratu.

Chapter Two

THE THROB OF DRUMS, WHICH HAD GROWN louder and louder as the *Siwara* edged her way up the long, narrow harbour, ceased abruptly the moment the first hawser was thrown ashore and made fast. Dido leaned over the rail and watched as small dark men in black cotton trousers darted about, attaching more cables to bollards on the quay, and hanging thick rope fenders between the ship and the dock wall. A taller man, white-haired and wearing elegant black silk clothes, stood with his hands in his pockets, apparently overseeing the operation.

"Why, there he is! My friend – my father's friend!" said Doctor Talisman, leaning eagerly over the rail. And, catching a pause between the shouts of the dock-workers, the doctor called out: "Manoel, Manoel! Ohé, Manoel!"

Looking up at the ship and her passengers, the white-haired man made a formal bow, and raised his hand in a ceremonial gesture of recognition and greeting.

"He doesn't seem *at all* surprised to see me," Doctor Talisman said, sounding a little quenched.

Indeed the man on the dock looked quizzical, as if his opponent in a game had made a move that amused him.

"Maybe he got a message on another ship from Amboina, and knew you was coming," Dido suggested. "How long was you there?"

"About ten days. I took passage on the first ship that sailed this way."

Now a companion-ladder was lowered, and the white-haired man came briskly up it and saluted the doctor with another low bow.

"My dear Doctor Talisman! (I assume that you *are* now a doctor?) Welcome back to your birthplace!"

"Manoel! Let me make you known to Captain Sanderson – Senhor Manoel Roy."

"The brave Captain Sanderson of the good ship *Siwara*, I know already." Another bow.

"And here is Dido Twite, who has come to Aratu looking for Lord Herodsfoot." Senhor Manoel Roy seemed a little astonished at this news. He took careful stock of Dido, who, as usual, wore long, wide trousers of dark blue duffel, a close-fitting pea-jacket with brass buttons, and a white shirt with a sailor collar. She was tanned as brown as a kipper, and her hair, much the same colour, had been cut close round her head by one of the sailors, for coolness and comfort.

Manoel asked: "May I inquire why you seek his lordship, my young sir?"

"It ain't me that wants him, mister, it's King Jamie, back in London town; and a tarnal long time we've been arter his lordship; all the way from Easter Island," Dido explained. "Is he here? On Aratu?"

"I have not met him myself, but I understand that, yes, he is – you will be happy to hear! Somewhere out in the forest, in the middle of the island. We shall have him sought for you directly."

"Thanks, mister!"

Captain Sanderson said, "We have another wee bit problem for ye, sir: a laddie, a naval officer, Miss Twite's companion, suffered a sore dunt on the heid yesterday, and now lies stupefied; and young Doctor Talisman here is of the opeenion that he is done for, unless the medical folks in your hospital here on Aratu can mend the wound in his skull. Can ye be of asseestance to us in this matter?"

"Oh, my dear sir! What an unfortunate misfortune! For the most grievous part of it is that our beloved and revered island doctor, affectionately known by all the citizens of Regina, died himself, only last week, of snakebite, and as of now we have no replacement for him!"

"Hech, noo, that *is* serious! What'll we do? The puir laddie is in a mortal bad way – isn't that so, Doctor?"

The Doctor agreed emphatically. "Yes, indeed it is. I just checked his pulse and breathing. Both are falling steadily and are now very low. I fear he will not live more than another five or six hours."

"Oh, *poor* Mr Multiple," Dido said sadly. "Can't *you* do something for him, Doc Talisman?"

Manoel Roy said: "I myself was about to suggest that very thing. Here in the town of Regina we can offer a fine hospital, and a group of nurses who know their business to a nicety, are skilled in the arts and duties of healing. All we lack is a surgeon. If you, Doctor Talisman, were prepared to undertake the task—?"

Doctor Talisman turned pale, swallowed, and said, "Well – if that is the poor boy's only hope – I suppose I can hardly refuse. I can only offer to try and do my best – I did study brain surgery in Vienna for six months – I have a basic knowledge – but will the people in the hospital allow a total stranger to come in and do this?"

"If I introduce you, yes, I am sure of it," Manoel said confidently. "I hold the position of Mayor and Harbourmaster and head of the Civil Guard in Regina town. Furthermore I am the Sovereign's brother. It is true that he – but never mind that. And – dear Doctor Talisman – you are not a complete stranger to us, after all. You were born in this land. When they hear your history, I am certain they will be glad to welcome you."

Doctor Talisman seemed doubtful still, but said, "Well, there is really no time to be lost, if we are to try and save him. May we have some men to carry him to the hospital?"

"I will arrange for that at once." Manoel retreated down

19

the ladder, and Captain Sanderson hurried away down the deck, looking harassed, muttering something about stores and cargo. Doctor Talisman turned to Dido and said: "Dido Twite: since it does not sound as if your Lord Herodsfoot will be found within the next few hours, if he is away in the forest – will you be so kind as to come with me to the hospital and assist me there – should that prove needful?"

"You mean," said Dido gulping, "with poor Mr Mully's operation?"

"Yes. That is what I mean. For all we know, the staff in the hospital may be old witches, with their heads wrapped in cobwebs and tools made out of sharks' teeth or bamboo splinters. Luckily I have my own surgical implements with me, so that is no problem."

Dido said: "Yus, of course, Doc, I'll help you, if that's what you want. Though I don't know a blame thing about doctoring; but I'll be glad to do anything I can for poor Mr Mully. He's been right kind to me. That looks like the fellows coming now with a push-cart; you better fetch up your cutting-tackle, Doc."

Studying them as they approached, Dido thought gloomily that the group of men on the quayside with the stretcher looked like mourners prematurely celebrating Mr Multiple's funeral. They moved and spoke to each other soberly; they were black-haired, brown-skinned, like the dock-workers, but much taller, and with sharply chiselled features. They looked as if they had been carved out of wood. Dido guessed that they were Angrians, whereas the dock-workers, much more cheerful and lively, were Dilendi or Forest People.

The stretcher had two wheels, like a rickshaw; two of the men pushed it, two pulled. Mr Multiple, still deeply unconscious, was lowered over the ship's side in a sling, and carefully positioned on a mattress stuffed with leaves, that rustled under him. He was motionless and hardly seemed to breathe.

Doctor Talisman, carrying a bag of equipment, slipped quickly down the ladder, closely followed by Dido, and they followed the stretcher across the wide stone quay. It was all inlaid, Dido noticed, with small oblongs of marble about the size of dominoes. They were either black or white, and were formed into patterns, squares, circles, and geometrical designs. Some of these looked like chess – or chequer-boards; others seemed to be designed for games that Dido did not know. It's no wonder Lord Herodsfoot wanted to come to this island, she thought; it all seems to be set up for games. Indeed she saw two men playing a dice-game on one of the patterned squares.

Shiny-fronted houses, blue-and-white tiled, lined the rear of the quay and rose, one above the other, up the steep hill behind. Some of the tiles formed pictures, women spinning, men fishing, or digging; others were merely flowers or stars. Dido followed the doctor up a narrow, steep, black-and-white paved street. The town seemed almost unnaturally clean, bare, and silent. The hush was eerie after the mutter of drums as the ship made her landfall. But of course it was early still. However, Dido noticed that they were watched, as they walked, through tiny grilled windows and iron-barred gateways, by silent, black-hooded figures.

This is a right spooky place, Dido thought.

Suddenly a small group a few yards distant down a side-alley parted, and a black-clad figure darted towards the stretcher with arms outflung.

"*My son! My son!*"

The voice had in it a mixture of rapture and appeal.

"Croopus! Now what?" muttered Dido.

Two more women now left the group and ran after the first. Dido supposed they were women, for they had black skirts down to the ground; but their faces were invisible, wrapped in black, with only slits for the eyes. Their voices were low, urgent, and concerned.

"No, no, Modreda! That sick man is not your son. Your son is far from here. Go back now. Go back to your home. You should not be on the street."

The woman sobbed and protested – but humbly, in a murmur, as if she did not expect to have any attention paid to her.

The man, Manoel, who had followed the stretcher from the quayside, now intervened. He spoke a few quick, harsh words in an undertone, marshalling the group of black-clad figures away down the alley from which they had come.

The men with the stretcher had gone steadily on, as if this was no concern of theirs.

But Doctor Talisman had paused, and while there was still a bit of distance between them and Manoel and the men in front, Dido said softly: "Doc Talisman! There's a thing I better say now while no one else is near by. Listen – you're really a *gal*, ain't you? Like me? Rigged out as a feller? No business of mine why you do it, but Mr Mully and me, we both of us twigged your act – at least I'm pretty sure he did – and, and I jaloused as how I'd better let you know. You got your own best reasons for doing so, I reckon. None o' *my* affair. I'm on your side, whatever it is – buckle and thong! Jist figured I oughta tell you."

Doctor Talisman's level stride paused, hesitated for a moment, then resumed its smooth swing. After a moment the doctor said, "Thank you, Dido. I appreciate your telling me. You are quite right, of course."

Manoel caught up with them again and told them, "The hospital is just at the top of the hill here, on the right."

What they had seen of the town so far was all dry, clean narrow alleys and white-washed walls, often as high as the

22

houses themselves. Many of the houses were tucked away behind walls, gates, and courtyards. All the house-fronts that could be seen were faced with glistening blue-and-white tiles. Some of these had recurring patterns like wall-paper, others were large pictures, battle-scenes, or ships, or mermaids, or monsters.

The hospital, when they reached it, was similarly set back. It lay behind heavy wrought-iron gates, a wide paved courtyard, and a colonnade of arches. Palm and locust trees made the courtyard shady. Outside the gates a black-clad group of people had gathered; they seemed to have learned, by some bush-telegraph, of the event that was about to happen; all their eyes were fixed on Doctor Talisman. They were all men, and looked unfriendly. Dido heard murmured words, curses perhaps? – as they passed in. Manoel acknowledged a few bows by an inclination of his head.

Inside, the hospital was impressively white, silent, and clean, with arched stone passages and paved cloisters, like a monastery. Perhaps it had once been one?

A group of women met them at the end of a cloister. Women? Dido supposed they were women. They had green robes down to their feet and immense square green head-dresses made of leaves – huge leaves, bigger than rhubarb or hemlock, giant leaves tacked together with threads of fibre.

Manoel addressed them in what Dido guessed to be the Dilendi language, using many gestures. Here and there she recognised a word or two.

"Now I must leave you," Manoel said to the doctor. "And so must the stretcher-men. Only medical staff are allowed in beyond. The nurses will not take off their headdresses while we are present."

Does Manoel know that Doc Talisman is a girl? Dido wondered. And that I'm one? After all, Manoel and the doc met before, in Bad Thingummy. Or are doctors allowed in here even if they are men? Maybe they don't have any women doctors?

Manoel and the stretcher-bearers left. Mr Multiple was wheeled away by the nurses, Dido and the doctor were led into a little clean, cell-like room where they were provided with large earthenware basins of hot water, smelling strongly of sage or ginger, to wash their hands, and offered clean towels and white smocks. Then they were escorted farther on into a large vaulted room where Mr Multiple already lay on a stone block in the middle of the floor. A frame, draped with more of the huge leaves, covered him, all but his head.

Dido began to feel slightly sick.

The hooded helpers now took off their leaf headdresses and robes, revealing themselves as small, thin, dark smiling women in white tunics and trousers.

One of them, with lively pictorial gestures that included putting the palms of her hands over her eyes, offered Doctor Talisman a twig, first nibbling on a similar twig herself. Talisman tested the twig with her tongue, bit off a shred of bark, then spat into a clay dish that the girl held out. She shook her head, smiling.

"What is that?" asked Dido.

"Narcotic. A very powerful one. My tongue went numb! It's to put the patient to sleep. But not needed now. He sleeps already."

A cane table on wheels was now rolled forward, with various implements on it. But Doctor Talisman, with a polite gesture of thanks, declined them and spread out her own tools, which were made of steel and glittered dimly in such light as there was, which, coming through tiny windows, was not very bright.

Doctor Talisman turned to the assistants.

"Luz?" she inquired. "O sol? Tem lume?"

24

"Nusa?" suggested Dido, remembering the Dilendi word for light.

One of the girls pulled a cord, which drew back a blind above, revealing a window in the vaulted ceiling. A ray of sunlight stabbed directly down on to the block where the patient lay.

"Ah, very good, just right—" Doctor Talisman turned to lay out her tools, but one of the girls touched her arm, to indicate that they had more facilities to offer. These were curved metal mirrors, shaped like shallow bowls, which caught the sunlight from above and focused it in beams thin and fine as needles.

"They can cut and cauterize besides giving light – how extremely clever."

Talisman tested the strength of one of the rays on her finger, then burned a thread of cotton from a bandage. "Excellent! Bueno! Now: let me see . . . Dido, please pass me those tools in order as I have laid them out. And, when I ask, be ready to pin back a flap of skin with one of these. Like that . . . Now this hair must be shaved off – thank you—"

Having stripped the bandages from Mr Multiple's head, the doctor indicated the short dark hair which had to be removed, and a girl skilfully shaved a patch of scalp with a slender white blade which seemed to be made from a seashell.

"Good. Are you ready, Dido?"

Dido nodded, gulping, and moved to where she could assist without getting in the doctor's way.

The ray of sunshine piercing through the roof-light had moved slowly across from one side of the space to the other before the doctor had finished her delicate, intricate task. At one point she said, "Ah, look. There is a spot of blood on the surface of the brain. Tweezers, please, Dido—"

25

And when she had lifted the tiny dark particle from where it swam, Mr Multiple suddenly stirred under the linen bands that held him and exclaimed: "Curse it, Windward, one of those be-damned mosquitoes just bit my noddle—"

"Hush, sir!" the doctor admonished him mildly. "You will be very well presently. Go back to sleep now! – You may let go of the flap, Dido."

She stitched up the wound in Mr Multiple's skull with a thread of grass, using a curved needle like that of a shoemaker. Then a pad of what looked like cobweb was laid over the scar.

"Put him to bed now, he will sleep for hours," Talisman told the nurses.

The patient was carefully shifted to a trolley and wheeled away.

A male voice was heard outside in the cloister and the women quickly resumed their green-leaf hoods.

"D'you think he'll get better now, Doc?" Dido asked.

The doctor was rinsing her hands in the ante-room. This time the hot water was scented with rosemary and lavender.

"Yes; I believe that his head will mend now. There may be a blank in his memory. But I do not think he will die."

"That's just prime, Doc. You are a one-er, and no mistake! If it weren't for you, poor Mr Mully'd be sharks' dinner by now."

"But I am worried that there may be trouble with the authorities over my doing this," said Doctor Talisman, pulling off the white smock and putting on her jacket again.

Now that Dido knew for certain that the doctor was female, the very possibility of her being a man faded into the realms of *im*possibility – all her movements, her neatness, her thinness, the cock of her elegant dark head, the

angle of her neck and jaw, seemed to proclaim her as
undoubtedly of the female sex.

Dido would have liked to ask the reason for this disguise.
Maybe it was just for convenience? – after all, Dido herself,
in her midshipman's rig, was often taken for a boy – and
there were plenty of occasions when this came in very
handy. There were places where girls were not welcome,
specially on a ship. And – on this island – it seemed as if
females were not welcome *anywhere*. Except with their
heads wrapped up in leaves.

"How long—" she began. She was going to have said,
"How long have you been going around in this turn-out?"
but as one of the nurse-girls returned to the room at this
moment, she changed her question to, "How long will Mr
Mully have to stay in the sick-bay now, d'you reckon, Doc?"

"At least a week, I'd guess, depending on how fast he
mends. Such an injury to the head inflicts a strong shock
on the whole system."

Dido frowned, pondering.

"Hmn. That may be a mite okkard. I'm supposed to get
back to Amboina with Lord Herodsfoot the quickest way I
can (supposing I can *find* the guy). As well as that, I reckon
Cap Sanderson won't want to dangle here with the *Siwara*
all that time – he'll want to drop his cargo and finish his
trip. And Cap Hughes on the *Thrush* will wonder what the
plague has happened to us."

She folded up her white smock and handed it, with
a nod, to the green-hooded nurse-girl, who was making
beckoning gestures.

"I think we are wanted outside," said Doctor Talisman,
and followed the girl.

In the cloister, Manoel waited for them.

"How did it go, Doctor?" he inquired civilly.

"Well enough – I think – I hope." Doctor Talisman's
tone was one of calm caution. "We shall know better after

27

he has slept and woken again. I shall go back and look at him this evening."

"Good." Manoel's tone suggested that his mind was on other matters. "I think it would be best if we now quickly left the hospital."

"Certainly. And I think we should inform Captain Sanderson that so far all is well—"

"I will send a boy with a message. Sanderson is busy taking on stores. In the meantime, pray come to my house, which is close by, and have some breakfast—"

Dido wondered if she was included in this invitation, and, if so, whether she wanted to accept. She was not sure that she liked Manoel Roy. He was too smooth, too bland, his tone never seemed to go with his words. His clothes were too neat, his hair was too white. His eyes were too blue. He's like a dummy, Dido thought, a big handsome doll made jist like a man, so everything works as it should, but – but—

"*Take care!*"

Dido was aware of something wildly jerking at her feet, a hand that grabbed her arm and spun her aside. Startled to death, she looked down.

Doctor Talisman, right beside her, was breathing fast but not at all discomposed; from her hand dangled a black-and-white snake. She had snatched it off the ground and cracked it like a whip. It was dead.

"Even here in the town you must always watch where you tread," she said quietly. "Captain Sanderson was most urgent in his warning – and he was right, is it not so, Manoel? The snakes here are a constant peril."

"Good sakes!" said Dido. "Thanks, Doc! I reckon I didn't figure to tread on one right here in the hospital. But, my certie! How quick you were, Doc! I owe ye for that – I'd a bin a goner."

28

"No need for thanks," said the doctor. "A medical training speeds up one's reactions."

Manoel, who had not commented on the incident, led them out into the street. Dido saw that the group of people waiting outside the gate had all left.

"Down the hill now," said Manoel. "This way, if you please."

He don't like me one bit, Dido thought. *He* wouldn't have cried millstones if that snake had done me in. Why? What bee's he got in his bonnet? He'll bear watching, will Mister Manoel Roy.

And Dido quickly changed her mind about returning to the ship, and decided to accept Manoel's invitation, whether it had been intended for her or not. But the way Doc caught that snake – that was really something! How could she have been so quick? I'd have said she was ten paces behind me—

The narrow cobbled roadway forked here; as they were about to go down the left turning they saw Captain Sanderson coming up the right one, accompanied by a sailor who carried Mr Multiple's duffel bag.

"The job's all done!" called Dido. "Doc here done a prime bit of work, and he thinks Mr Mully may come to and be as right as a trivet."

Dido had nearly said *she* thinks; I better watch my tongue, she scolded herself. It had become so natural to think of Doctor Talisman as a woman; she now felt as if she had done so all along.

"Aweel, aweel, I'm rejoiced to hear that," grunted Captain Sanderson. "Now we must conseeder what's best to be done."

"Come and have breakfast at my house while you talk it over," invited Manoel.

Sanderson accepted, and the sailor was sent on to the hospital with Mr Multiple's gear while the others turned down the steep hill. Over the high white walls tropical greenery could be seen – a feathering of palm fronds against a gable, rich-leaved spiny branches behind iron gates, blue-flowered creeper dangling over roofs and chimneys. And huge red or white flowers the shape of thistles but the size of chimney-pots. The air was spicy with a dozen tickling scents, blown on the warm breeze. The distant drumming had started up again, Dido noticed.

"Windy up here, ain't it," she said.

"Wind always blows on Aratu," Manoel said. "Which means the climate is never intolerably hot. But the wind makes people irritable. Here we are."

They walked through one of the wrought-iron gates – which was locked, Dido noticed, Manoel had to unlock it with a key – into a pebbled courtyard where water from a spout trickled into a large stone basin among pots of glossy-leaved shrubs with purple-and-white flowers. In a pillared arcade at the far end of the court stood a cane table and chairs. A fragrance of coffee drifted through an open door.

"Ech, now, that looks comfortable," said Captain Sanderson, and made for one of the chairs. Dido, two paces behind him, heard a dry rustle in the shadows of the pot-plants and, turning, was just in time to notice another of the small pearl snakes slither purposefully towards the Captain's foot. She glanced round rather wildly, saw a riding-crop on the table, snatched it, and gave the snake a whack, severing the pearly head from the black body.

"Neatly done. You learn fast," said a cool voice behind her and Manoel, taking the riding-crop from her, used it to flick the body of the snake into the flower-pot. "Tonto!" he called. "Bring coffee!" and a boy appeared from indoors with a tray of coffee and rolls. Manoel jerked his head towards the snake in the pot, and the boy removed it.

"Excellent coffee, sir," said the Captain, not a bit discomposed by the incident. "Now: what's tae be done about this

30

puir laddie in the infirmary? I canna stop for him here past my usual embarkation day for I've commissions on other islands, ye ken; I must be on my way. Can the lad be taken back on board – cared for on the ship?"

Doctor Talisman looked doubtful. "I'd not advise that; not for a few days – in case he took a turn for the worse. Best he remain here for a week at least. When will another ship call in here?"

"There's the *Wamena* – in three weeks' time—"

"But what about Lord Herodsfoot – and the games?" said Dido.

"Games?" Manoel's stare at her was half puzzled, half scornful.

"Have ye not met Lord Herodsfoot?" Sanderson asked him.

"No. I was at the southern end of the island when he arrived. I heard some crazy tale, from my house-boys, of a strange Englishman who cares for nothing but roses, insects, and chess. And dice."

"Dice!" said Doctor Talisman with a sudden grin. "That takes me back to Bad Szomberg – does it not you, Senhor Manoel?"

Manoel frowned, as if he did not care for such memories.

"Do folk gamble much on Aratu?" asked Dido, thinking of the checkerboards laid out in the cobbles of the quay. And there were similar ones here, in Manoel's black-and-white pebbled yard, she had noticed.

"Havers, yes!" Sanderson said. "The isle's known to traders as Dice and Spice Island."

Manoel frowned again. "It is true, the Angrian townspeople indulge in dice games. And the Forest People have their own diversions – the Hyena game is one—"

"How do they play that?" asked Dido.

"With throwing sticks – tabas – and a spiral board, mostly drawn on the ground, in the earth. The game is to 'send

31

your mother to the well' and get her back again. You throw the tabas and add up the value of your throw, and move your piece (mostly a nut or a cowrie-shell). At the well she must wash the clothes – taking so many throws – and then return to the village. There are many dangers. If she does return, the mother becomes a hyena."

"Does she, indeed?" said Doctor Talisman, much interested.

But Captain Sanderson, anxious to have his problem solved as soon as possible, said: "Dido, it fair fashes me to ask it, but I'd be greatly obliged if ye would go off into the forest at once and find Lord Herodsfoot and bring him back so that we can sort this matter as fast as possible. I'm afeered we'll have to leave poor Mr Multiple behind, but I ken weel we'd leave him in good hands with Doctor Talisman here. I've little seerious alarm on his account now – that's if we get a good report on him this forenoon – so will ye set off directly after Herodsfoot?"

"O' course I will, Cap – so long as there's no objections," said Dido, giving a swift glance at Manoel; somehow she felt he might well raise objections to anybody else's plans. But he said nothing, he seemed wrapped in deep thought.

"Reckon I'll need a guide – someone to take me to where the old gager's got to," Dido went on.

"That can be arranged," Manoel said slowly. He called the boy Tonto and gave him instructions. Tonto nodded and ran off.

"I suppose Dido will be safe enough on this errand? How do matters stand in the island now?" Sanderson asked Manoel: "I've not put in here for six months." Suddenly he looked a little doubtful as to the wisdom of sending Dido off into the jungle.

"Just now," Manoel said, seeming to choose his words with care, "just now things are quiet. Luckily. But the people feel the need of a leader."

"I thought you said, Cap, that there was a king on this island?"

Manoel looked affronted. "There is," he said coldly. "Our Sovereign. John King."

"Where does *he* hang out?"

"He has his royal residence at the southern end of Aratu – on Mount Fura. In Limbo Lodge. But he is a sick man. He is little seen by the populace."

"The populace of this island," Doctor Talisman explained to Dido, "consists of the rather sparse remnants of the Angrians, who came and annexed Aratu four hundred years ago. Most of them left fifty years ago, when the island became independent, and returned to Angria. The rest live in this town. The Forest People call them Los Outros. The Dilendi people live in the forest, which is their natural home (when it has not been cut down and turned into spice plantations)."

"You are well informed about the island," Manoel said stiffly to the doctor.

"Of course! I know all that I have been able to find out! Haven't I been reading books about Aratu, any that I could find, since I took a fancy to come back here?"

Dido was interested. "And do the folk get on well together – the Dilendi and the Angrians?"

"Eh, well, there will be a bit of a skirmish from time to time," said the Captain. "Is't not so, Senhor Manoel?"

Manoel made an affirmative grunt. It seemed to Dido that he was not all pleased to have island matters discussed. Then she suddenly remembered something. When Doctor Talisman had asked if the hospital people would allow her to operate on Mr Multiple, Manoel had said, "I am the Mayor and Harbourmaster and Leader of the Civil Guard, *and* the Sovereign's brother." Something of that kind. Had he not?

That's a bit rum, Dido thought. If he's the *brother* of this

Mister John King, who rules the whole shebang, you'd think he'd have a fancier job than Harbourmaster. You'd think he'd be Prime Minister or summat like that.

Maybe the brothers don't get on with each other?

Dido poked about in her memory, trying to recall something else that Captain Sanderson had told her about John King. He was an Englishman – that was it – who had been thrown out of England, more than forty years ago, for revolutionary activities. He had been involved in the nefarious Pimlico Plot, an attempt to blow up King Charles the Fourth, and had been deported – that's right, he had been deported along with his younger brother. But they had escaped from the ship that was transporting them to the convict settlement of New Cornwall and had made their way to Aratu. Had started spice plantations and had done very well there, grown rich. And, of course, had never gone back to England, where they would be thrown into jail. But – wait a minute, Dido thought – that don't jell. Or not quite. Because this feller, this Manoel – he used to meet Doc Talisman and her Dutch adopted father in Europe, at all those gambling places. Not in England, though. Bad Whatsitsname, in Hanover. And it's true he didn't seem at all keen on being reminded about those times. Maybe his big brother don't care for him gambling. Maybe Manoel's one of those crazy gamblers that can't stop.

Dido knew all about those. Her own father, once he heard the rattle of the dice, was lost to the world, so long as he had a sixpence on him. And even when the sixpence was done he had been known to gamble away his wig, his shoes, his cravat – everything but his precious flute. Talisman had said – Dido remembered – that Manoel was not such a lucky gambler as her adopted father. Maybe he had to give up going to Europe to play games of chance; maybe the dibs ran out, Dido thought. Maybe that's why he don't like talking about games. Maybe he had a grudge against Talisman and her lucky pa?

Talisman, unaware, apparently, of these undercurrents, had gone back to the subject of games. "Do you remember, Manoel, how we used to play cottabos in Naples?"

"Cottabos? What's that?" asked Dido.

"Oh, it is an ancient Roman game – or perhaps Greek, I am not sure which. Very ancient, at all events. It is a game of skill, not chance. We could play it now—"

To Dido's astonishment, Talisman jumped up and walked to the other end of the courtyard, whistling, as a boy might, an odd little three-note melody with a lilting refrain. She's real happy to be back here, Dido thought. It's as if it just hit her. But don't she *know* how much she's annoying Manoel?

The doctor stooped and picked up, as easily as if it had been a plate of fruit, the heavy marble basin into which the fountain played. It was at least a yard across, and thick in proportion, and full of water, but she carried it across the courtyard without the least appearance of strain, then sank to her heels and set it on the floor by the table without spilling a drop.

"There!" she said. "Now, Manoel, we need some sea shells."

Captain Sanderson had been gaping at the doctor, open-mouthed, in silence, but Manoel, with a scowl, walked into the house and returned in a moment carrying a basket of shells, pearl, pink, and slate-colour. He stared at Talisman, frowning, as if revising his thoughts about her.

"My word, Doctor-lad," said Captain Sanderson, "I'm thinking ye must have muscles on ye like ships' hawsers! I couldna lift that basin – even *without* the water that's in it."

"Oh, it is just a knack," said Talisman lightly. "There is nothing to it, once you know how. Thank you, Manoel, those shells are just what we need."

35

She set the shells afloat on the surface of the water.

"Properly, of course, we should use wine, but it is a little early in the day for that! Coffee will do instead."

With a lightning-quick turn of the wrist she flipped a spoonful from her coffee-cup into one of the floating shells. The brown liquid seemed to pour across in a clear, spiralling curve, a continuation of her arm and wrist, sinking the shell neatly to the bottom of the basin.

"Mighty neat, young fellow!" said Sanderson. "Ye'll no find me such a hand at the sport."

Instead of arching clearly down, the coffee jerked out of his cup like a blurred hieroglyphic, but enough of it reached its target to tip and drown another of the pink shells.

"Now you," Talisman said to Dido.

Ever since helping with Mr Multiple's operation, Dido had felt that the bond of friendship between her and the doctor had warmed and strengthened; and the encouraging look she now received from Talisman gave her confidence; hardly troubling to take aim she tossed the contents of her cup so smoothly that the shell into which it fell bobbed gently on the water but remained afloat.

"What does that score?" she asked.

"It's an omen," said Doctor Talisman gaily. "An omen that you will live to play another day. Now you, Manoel."

Scowling, Manoel, in his turn, flipped some of the contents of his cup. But he did so unskilfully, and the liquid, instead of flying neatly to its target, seemed to hover in mid air and splashed across the basin, sprinkling all the shells but sinking none of them.

He flushed a deep angry red, but Doctor Talisman (perhaps to distract attention from his failure?) cried out: "Oh, dear heavens! I have just remembered that I left my notebook in the theatre-room at the hospital. I must go back and get it directly."

36

Dido said: "Don't you stir, Doc; I reckon you need a lazy, after that long job you did on Mr Mully. I'll go for your notebook – you take it easy – I'll be back in a brace of shakes."

"The guide will be here in a moment to take you to Lord Herodsfoot," Manoel reminded Dido coldly.

"I'll be back by then – it's nobbut a step to the hospital."

Dido darted out of the courtyard and ran back up the hill. At the hospital she had to knock for admission, but the green-hooded portress evidently recognised her, unlocked the gate, and let her in.

"O livro?" said Dido hopefully, and made a shape with her hands, demonstrating its smallness.

The portress nodded and, gesturing for Dido to wait in the courtyard, went away into the interior of the hospital. Waiting, Dido heard the patter of footsteps behind her, and whirled round, not wishing to be taken by surprise, remembering there were sting-monkeys as well as snakes – she had not seen one of those yet. But in the road outside the gateway was a black-haired girl of about her own age and height, who gasped something and made a beseeching gesture – "*Let me in!* For mercy's sake, let me in!"

Her desperate need was obvious and, without waiting for permission, Dido twitched the gate open again. The girl slipped silently past Dido, shutting the gate behind her, then vanished through one of the many dark doorways leading away from the cloister.

One of the nurses? Dido wondered. But she looked young for that. In bad trouble, anyway.

Next moment the reason for her terrified speed became plain. A group of men in black uniforms and silver badges, armed with clubs and long curved knives, strode up the hill, looking this way and that, plainly in quest of some quarry. As they reached the hospital gate, the portress returned with Doctor Talisman's little notebook. The leader of the group of Civil Guard (for such Dido guessed them to be) rapped on the gate and put some question to the portress. She shook her green-wrapped head decisively and – after some searching looks at Dido – the party of men went on up the hill.

Now I'm in a fix, thought Dido. Should I tell the portress about that gal who bolted in here? But the gal seemed scared to her marrow, poor devil. And I didn't care for the looks of those fellows. But will it mean trouble for the portress?

She took another survey of the hospital. It seemed a huge old place. Most of it don't look as if it's used at all. I reckon there's a plenty places where that gal can hide herself till the trouble's over.

I'll not tell on her, Dido decided.

She made thanking gestures to the portress, left the cloister, and heard the gate clang to behind her, then walked rather slowly and thoughtfully up the hill, giving the guards plenty of time to get ahead of her.

But when she reached Manoel's house it was plain to her immediately that something had gone badly amiss. The gate stood open – whereas she had heard Manoel lock it behind her when she left for the hospital – and the court-yard was empty. It had a bereaved, untidy look, as if something unexpected and nasty had recently taken place there.

"Hilloo?" called Dido. "Doc Tally – Cap'n Sanderson – anybody about?"

She walked to the table and chairs, which were all askew. A cup had fallen into the stone water-basin.

"Where's all the folk?" Dido called again.

Captain Sanderson emerged from the house. He looked pale, shocked, and angry.

"The Civil Guard came," he said. "They arrested Doctor

38

Talisman for illegally performing an operation in the hospital without proper accreditation."

"Blimey! Couldn't Manoel *stop* them? I thought he was the boss of the Guard?"

"There seemed to be some misunderstanding. It's a good thing you weren't there or they would probably have pulled you in too for helping the doctor. Manoel has gone off to find a lawyer to help Doctor Talisman – he was very angry, but he said things would sort themselves out. He said you had better go off to the forest with Tylo here, and the trouble will probably have died down by the time you come back."

"But poor Doctor Tally!" Dido was horrified. "Just after she – he – had done that long hard job too—"

"The doctor did not seem too concerned at being arrested," Sanderson remarked. "He said a night in jail was no great matter."

"Where is the jail?"

"Up at the top of the town. Another disused convent, I fancy. You will pass by it on your way to Sorgu. Tylo here is a forest boy; he will take you there. You had better leave at once, in case they come back. I must go down to the ship and carry on with unloading."

"Who'll go to see how Mr Mully is getting on?"

"I will try to do that later," said Captain Sanderson, looking harassed. "Or you can, if you get back in good time with Lord Herodsfoot."

"Come quick now, Shaki-miss," said Tylo, the boy who during this talk had been standing quietly, staring down at the stone bowl of water. "Is need to start walk our journey from town. Horses meet us."

"Chop-chop, I'm a-coming! What does Shaki mean?" Dido asked the Captain.

"I think it simply means Foreign Person. I just hope that you find Lord Herodsfoot without too much difficulty," said Captain Sanderson, sounding worried to death. "Manoel ordered horses to meet you at the edge of town."

"Going in style, eh? So long, Cap; keep your mains'l trimmed," said Dido, and followed Tylo from the yard.

She still carried Talisman's notebook.

Chapter Three

"TYLO," SAID DIDO, "WHY DOES EVERYBODY in this town wear black?"

Tylo smiled, with a flash of large white teeth. He was a golden-brown boy, short, about Dido's height, with short curly black hair. A Forest Person. His costume, like that of the small men on the dock, was close-fitting knee-length black cotton trousers and nothing else.

"Why? Because, treetime back, old Sovran King John he lose he wifie, Erato. Much-loved wifie. So, says he, *all* now grieve till I say quit grieving."

"And he hasn't said that yet?"

Tylo sighed and spread out his hands. "Old Sovran King John very very sad sick man."

"How long is treetime?"

"Till djeela tree grow fullsize."

Since Dido had not the least idea how long a djeela-tree took to grow, this did not help.

"What is a djeela-tree? Are there any round here?"

Tylo shook his head. "Not in town. In plantation – djeela-trees much costly. Nobody allowed to grow them, only old Sovran King John."

"Yus," said Dido. "Now I remember Captain Sanderson talking about djeela spice. It costs twenty guineas for a thimbleful. No other islands have the trees, only Aratu . . . And John King brought the seeds from no one knows where. Is that right?"

"Right as rainbow!" Tylo grinned again. "Only us have djeela, and only Sovran John grow djeela-tree. Anybody else plant djeela-tree in backyard, he quicktime thrown off Cliff of Death."

41

"Croopus," said Dido. "What's the Cliff of Death?"

"On Fura Mountain. Nineteen hours' walk from Regina town."

"This town where we are now?"

"Yes, Shaki-miss. Sovran King John live on Fura Mountain. In Limbo Lodge."

"I guess you know the whole island very well?"

"Like palm of my foot!" he said cheerfully. "Tylo, everybody say, optimus guide! Zehr gut, molto bene, oh la la, bueno bueno, speak all language much perfect!"

"And you know where Lord Herodsfoot is just now?"

"Mylord Oklosh?" For some reason, Tylo burst out laughing at the very thought of Lord Herodsfoot, then covered his mouth with his hand, slipping his eyes away politely, and added, "Easy go there for me, Shaki-miss, go to Sorgu dream-easy. Lord Oklosh now sitting outside the house of my father's Sisingana. He Halmahi."

"Sisingana?"

He thought, and explained. "Father's father's father."

"Your great-great-grandpa?"

"Golly-likely."

Dido found that when Tylo was not certain of an answer, this was the phrase he used. It seemed a handy one to her. When she asked how long it would take to reach the Sisingana's house, Tylo said, "Four hour, golly-likely. Forest very thick, there-a-ways. If rain come, thicker. Take longer. Through night, maybe."

"Does much rain fall here?"

"Now-and-now. Then-and-then."

This talk had brought them to the top of the hill, where the houses of Regina town stopped, and a dirt track ran on across a hillside mostly covered with low-growing shrubs. Looking back, Dido saw how the town fell away steeply behind them, white-roofed houses set snugly like ivory dice among green plumy trees, and the harbour at the bottom like a blue keyhole, with the *Siwara*, a toy ship, tethered against the dock. There seemed to be a tremendous amount of activity on the dockside; hundreds of tiny black figures the size of ants rushed back and forth.

"How hard they are working down there," Dido said, and Tylo, frowning, made no reply for a minute, then said, "Maybe storm come. We best get on our way. Here bring-come horses."

The horses, led up another track by a wizened old man, were small, sturdy animals with shaggy coats; Dido had never ridden on a horse in her life and hoped the beasts had calm dispositions. Hers, luckily, appeared to have a placid nature, to know its business, and be willing to follow Tylo's mount.

They were equipped with saddle-bags which Dido hoped had food in them; she had eaten rather a scanty breakfast in Manoel's house, where she did not feel welcome, and the prospect of a four-hour (or longer) ride to their desti-nation and then the same ride back to Regina town sounded like a long day's excursion. Specially if they were obliged to stop overnight.

Also in the saddle-bags were gauze mosquito-nets. "You want, for forest," Tylo said, showing Dido how to wrap it round her. "Many-many bugs, very bitey."

"What about the sting-monkeys?"

He laughed. "Follycub? You no hurt follycub, he no hurt you. Scared of shadow – always frightened. There, now – see?"

They were passing a large gnarled, grey-leaved tree, standing solitary at the side of the track. Among its branches Dido could see a lot of energetic carryings-on as they approached, small creatures about the size of rabbits leaping from bough to bough and chattering shrilly.

"Watch-see-now," said Tylo. He dismounted, holding his reins, found a fist-sized stone, and hurled it into the tree.

43

Instantly, with wild shrieks and shrill yammerings, the whole population of the tree leapt out of the branches and fled away in terror over the scrubby ground. They were, Dido saw, small whitish-grey monkeys with long feathery fur and active plumy tails. Their faces, black-ringed, were triangular, and their large eyes pale blue.

"He sting you only by bad chance," Tylo explained, remounting. "And just as well, by golly, for if he sting, you die."

"Golly-likely?"

"No. You just die. You got kandu nuts?" Tylo asked, evidently reminded by this of the other peril they were liable to encounter.

"Kandu nuts? Oh, *scrape* it," Dido said, remembering that Captain Sanderson had advised always carrying some as a precaution against snakebite. "When I left the ship I didn't expect to go gallivanting straight away into the back o' beyond."

"No matter. I got, in saddle-bag." Tylo looked ahead along the track, frowned, and said, "Here-now we got ride quick. You golly-likely ride quick, Shaki-miss? Like this?"

He kicked his pony into a fast canter, and Dido's followed. In fact she found this easier than trotting, which was very bumpy. She stuck on grimly.

"Yes, all rug!" she called. "But what's up, Tylo?"

He made no answer, but kicked his pony on even faster. They galloped at full tilt past a group of people under a tree. Dido was so occupied with sticking on to her mount that she did not see what was happening, but heard a lot of shouting and then one thin, piteous wail, quickly cut short. Next minute they had passed some craggy rocks and were out of sight round a bend in the track. The road began to slope downhill into a valley full of trees; Tylo slowed to a trot, then to a walk.

"What was *happening* back there, Tylo?" Dido demanded.

"Bad business, Shaki-miss. Not our do. Only best ride past, ride away quick."

Dido thought, with deep worry, which for the past hour she had been trying to push to the bottom of her mind, of Doctor Talisman, hauled off to jail by that tough-looking party of Civil Guards. What was happening to *her*?

"Where is the jail, Tylo?" she asked. "My friend is there."

"Soon we come."

The road ran down into a dale where trees grew close together, planted in orderly rows. Some were tall, green, and feathery; others were thickly covered with dark-red flowers. The sweet scent that came from them was so powerful that, although Dido enjoyed it at first, after a while she found it almost too much, too painful; breathing became hard work.

"Jail," said Tylo, nodding towards a large building in the middle of the grove. "Not name Jail though. We call, House of Correction."

The House of Correction (a title which Dido thought even nastier than jail) was long and white, with narrow barred windows and a wall round it. A few Civil Guards lounged about the entrance. Others could be seen near wooden huts scattered among the trees.

Dido thought about Doctor Talisman. Was she in that building? What was happening to her? Would there be a trial? A judge?

"Now you listen me, Shaki-miss," said Tylo, when they had ridden on towards the end of the valley, were still among the planted trees but not in sight of the House of Correction. "You want leave word for your friend? She soon be free again, Shaki-Manoel he soon fix, you say you know that?" Evidently Tylo was not fooled by Talisman's disguise.

"So Cap Sanderson said . . . but *can* you leave a message there, Tylo?"

He grinned cheerfully. "Everbody know no-harm Tylo. One guard my father's sister's son. Not much Forest Person there, but some. You wait here, Shaki-miss, I leave talk-message. You got word-paper-speak?"

"No. I've no paper on me. – Wait, though – yes, I have."

In her pocket she had Talisman's little notebook. She pulled it out and leafed through it to see if there were any blank pages. At the front, in neat elegant script, was the name Jane Talisman Kirlingshaw. Then followed beautifully drawn little diagrams and numbered instructions. Then what looked like patterns embellished with little figures, some human, some animal. Then lists of herbs and medicines. At the end were a few empty pages. Dido tore one out and wrote (luckily she had a pencil stub), "Yore book is safe. Hop you are all rug. Hop to see you soon. Dido."

"There." She gave it to Tylo, then, for safety, tucked away the notebook inside her waistband.

"Now, Shaki-miss, you stay here. Just here. Soon back."

Tylo turned his pony and, following the track along which they had come, was soon out of sight.

Dido dismounted, threw her pony's reins over a branch so that he could graze and sat under one of the red-flowering trees (Tylo had told her they were clove trees) keeping a vigilant lookout for pearl-snakes and sting-monkeys. She could hear some monkeys in the branches overhead, jabbering at each other, but she did not interfere with them, nor they with her.

After twenty minutes or so she began to feel desperately thirsty, and looked in the pony's saddle-bag to see if it contained water. There were bread-rolls and squashy dried figs and a water-bottle, but it was empty. Nothing to drink. Not far away, though, Dido thought she could hear water running. Maybe there's a brook, she thought. I won't go far . . .

Through the trees she could see that the side of the

valley rose in a steep rocky wall. That was where the sound of water came from. Walking in that direction, Dido saw a little waterfall, spouting down between rocks into a pool below. The very sight of the white spray made her throat feel even dryer.

She hurried on, then came to a startled stop, when what she had taken for a rock at the side of the pool moved and lifted its head, and she realised that it was a man sitting on the ground, wrapped in some kind of brown, muffling garment. Now Dido could see two gaunt bare feet like those of a scarecrow extending stiffly from the draperies. He flung back a fold of cloth from his face, and extended a flat wooden bowl, crying out in rusty Angrian: "Alms, Senhores! Alms, for the love of heaven!"

Dido saw with dismay that he was blind. Jist the same, she thought, this is a mighty queer place for a beggar to choose as his begging-patch – ain't it? He can't expect many customers to pass by here? Still, best give the poor cove a couple of pennies . . .

She fumbled in her pocket, where she had a few tiny coins. She was about to drop them into the begging-bowl when the beggar grabbed her by the arm and jerked her off her feet. She yelled, and knocked the man's hands away from her throat. They rolled together on the ground. Dido had managed to twitch herself away, when the man pulled a long, glittering knife out of his draperies.

Don't I jist wish Tylo was here, Dido thought, pulling away to avoid the long eager blade which was wriggling its way towards her throat; why the plague did I ever leave the track? With a quick wriggle and twist she flung herself sideways out of the blind man's grip and kicked the knife from his hand; it whirled away and fell into the pool.

The blind man made no attempt to go after it; he raised his voice in a high cracked yell that set the monkeys in the trees to screeching and gabbling.

"Ohé! Ohé!" As if in instant answer to his call, two Civil Guards came strolling out of the grove. They carried pistols and wore an irritated air, as if they objected to being disturbed. They looked disapprovingly at Dido. One was fat, one thin. They were Angrians, tall and flat-faced.

"Hola," the fat one said, "what goes on here?" And at once the blind man broke into a torrent of explanation in the Dilendi language.

"Hey," said Dido. "What's he telling you? I was putting money into his bowl when he went for me with a knife—"

"You, girl, you come with us; come to our hut, wait for Capitan," said the thin guard. "We see no knife."

"Wait for Capitan hear what you say. Yes, you come now," said the fat guard.

They marched Dido through the trees, prodding her with their pistols. The blind man, meanwhile, melted away into the shadows of the grove. Dido cursed herself in several different ways; *why* had she not followed Tylo's instructions? Supposing the guards took her back to the town and found out that she was the girl who had helped Talisman with the operation? Then a whole lot of time would be wasted . . .

"Where are you taking me?" she said slowly and carefully.

"We put you in the hut, Shaki-girl; till our relief come and tell Capitan."

The hut, when they reached it, was small and wooden; outside it, two stools and a bench with a jug and cups on it suggested that the guards had been enjoying a morning snack of palm wine. Dido wondered if they had a regular arrangement with the blind cut-throat who passed on to them any promising prey. He, Dido thought, was not Angrian, but not a Forest Person either; a mix, perhaps.

"I have no money," she said loudly.

"We see. That we see."

They turned out her pockets and appropriated the few

48

coins they found. Dido was thankful that she had stuffed Talisman's notebook inside her shirt.

"What's this? What's this, Shaki-girl?"

This was a folded velvet cloth, embroidered over with lines, and decorated with beads and sequins. It had been bequeathed to Dido by Mr Brandywinde, the drunken steward of H.M.S. *Thrush,* who had died of too much grog earlier in the voyage.

"That? It's a game – you can use it for chess or fighting Serpents—"

"No, no," they contradicted. "The game you play on it is Senat. *We* know. You have game pieces, you got?"

"No, I don't. You can use black and white stones."

"We know. We know that."

One of the guards fetched a handful of white pebbles. The other opened the hut door.

"You stop in there, Shaki-girl, till Capitan come." Then he looked over Dido's shoulder into the hut and giggled. Both men were more than a bit drunk, Dido reckoned. "Oho – we have a friend in here, Andu," he hiccupped. "The Shaki-lady has a furry friend to keep her company."

"So?" The other guard came and looked through the door.

"Ah, so. A friend, a furry friend."

Dido did not care for the sound of this.

"Our furry friend will not trouble you if you stay quiet. Keep still, and he will not trouble you."

"*She,* idiot! It is a female. We will give her a drink. Females like to drink!"

"Ah, they do! Indeed, indeed they do!"

Hiccupping with laughter, the two men sloppily filled a bowl with palm wine and set it on the hut floor.

"Now: just keep still, Shaki-miss, and no harm will come to you."

"Remember poor Tonio?" the fat guard said in a thoughtful tone.

"Yes, the poor lad, and how he turned blue?"

"He swelled up and turned blue; he took a week screaming and dying."

"How he did scream."

"May he rest in peace," both men said. "Into the hut, Shaki-girl; watch out for the furry friend."

The door slammed behind Dido. Outside it she could hear one of the guards saying, "Now: you can be black and I shall be white."

"*No*, caramba! We shall shake the dice for it." They began to quarrel.

Dido stood quite still, looking hard about her. She let her eyes grow accustomed to the dusk inside the hut.

It was tiny, and completely bare: dirt floor, wooden walls, two slit windows, high up, which let in a red light filtered through the clove blossoms. The floor and the corners were in shadow. As Dido stood quietly, leaning against the door, she thought she heard a shuffling, scraping sound in one corner. Looking attentively in that direction, moving her eyes only, she began to interpret the huddled shadow, and saw a frill of white fur, a darker triangle of face, two pale eyes. It was a sting-monkey, flattening itself into the angle of the walls. It was terrified.

It's as scared of me as I am of it, thought Dido. Jist so long as it don't panic . . .

She stood as still as a post, trying to send mental messages to the creature. I'm harmless, I'm friendly. I won't hurt you if you don't hurt me.

It's their tails, she remembered Captain Sanderson telling her. Docked of its tail, a sting-monkey would be as harmless as a kitten. But they are nervous. They flick the tail over their shoulder, like a scorpion – that's why they

50

are sometimes called scorpion monkeys – and, if the sting touches you, you're done for. Dead as mutton.

Dido swallowed. She was still just as thirsty as she had been before. Thirstier.

So – it seemed – was the monkey. She could see its whiskers tremble, as it smelt the liquor in the bowl. By infinitesimal, creeping stages, it began to inch its way forwards towards the drink it craved.

What's that liquor going to do to the beast? Dido wondered. A cold trickle of sweat began to creep down between her shoulder blades.

The monkey suddenly jumped forward, put its face down to the bowl, and began to drink in audible, splashing swallows.

If only I had something to bash it with, thought Dido. But there was nothing in the hut, nothing at all.

Outside, the voices of the two guards grew louder and louder, as they argued about the game.

The monkey had finished every drop in the bowl. It picked up the bowl in its two slender little black hands, tilting to pour out the last trickle. Then it dropped the bowl, which broke. Then it began to bounce up and down on all four feet.

As if it were dancing, Dido thought. Croopus! The beast's as drunk as a fiddler.

The monkey began to whirl round and round. Its tail flew out like the sail of a windmill. Dido flattened herself against the wall.

The men outside could evidently hear something of the monkey's actions. One of them called: "Are you well, Shaki-miss? Why don't you lie down and go to sleep? *Hic*! Capitan won't come along for some while yet—"

Dido had no wish at all to go to sleep. But perhaps the monkey will dance itself into a stupor, she thought.

Outside, the voices grew higher.

"Ah pig! That was the last of the wine you swallowed!"

Dido heard the thud of a blow, yells, and the crash of breaking pottery.

Now, inside the hut, another small noise was making itself audible – the very faintest dragging, as of a finger being stroked on polished wood. At first it was hard to locate, because of the row outside, but soon Dido realised that it was coming from her right-hand side. She slanted her eyes in that direction without moving her head.

She was not long in suspense about it. From the corner of her eye she saw it coming – the flat, gleaming diamond-shaped head, with its metallic grey shine, the lean, whiplike black body. It slid along the wall, not fast, not slow, making obliquely for Dido's foot.

This hut, thought Dido, is like a perishing zoo. It's a wonder those fellers out there don't charge for admission.

It was not possible to stand any stiller, but she tried to do so. At the last minute the snake changed direction slightly so that only its final two-thirds, a quivering, tensely drawn-out spring, poured across her foot. Its motion was always indirect, on a diagonal, like an endless series of interlocking S's, casual-seeming, but purposeful.

It was making for the monkey, whose antics were beginning to slow down.

Do snakes eat monkeys? Dido wondered. Do monkeys eat snakes? I'm getting hysterical, there's too much action hereabouts, guards bashing each other with stools outside, and a special Benefit Performance in here, loser gets a shot of poison, winner gets the freedom of my ankle.

The snake was circling the monkey warily. There was a short tactical pause, then an involvement so quick and so complete that Dido could not decide which had been the aggressor: the snake's metallic coils flicked to and fro, the monkey's tail whipped, curled up, whipped again. If I weren't a coward, Dido thought, this'd be the moment to

jump on both of 'em, hard . . . and get a jab in each ankle.
If I had a stick, anything but my bare hands . . .

Her hands were behind her. She had kept them there,
gripping the doorpost, distrusting their steadiness. The
wooden jamb moved slightly as her fingers drove against
it. She gave it a push sideways, her heart suddenly leaping;
a section of it came away. With a swift, resolute tug she
had a three-foot joist in her hands, rotten at one end.
Ignoring the cloud of ant-infested dust that fell on her
ankles, she held her weapon coolly, watching until the
deadly skirmish on the floor came within reach; then she
beat down with all her strength, striking for the snake's
head, which gripped the monkey's hind leg. The snake
twisted away, writhing – she thought she had missed it, but
it twisted back, coiled and re-coiled in agonised jerks—
The monkey lay limp in death.

Now – don't wait – the door had given, moved behind
her when she pulled out the length of doorpost. She gave
it a cautious shove, another, more violent – and burst out,
coming face to face with Tylo.

"What – wherever—?"

"Come away, *quick*! *Quick*, Shaki-miss! Not good here!
Those men – imrit shash jailosh—" He fell into the Dilendi
language, evidently expressing something too bad to be
said in English.

"One of them hit the other on head, so I hit *him* with
handle of gun—"

He nodded to where the guards lay collapsed among
the wreckage of their jug and cups. The hot sun was
drawing winy steam from the shards of earthenware.

"You look very sick, Shaki-miss – what in there with you?"

"Oh, just some wild-life," said Dido, gulping. "I'm sorry
I didn't stop where you told me, Tylo. I was so thirsty – I
went to drink from the brook. There's a blind man somewhere – let's get away from here!"

She snatched up her velvet game-cloth which lay among a scatter of cowrie-shells.

Tylo tugged her, at a run, back to where the horses were tethered. No blind man was to be seen. Perhaps he had gone back to his station by the waterfall.

"You still thirsty – here—"

From the ground, Tylo picked up a hard brown fruit the size of a turkey's egg, which he expertly cracked on a stone, splitting it in two. Each half contained a mouthful of juice protected by a layer of white pith.

"Drink, quick—"

"That's prime," Dido said, gulping. "If I'd only known!"

The juice was sour, fresh, wonderfully thirst-quenching.

"Next stream we fill our water-bottles. That enough? Now we ride, gallop-quick!"

Chapter Four

THEY RODE UNTIL DUSK THROUGH HOT, SLEEPY forest. The island, Dido learned from her companion, was like a great wedge, tipped upwards towards the south. Mount Fura was the highest, southernmost point; and not far below the highest peak of that was John King's royal residence, Limbo Lodge.

"Why's it called that? That's a funny name," said Dido.

"Well I dunno, Shaki-missie. Old Sovran King would have it so. After he wifie die, that's where he mostly stay. Would come to Regina town no more. Too sad, see? And throw his girl-child off Cliff of Death in clay pot."

Dido's blood ran chill.

"Why did he do *that?*" she demanded, when she got her breath back.

"Too much she make him remember wifie."

"Seems bad luck on the girl-child."

"Ah well, see, Shaki-miss, Outros people not want girl children. Not at all! No value."

"Is that why gals have to wrap up their heads?"

He nodded. "In town, hate gal. Among us, Forest People, *most* different. For us, girl-child bring good luck. When she grow, she be Kanikke."

"What's that?"

From Tylo's explanation, Dido learned that, among the Forest People, who did not live in settled villages, but kept moving around, the men were Hamahi, guides, or record-keepers, while the women became Kanikke, witches, and dealt with the practical affairs of life.

"How do the men keep records?"

"You see, you soon see, when you see my Sisingana."

55

"So the town people, the Angrians, hate gals and the Forest People love them."

"Is so, is so."

"And the Civil Guards are town people."

"Is so, golly-likely."

Croopus, thought Dido, I just hope Doc Talisman keeps fooling those guards that she's a boy.

But she didn't fool Tylo. That's rum . . .

"What happened at the jail, Tylo? Did you see Doctor Talisman? Did you give her my message?"

He laughed. "No, I not see. But she, Doc Talisman, top-high Kanikke! She soon be out of that place. They – those Guards – fright-scared of that Shaki-lady. She got mighty strong nooma."

"What's nooma, Tylo?"

A kind of magical power, nooma seemed to be, Dido gathered from his explanations. She was somewhat startled, then remembered Talisman's amazing feat of lifting the heavy marble basin full of water. Could something like that have happened at the jail?

Dido and Tylo had long since left the orderly plantations and were now making their way through true forest, the vegetation packed and juicy around them, creepers and ferns solidly filling up the spaces between the big trees, which towered high above, their crowns, and the sky itself, out of sight above dense foliage. Even the birds and monkeys sounded far away, hundreds of feet overhead, and the path snaked its way through silent green twilight.

Dido supposed there *was* a path; Tylo seemed quite certain of where he was going and kept on at a steady pace. Then Dido began to notice a small white bird with a pink tail and crest which, from time to time, perched on a bough above them, chattered out a short, shrill song, then flew on ahead. Sometimes it lit on the brow-band of Tylo's horse.

"Is that the same bird each time?"

"Is so, Shaki-miss. Memory-bird. You tie knot in rope, throw rope in water, memory-bird stay with you when you want."

The memory-birds, Dido learned, each had their own zone. All Aratu was divided into memory-bird zones.

I wish I could get hold of a memory-bird, Dido thought; they sound right useful. Not that there was any shortage of other birds at this point. But they were mostly out of sight. The trees in the spice-plantations had been bustling with gaudily coloured parrots and parakeets, and no doubt they were here too, but high up, invisible. Once or twice Dido, with a thumping heart, noticed a huge snake, twining in among the branches, but there did not seem to be any pearl-snakes in the forest.

"Pearl snake, he stay near sea, near nutmeg-grove," Tylo confirmed. "Only tree-snake in forest."

"I don't know as I like these any better," said Dido, regarding a twelve-foot specimen winding its muscular way up a vertical tree-trunk.

"You leave him alone, he leave you."

"I'll do that."

Presently Tylo's memory-bird changed its call. Instead of the short song, it let out sharp warning shrieks.

"Rain come soon. Best we find shelter-place for sleep-night," said Tylo.

"I'd have thought these trees would shelter us."

"Oh, no, Shaki-miss. Best we find a wocho."

A wocho, Dido learned, was a house where Forest People had lived but moved away. Soon Tylo found a clearing with two huts which consisted of thatched roofs on legs.

"No walls?"

"What need?"

"To keep out snakes?"

Tylo explained that if you said the proper charm before going to sleep, no snake would trouble you.

The wocho roofs sloped down to deep, overhanging eaves. One house had an earth floor, the other a kind of deck, knee-high above the ground, made from palm fibre laid across joists.

"Ponies in there," said Tylo, and tied them up in the first wocho with an armful of fodder apiece. "Now we go sit here on deck—" and he gave it a poke to dislodge any ants or scorpions that might be lodging among the fibre.

They had not been any too soon in taking shelter; the memory-bird was entirely correct in its forecast. The air turned grey. The forest gave a loud moan. Then the trees at the edge of the clearing vanished from view; a thunderous noise, a mixture of rattle and roar, swallowed up the whole world; the ground outside the hut looked like a battlefield, with water pouring down and water leaping up, bouncing off the dry earth.

Mercy, thought Dido, how can anything stay *alive* under that deluge? It's a mighty good thing we're here and not out there! She turned to say this to Tylo, but realised that he could not possibly hear her, it was like trying to make herself heard through the yelling, shouting, and screaming of a huge multitude. Every now and then there came a flash of lightning across the gloom. Too bad we didn't take out the grub from the saddle-bags, Dido thought, we could have had us a picnic; but I wouldn't venture out in that downpour, even to the other hut, it'd flatten you out like a pastry. The rain cascaded down the stout leaf-roof above them and poured off the eaves in a solid sheet. It's like windows made of water, Dido thought.

The storm raged all night, then stopped as suddenly as it had begun. The forest was sodden and dripping and, because the drenched foliage hung straight down, a good deal lighter; patches of sky were visible. The birds in the treetops were shrieking joyfully as if astonished at being still alive.

"We late, now we eat as we ride," Tylo said, and gave Dido a hunk of corn-bread with figs stuffed into the middle.

They rode fast, munching, through the forest which now became thinner and more open giving way to dispersed groves, then to shrubby savannah-land. Descending into a valley they saw a larger grove of taller trees ahead of them. The memory-bird, satisfied, let out a broadside of chirrups, then flew fast and disappeared among the trees.

"My Sisingana's now-place," said Tylo.

The sun in the east was dazzling; sparks and flashes of light tossed and flickered from every wet surface; but Dido, peering ahead, could see two large dwelling-huts in the middle of the shady grove, and, she thought, figures seated in front of them.

"What is your great-grandfather's name?" she asked.

"Name he *known* by is Asoun, but real name known only to him."

"I see," said Dido, though she did not, quite. Still, she thought, if he wants to keep his moniker to himself, I reckon that's his business.

"Is the other cove that's sitting with him – is that Lord Herodsfoot?"

Tylo gave the chuckle that always seemed to follow any thought of his lordship. "Mylord Oklosh! Yes, that him."

Well, thank goodness for that, thought Dido. At least there's one thing that's worked out to order.

It had not quite worked out yet, though.

For as they entered the grove, Dido heard a piteous wail from overhead, somewhere to their right. Visibility was less dazzling now they were in the shade of the grove; she scanned the dusky foliage high above them and caught sight of a small somebody at the end of a leafy branch, who called out frantically: "Aie, *aie!* Help me, help me! Help, *please!*"

Was it a monkey? No, it was about the size of one, but human, and absolutely petrified with terror.

"Oh, Tylo! What shall we do, what *can* we do?"

Gliding up the tree, twining round and round the trunk with formidable strength and speed, was one of the large snakes they had glimpsed as they rode through the forest.

"Can we pull it down by the tail?" cried Dido, sliding off her mount.

"No, *no*, Shaki-miss! He strangle you at once dead, shock-shock quick!"

Dido did not waste time asking any more questions, she acted. Far away, long ago, in the streets of Battersea, London, she had more then held her own against mobs of enemies wielding bottles and brickbats. Now she snatched up a hefty stone from the ground and hurled it with certain aim and ferocious force. The stone struck the snake's head, and a shudder passed through all its shining spiralled length. Grabbing another stone, Dido flung it with equal fury. The snake loosed its hold of the tree-trunk and fell to the ground in a twist of writhing coils. When Dido let fly with a third stone, the snake waited no longer but made off, discouraged and affronted, seeking for easier pickings.

"My word, Shaki-missie!" said Tylo, hugely impressed. "You number one thrower!"

Without answering, Dido went up the tree. A mere tree was to her a simple matter, due to all the time she had spent in the rigging, first of a Nantucket whaler, then of H.M.S. *Thrush.*

"Don't you be scairt, I'm a-coming!" she called. A faint whimper was the only reply. The tiny girl she had come to rescue was huddled in a cluster of shorter branches at the end of a long upward-pointing bough. Now the cause for her venturing up so high was also visible: bunches of bright-red fruit about the size of grapes or cherries. Her face and hands were splashed with their juice and she had a large grass-fibre bag half full of berries.

"Hang on, liddle 'un – that's the ticket," Dido said encouragingly. The small girl gave her an amazed look, half alarmed, half trusting, but after a moment or two allowed herself to be helped down the branch and back to the main trunk of the tree. Here, she regained all her own tree-climbing confidence, and slid nimbly down to the foot of the trunk, where Tylo was dancing up and down.

"Yorka! Yorka! Wicked child! Ahash oho toohooli!"

Dido understood that he was giving her a terrific scold in the Dilendi language, but that she was defending herself vigorously. What was she to do, what was she to do, with the two old gentlemen so busy, and no breakfast meal ready for them when they would have finished their sacred business, and Uncle Desi away catching fish in the river? Of course she had to pick some djeela fruit!

"Oh, are those djeela fruit?" inquired Dido. "I thought no one was allowed to grow djeela trees except John King?"

Tylo gave her a quick glance, both embarrassed and reproving.

"Never mind that for now, Shaki-miss! I explain you later. Yorka tells my Sisingana singing Lord Oklosh world-beginning mystery song. Very long song, must sing sunrise to sunrise. Can not stop song till finish. Lord Oklosh putting song into word-paper-speak. Must, must wait till finish. Near done now."

"Massy me," said Dido. "A song that lasts twenty-four hours!"

Now indeed, coming closer, they could hear the Sisingana, who sat in front of his house, partly chanting, partly telling a long saga – Dido caught a word here and a word there, about the living world, the great cloud-beast-mother that carries us on her back, the moon and the sun, her sisters, the shadow-people who live underground. How they were all born, where they are all going. To tell this story truly would take a hundred hundred treetimes. And our own island, Aratu, is the centre of the whole mystery, the heart of the cloud-beast-mother. And the centre of our island is the twelve ghost-stones. Nine are already fallen. When the last three fall, then comes the dark after which there will be no sunrise.

The Sisingana's strong, vibrating voice began to slow down, then came to a stop. An insect like an outsize cricket emerged from his great mass of silvery beard and chirped lustily.

"Is finished!" said Tylo. "Longlegs clockfly say so."

The Sisingana had a broad brown benevolent face and the blackest, deepest eyes that Dido had ever seen. He wore a cloak of silvery pale djeela-flowers, which were hooked at the end of the petals so they clung together. He had been sitting cross-legged while giving his lengthy recitation, but now he stood up and stretched. His movement reminded Dido of Talisman. She noticed that his hair and beard were soaking from the storm. He must have been sitting out here telling his story through all that downpour . . .

Dido turned to look at the other old gentleman and received a shock. Somehow she had always assumed that Lord Herodsfoot was elderly, from what she had been told about him and the things he chose to do. Would you expect a young person to wander all over the world looking for roses and dice-games and grasshoppers? Hardly! But Lord Herodsfoot was indeed quite young, about the same age as Lieutenant Windward of the *Thrush*. Dido reckoned, and Lieutenant Windward was only thirty-five.

Herodsfoot had a thin, pale, acute face, and fair fuzzy hair – hair so pale that it was almost white, which was why the child Yorka had mistaken him for an old gentleman.

Also he wore tortoiseshell glasses perched on the end of his nose, which made him look serious. And he had been frantically scribbling in a small thick notebook all the time and the Sisingana was chanting his tale of the world. Herodsfoot, like the Sisingana, was completely drenched, clothes, face, and boots, but he had managed to keep his notebook dry by pulling a huge green waterproof leaf over his head and shoulders, and protecting the notebook under its folds.

"Why the plague didn't they go indoors?" Dido asked Tylo later.

"Oh, my Sisingana would never allow an Outros person into his house."

"*Why?*"

"Infection. Not body-germ – soul infection. Only have Shaki-lord sit outside there, Sisingana will have to wave feathers four days to drive away soul sickness."

(And, indeed, all the time that Dido was in the forest, she never set foot inside a Forest Person's house – unless the owners had already left, as when they sheltered from the storm in the deserted wocho.)

Now Dido approached Lord Herodsfoot, who was carefully studying his notebook to make sure that the rain had not blotted any of the writing in it. Of his soaked clothes he seemed oblivious. Dido noticed that what he had put down in his notebook was not ordinary writing, but pothooks – some kind of shorthand.

"Yes, well, I think I have it all," he said, addressing Dido as if she were an old acquaintance. "It was a great piece of luck that you did not arrive any sooner."

He had not shaved for a couple of days; his face was covered with pale stubble so that, with his damp pale hair, he looked like a wet dandelion clock.

"Lord Herodsfoot, you're wanted back in London in a hurry! I'm sent to tell ye."

"Oh, good heavens, now why?"

Lord Herodsfoot rubbed his damp head. He had a wide, lively mouth. When he smiled, it seemed to extend right across his face, from ear to ear. His smile was very friendly.

"King Jamie wants ye badly. We got a message at Tenby," said Dido, feeling somewhat aggrieved at this matter-of-fact reception, as she thought of what a long distance, and long time, she had been travelling in search of this man. "King Jamie is mighty poorly. Cap'n Hughes, of the *Thrush*, is waiting at Amboina to fetch ye back to Lunnon town."

"Oh, bother King Jamie! Is he really sick? Or just bored?"

"That, I couldn't tell ye. Not having the pleasure of His Majesty's acquaintance."

"Do you think I *really* have to go?" Herodsfoot asked, as seriously as if Dido were the Prime Minister.

"If King Jamie himself wants you – maybe you could go by the North-West Passage – that might be faster—" Dido was beginning when the little girl, Yorka, came to them with a large bunch of feathers. Her aim was to indicate to them politely that they should move a bit farther away from the Sisingana's hut, into which he had retired and was now taking a much-needed nap.

The uncle, another broad-faced, smiling man, had returned from his fishing excursion, evidently a successful one, for he had a basket of what looked like large river trout.

He and Tylo were lighting a fire by blowing on a piece of tree-fungus, which slowly became incandescent. The fire was not laid on the bare ground but contained inside a hearth made of piled-up stones with a knee-high kerb around it to prevent sparks from flying out. When Dido asked about this, Tylo explained that the soil of Aratu was very combustible, being mostly peat. Once or twice in the island's history there had been disastrous fires, and the

Forest People were afraid that if a fire ever got out of control, the whole island might burn up.

"Like what happened on Mount Ximboë. That once island like this one, many tree-length from here, far towards place of cold white sea; and it burned up and all the people died. So now always we keep fire in fire-box."

The roasted fish were accompanied by roots dug from the ground, beans, delicious bark-bread, sandwiched with peppery leaves, and the djeela fruit which were the best food Dido had ever tasted.

"No wonder John King wants to keep them for himself!"

While they ate, Lord Herodsfoot told Dido more of the history of Aratu, about which he seemed to be very well informed.

"The Angrians came here from Europe about four hundred years ago. That was a time when a lot of European countries were grabbing other people's lands. The Angrians took over, driving the Forest People into the middle of the island, and they built their port, Regina, and planted spice plantations. The pepper trees were here already, but they brought nutmeg and cloves and many others. But then the Forest People, very slowly, but powerfully, began to fight back."

"How did they do that?"

"They began casting spells, to make the Angrians homesick. One of them went:

Spirit of our grandmother, Aratu-land
Make the incomers mourn for their own place
Make them sad in their hands and feet
Their eyes, their mouths, their private parts
Stab them in their thoughts
Trouble them east, west, south, and north
Make their stomachs long for their own fruit, own fish,
Oh, make them get in a ship and sail far away

To Angria,
To their own, own home
To their own, own home."

"And did the spell work?"

"It did indeed. In the course of the last hundred years, nearly all the Angrians migrated and went back to Angria, or to South America. And the ones who stayed behind have grown very sad and peculiar."

"They hate girls, don't they," Dido said, remembering what Tylo had told her.

"Yes, and they hate sport and anything cheerful. Because of the spell. They have become very glum and puritanical. They used to be fond of playing games, but now they think that is sinful. They disapprove of me, because I am looking for ancient games for King Jamie. They look down on any sort of amusement."

"Soon they all go," said Tylo hopefully. "By and by, by golly."

"In spite of this disapproval," Herodsfoot went on, "many of the Angrian men are addictive gamblers. Cards, dice—any form of betting they can't resist."

"But tell about John King. Why did the Angrians let him come and take charge here? He was English, wasn't he?"

"He very strong mind," said Tylo.

"King came to this island when he was about twenty years old," Herodsfoot said. "He had his younger brother, Paul, who was sixteen. And a pocketful of djeela seeds. No one ever learned where he got those. The convict ship from which he escaped had stopped at various ports. King started growing djeela trees and trading spices in a small way, but soon grew rich. And by that time the Forest People's curse was affecting the Angrian settlers very strongly, so they were devilish down in the dumps, and glad to have King take over the running of the island, which he did very capably. He adopted an island girl whose parents had died of snakebite, and called her Erato and had her sent to school and taught music. And then he married her. She had a very beautiful singing voice, I'm told."

"Like sunrise bird," said Tylo nodding.

"You heard her? No, you couldn't have. She died twenty years ago."

"My father hear her. Gardener to Sovran King. Live those days in Asgard Hall. Now House of Correction. When Erato die, old Sovran John move to Mount Fura. And threw his baby off the Cliff of Death."

"No," suddenly put in Uncle Desi, who up to now had remained silent, munching his bark bread. "Not Sovran John. His brother Paul throw baby."

"How do you know *that*?" asked Lord Herodsfoot, very interested. His glasses slipped off his nose, and he shoved them back by one ear-piece, causing little Yorka to let out a shriek of wrath.

"No! No! Not do so! You break again, no more tinnel-stalk!"

"Oh, I'm terribly sorry, Yorka! She has had to mend my glasses half a dozen times while the old boy was singing his story," explained Herodsfoot guiltily. "It was so very exciting."

"My father's sister see Paul throw baby. She, picking sing-plums up sing-plum tree, see Paul King put Jane-child in clay pot, throw off mountain. Time of the onda."

"That's the tidal bore that comes past every time Mount Ximboë erupts," explained Lord Herodsfoot. "But this is very interesting. If Paul King really did throw his niece into the sea, it gives one quite a different notion about him. He has changed his name to Manoel, by the way," he explained to Dido. "Manoel is an Angrian name; he is friendly with the Angrians and wishes for their approval. I used to get on tolerably well with the fellow but – throwing his niece off the cliff – no, no, really one can't countenance a thing like that."

"But – Lord Herodsfoot—" said Dido, puzzled.

"Oh, do, call me Frank! My name's Algernon Francis Sebastian Fortinbras Carsluith, but all my friends call me Frank."

"Frankie, then. Thanks. Mine's Dido. But—in the town—when we saw him—Manoel didn't seem to know you, acted as if he'd not met you."

"Oh, that's because, in the days when I knew him, I hadn't come into the title yet. I was just the Honourable Algernon Carsluith when I used to come across Paul King in gambling towns like Bad Szomberg. Of course I was doing research then for my doctorate degree in Loaded Dice."

"Oh, now I get you. He don't know it's you. Did you come across Doc Talisman too?"

Herodsfoot had only vague recollections of a Dutchman, Van Linde, who upset the casino managers by his phenomenal luck. He did not remember a little girl. Maybe she was a boy then, Dido thought. Maybe she always dressed as a boy, to get inside gambling halls, or because it made travel easier.

"But why would Manoel throw the baby into the sea?"

"Maybe, like the Angrians, he hates girls."

But Uncle Desi said no, it was because, if the girl-baby were out of the way, then when John King died his brother Manoel would take over his position as ruler of the island. "Or, that is what he hope. Maybe soon he throw his brother off Cliff of Death. Or hope Outros people do so. For now Sovran John don't give his brother no more money for travel. He can't go away, must stay here on Aratu."

Dido found this story extremely interesting. Twenty-odd years ago Doctor Talisman had fallen off a cliff, had been rescued by a trading ship, taken halfway across the world, and brought up in Europe.

It's a rare funny thing, thought Dido – that, if Doc Tally is John King's daughter – and her story does seem to fit into that one like a foot into a shoe – it's a mighty havey-cavey thing that the very cove, her own *uncle*, who chucked her off the cliff, should meet up with her years later in a gambling town in Hanover.

Or is it so havey-cavey? Was he looking for her? Does it all hang together? Suppose brother Paul – or let's call him Manoel if he's changed his moniker to that because it sounds more Angrian and he wants to be all pals with them – suppose Manoel, after he chucked the kid into the sea, suppose he heard tell about the Dutch vessel a-sailing by that picked up the young 'un. Suppose he goes to Holland and hears of a girl-kid being rescued by this Van Linde? We know that, in those days, Manoel made a plenty trips to Europe, gambling. (Where did he get the dibs to gamble? Well, brother John was doing right well from all those djeela trees; maybe he got the mint sauce from generous brother John). But then brother John clams up. Manoel has to stop home. But he'd met young Tally at one of those gaming places and given her the notion of coming back to Aratu to take a gander at the place she come from.

Now *why* does Manoel do that? Why does he want her back here?

Right from the start I reckoned that Manoel would bear watching, Dido thought. In my book he's as twisty as a corkscrew. He knows that Tally is Old Sovran King's daughter, what's he planning?

"Frankie," she said urgently, "we must hurry us back to Regina town."

At this moment old Asoun, the ancient Sisingana, woke from his brief nap and came rolling impressively out of his wocho.

"I hear the drums," he said. "They send a message."

He spoke in the Dilendi language, but Dido by now was beginning to pick up a fair number of words.

"Drums?" She was puzzled. "I don't hear no drums, your honour."

Yorka, now the meal was finished, had come to sit leaning comfortably up against Dido in order to teach her a game played with four blades of grass and two snail shells.

"Great-great-grandpa can hear drums when no one else can," she explained.

"Drums," repeated Asoun. "Drums tell me two things. The clever Outros lady has escaped from the House of Correction."

"Oh, bully for Doc Talisman!" cried Dido joyfully. "We might'a guessed they'd never keep *her* buckled up for long! But I wonder where she's heading? I hope she'll come this way. She knew I was under orders to look for Lord Frankie – and she'd not want to stay in the town in case there was trouble about Mr Mully – unless she'd go back to the ship?"

"No," said Asoun. "For the second drum-message relates to the ship. The City Guards have taken the ship."

"*Taken* the ship? Why, in mussy's name?"

Asoun waited for a few moments, listening to inaudible messages.

"Is so, often," whispered Yorka. "He hear drum from all over."

"Who does the drumming?"

"Other Hamahi. All over forest."

Like the memory-birds, thought Dido. A network of drum messages all over the island, heard only by some. Pretty smart, that. Those Angrian coves had things really stacked against them when they tried to take over this place.

Asoun was ready to speak again.

"City Guards took ship because djeela-pods found in

cargo-hold. But Captain said he never put them there. Very angry. Said it was a plot, a trap. Guards take no notice. Unload his cargo."

"Why do that?"

"They want ship. Take out to sea, make for Manati harbour."

"So Cap'n Sanderson's cargo was just left lying on the dock? He won't be best pleased about that."

"What was the cargo?" Lord Herodsfoot inquired.

"Tea. Sugar."

Dido thought of the savage rain last night beating down on sacks of sugar, on chests of tea.

"Where *is* Cap'n Sanderson?"

"Gone to ask audience of Leader John King."

"Humph," said Herodsfoot. "He'll be uncommonly lucky – by what I hear – if he gets to see King on his mountaintop. Not even his brother gets to see him these days – if what I'm told is true."

"Poor Cap. He'll be really wild," said Dido. "First, having some scallywag plant a load of djeela pods on him; he'd never be such a jackass as to take those on board. And second, having his ship pinched! That's the limit! I lay it'll be a while afore he comes to Aratu again."

"But in the meantime," said Herodsfoot, sliding his glasses up his nose and evoking a warning shriek from Yorka, "in the meantime it somewhat lessens our chances of getting *off* the island. In the near future, at least."

"Yus. That's so," agreed Dido, pondering. "Tylo – what'd we better do? It's late in the day, now, to go back to Regina town – and if we did go back, what's the point? There's no ship and no captain—" And the Town Guards may be waiting to collar me too, she thought, for helping Doc Tally with the operation. Croopus! Poor Mr Multiple in the hospital! I just hope he's coming along as he ought, that

71

they are taking good care of him. After all, none o' this is *his* fault.

Tylo considered.

"Might be better try go see old Sovran John King."

He sounded rather pleased at the prospect.

"*Have* you ever seen him, Tylo?"

He shook his curly head. "Only across river-gorge, he sit in garden of Limbo palace. Very old man, white hair. And hard to make hear voices. That I know."

"King is very deaf," confirmed Herodsfoot. "I heard that too. All his personal staff are issued with notebooks; they have to write down in their books anything they want to tell King, or ask him."

"Tough luck if you can't write. Or can't spell."

It was a lucky thing for John King, Dido thought, that his deafness had come on *after* his wife Erato died. If it was her singing voice that he so specially loved. Would have been hard on him if he grew so deaf he couldn't hear her sing.

"What did she die of – King's wife?" she asked Tylo.

"Snakebite."

"Too many snakes on this island. You'd think he'd want to leave, after that."

"Rich here," Tylo pointed out. "Djeela nuts. And kw'ul."

"What's kw'ul?"

He made gestures with his fingers. "What Shaki-misses like to wear round neck."

He pointed to little Yorka, who had a necklace of shiny brown nutshells. They hardly seemed worth braving snakes for.

"How long will it take to get to this Limbo palace?"

"Two night in forest. Best we start chop-chop now. And Sisingana need peace."

"You agreeable to that, Lord Herod – Frankie?"

He sighed. "While grieved indeed to terminate my

72

pleasant visit with the venerable Asoun, who had promised to teach me the game of King and Crocodiles (which sounds to me remarkably like the ancient Saxon game of Hnefatafl) I believe we had best set out with no delay. Asoun did mention that we were in for a spell of unchancy weather."

"Unchancy! If that means a shower like the one last night—"

Little Yorka, jumping up and down, squeaked, "I can teach the Shaki-lord King and Crocodile! Oh-oh! I can teach!"

"Can you, my dear?" said Lord Herodsfoot, looking down at her kindly. "But you would not want to take a long wet trip through the forest, would you?"

"Not? Why not?" The forest was where Yorka lived, she pointed out. It was her home.

"Well, let her come," said Tylo. "She can help me find the way to the Quinquilho Ranch, where we spend our first night. Belong to Angrian family, Ereira."

"Will the Ereiras want us staying with them?"

"No," said Tylo, "but must give bed to traveller."

"They have strict rules of hospitality," Herodsfoot agreed.

So they set off without delay.

Herodsfoot had had another guide, a boy called Senu, to lead him to the grove where Asoun at present chose to live. Since his services were no longer required, Senu declared his intention of going off to the Kulara Place for a cleansing, and loped away at once up the side of the valley.

The others mounted their fed and rested mounts; Herodsfoot had a little fleabitten grey pony, and Yorka rode in front of Dido (though she said proudly that on foot she could keep up with any four-footed beast).

73

"Still, no need to walk when you can ride," said Dido. "Where are your mother and father, little 'un?"

Her mother was dead, Yorka explained, fallen from a tree when a rotten bough broke under her. Her father, a Hamahi message-sender and record-keeper, was somewhere in the forest; she saw him now and then, but spent more time with her aunts, and with great-grandfather Asoun. She turned round to call the old man a last goodbye, but he was busy waving infection away from his door with a bunch of feathers, and did not heed her.

"He will do that four days now."

"What's that cleansing place where Senu's gone?"

"It is the Place of Stones, the twelve great stones that our Sisingana spoke of in his story. Nine are fallen, three still stand," Tylo explained. "We go there to be made clean of trouble or curse."

"Dear me!" said Lord Herodsfoot eagerly, pushing up his glasses, at which Yorka gave a warning growl. "I should dearly like to see that place! There is a game called Twelve Stones, played by the Twi people—"

"Well," said Tylo, "we sleep tonight at Quinquilho Ranch. We could perhaps cross Honey river tomorrow by the ford, and pass Place of Stones."

"Splendid! Splendid! Do you know the history of this place?"

"Is old, very old. Many thousand treetime. Stones come from who knows where? Not island stone. Who knows how? Too heavy for men to lift. Under every stone a man's headbone buried."

"A skull."

"Is so. But one headbone gone."

"Who took it?"

"No one know."

Nor could they find out from Tylo exactly when the skull had been taken.

"Some treetime back," was all he could tell them. People did not often visit Kulara, the Place of Stones, because, unless you had a real need for cleansing, the Place was likely to send you away loaded with more trouble than you had brought with you.

The Place discouraged casual visitors.

"Some say, why not old Sovran John King go for cure from hearing sickness."

"Well," said Dido, "why don't he?"

"Maybe stones don't help him, he not Island man."

"He would have to believe in them," said Herodsfoot thoughtfully. "But if he married an Island girl, he must have shared some of her beliefs."

All the way along, as they rode, Yorka was telling Dido about the plants in the forest.

"Not one, *not one* single tree, in the whole forest, but happy to help us. See, those berries make wash-paste; this creeper just right to weave bags; that tree make table or stool, that fruit very good for flavour meat when you cook. These leaves keep you dry when rain come."

In exchange for this information, Dido told Yorka about the streets of Battersea, London, where she had gown up, the beggars, thieves, cut-throats, lords and ladies in their carriages, market stalls selling food, household goods, and toys, the street singers and jugglers. Yorka was polite and interested, but she made it plain she thought that Battersea sounded like a dreadful place – where you had to *pay* for food!

"Wouldn't you like to travel and see other places besides Aratu, Yorka?"

"No. I wholly love our Forest. Don't want anywhere but here."

Yorka had not even been as far as Regina town, and had no particular wish to do so. She said it sounded like a dismal place full of bad tempered people.

"Tell about this Quinquilho house where we are going."

And none too soon, either, thought Dido, for though they were now back in the true forest and could not see the sky above them, even the dim tree-light was dwindling fast, and ominous growls of thunder and flashes of lightning every now and then made the horses start and whinny.

"Quinquilho not a wocho. House built by Outros people ten treetimes back." Yorka pushed her lip out disdainfully. Dido gathered that she, personally, would prefer to spend the night in the forest rather than lodge under a stone roof with this gloomy Angrian family.

"They got nowhere they want, nothing they do."

Dido pondered.

What *do* folk want? Frankie Herodsfoot there, he wants to find more and more games. And plants and stories. Doc Talisman wants to cure sickness. Cap'n Sanderson wants to sail his ship. What do I want? I want to go back to Battersea and find my friend Simon and see what's happened in London Town.

"What do you want, Yorka?"

"Be a Kanikke. Like my mother's sister, Aunt Tala'aa."

"What do Kanikke do?"

"Magic. *Good* magic," said Yorka firmly. "Bring rain. Make fish grow big in river. Send away the Drought Woman. Sing Whispering Song, melt trouble fire. Write name in sand, keep away Never Week."

"You can learn to do all that?"

"By and by. In treetime. Now," said Yorka, "here we come Quinquilho. Ereira family. Don Enrique. Dona Esperanza. Hear dogs bark."

Her quick ears had caught the sound, far away. The dogs sounded very savage.

"Hope they're tied up," said Dido.

"Dog won't ever bite naked person, you know that?"

"Well," said Dido, "I don't aim to take off my britches

and jacket just to find out if that's a true tale. It's too cold by half, anyhows."

The temperature had shot down. Now the travellers were out of the forest and in a large cleared space of spice plantations. There were grape vines also. The smell of spice tingled on the cool evening air. Ahead of them was a solid stone house, enclosed by walls, approached across a paved yard. The dogs, raging their heads off, were behind a fence, Dido was thankful to find. A bent, aged man, muttering what might have been either blessings or curses, arrived and led their horses away to an open-fronted stable. A sour-looking elderly woman appeared. She seemed a little put out at their arrival, but, nevertheless, invited them to come indoors.

Chapter Five

THE HOUSE SEEMED TO BE IN A STATE OF subdued commotion, Dido thought, as they followed the old woman through the ice-cold stone arched passages to a cavernous dark kitchen as big as a ballroom. It contained a large bare table and several stools, besides many shelves holding enormous platters and dishes. No other inhabitants of the house were to be seen, and yet there was an atmosphere of hurry and trouble; somewhere in the distance they could hear hasty footsteps; and the clamour of raised voices, and the clatter of pots or pails suggested that some domestic crisis was taking place.

Dido shivered. Despite a wan fire alight in the huge old cooking stove, the kitchen seemed not much warmer than the yard and orchards outside. Yorka's dead right about this place, she thought; there's summat about it that gives you the chill heeby-jeebies.

Lord Herodsfoot glanced around him with interest and remarked in a low voice: "This must be one of the oldest Angrian mansions in the island, several hundred years old, I'd guess."

"Feels like it's never been properly warmed since it was built," Dido whispered back.

The grey-haired woman who had led them in now made off through a doorway with some muttered explanation: "Later, food will be brought. Now you will have to excuse me . . ."

"This is a good time for you to show me the King Crocodile game," Lord Herodsfoot suggested hopefully to Yorka.

He took a half-burned stick from the fire and was about

to draw a game-square on the white scrubbed flags of the floor, but Dido, guessing that this would not be at all well received by the housekeeper, pulled her embroidered game-cloth from her pocket. "Here, you can use this; some-one's been scrubbing those flagstones all day."

Herodsfoot's eyes lit up at sight of the cloth. He exclaimed; "Why! That is an original game-board cloth, probably from ancient Persia; it may very well date back to the reign of Chosroes II! It is a most rare and valuable specimen. Where in the name of wonder did you get it, may I ask?"

"It was left me by a feller called Brandywinde who died," Dido explained. "And dear only knows where *he* laid hands on it – if ever there was a jammy-fingered rapscallion, he was the one! Anyhow I reckon it'll do for young Yorka to show you the rules of the crocodile game – you can just turn the cloth face down."

But Yorka, unexpectedly, would not allow this.

"Many, many spirits of dead people in this house," she said, shivering a little as she stared about the gloomy kitchen. "Play games by day, very well, pleases the ghosts, they enjoy to watch. But at night, in darktime, no! they come play too, take us back with them when they go home."

"Oh? Is that really so?" said Herodsfoot. "Then certainly we must not play. But it does not look as if anybody is going to come and take care of us for some time. We might as well make ourselves comfortable." He sat on a stool. "Won't you sing one of your songs to us, Yorka?"

Yorka sang, in a soft threadlike little voice:

"If there is a girl-child soon come to this house
O, o, o, I fear her tasks will be many and hard
O may the waterpot be light on her shoulder

79

O may the needle not prick her finger too hard
O poor little sister I wish you well!"

"Do you know any songs?" Herodsfoot then asked Dido.
"Only the ones my pa used to make up." She sang:

"Oh, how I'd like to be Queen, Pa,
And float in a golden canoe
Sucking a sweet tangerine, Pa,
All down the river to Kew."

Dido sang quite loud and cheerfully, thinking of her father, and what a bad parent he was, except for making up songs, and the grey-haired woman came storming back into the kitchen.

"What devil's music is that?" she hissed, giving Dido a ferocious look. "How dare you raise your voice in impious song while the young senhora is in such trouble? Be quiet at *once*! If you make any more noise you will have to go back into the forest, and you will not like *that*, for it is raining as hard as ever."

Indeed they could hear the rain lashing down in the paved yard outside, and the gale howling against the stone-mullioned windows.

"We are indeed sorry for your trouble, senhora," said Herodsfoot politely. "We did not mean to offend. But what is the matter? Can we be of any help, any use, in any possible way?"

"In no way!" she snapped. "The younger senhora, Meninha Luisa, she is about to give birth at this time. But the birth is a hard one, and the child a long time coming. The young lady is in much pain. No one can help. If we only had a doctor! Instead we have a parcel of useless idle-mouths who will be wanting food and beds, and have no more sense than to *sing* in this house of calamity!" And taking a cauldron of hot water from the range, she stomped out of the kitchen again.

"Well; there *is* a doctor," Dido said sadly, "but dear knows where she has got to. Don't I jist wish she were here with us!"

Her words went unanswered, for at this moment a personage who must be the lady of the house entered the kitchen: an extremely grand, white-haired senhora, thin as a broom-handle, with a pale, flinty face, pale eyes, black clothes, and a black lace headdress spangled with large pearls draped over her brow.

"I understand you are Milord Herodsfoot?" she said to his lordship with icy civility. "I have heard about you from my cousins in Regina City." He bowed. "And these will be your servants, no doubt." Her eye swept over Dido, Yorka, and Tylo without pausing. "I regret that you find our house in some confusion, and that you were shown into the kitchen. My daughter Luisa . . . is unwell. But you, senhor, should not have been left in this room. Your servants . . . may remain here. You, sir – pray come with me – do me the honour of accompanying me to the Sala where a meal shall be served for you."

"That's uncommonly kind of you, ma'am," said Herodsfoot, standing his ground, "but I beg you won't trouble yourself with entertaining me. I'm sure you wish to be with your daughter. And I shall do very well here with my companions."

"Your compan—" She stared at him as if he had asked to be accommodated in the pigsty. "Most singular! You prefer to remain in the kitchen? Oh – very well – if that is your wish. The meal shall be brought to you here . . . in the course of time . . ."

And she swept severely away, without another word.

Herodsfoot gave Dido a rueful grin, pushing up his glasses. "Bless me, what a tartar! Lucky she's not the one

81

passing out vouchers for the Royal Garden Party at St James's. We'd none of us be invited— Oh, may the foul fiend fly away with these glasses! Yorka, I'm afraid the earpiece has broken again—"

With a suppressed wail, as if this were the very last straw, Yorka received the broken spectacles from Herodsfoot and looked around her for mending materials. But nothing in the bare, cold kitchen seemed to strike her eye as being at all suitable. Shaking her head sorrowfully, she tucked the glasses into a little pouch containing seeds and grasses which she carried at her waist.

At this moment an elderly man in black breeches and a striped apron came in carrying a tray and – rather to their surprise – proceeded to serve them a meal, which was unexpectedly good: thin, bitter soup, pancakes, some game-bird roasted with rice, peppers and garlic, and cups of hot drink served in small metal cups.

"Maté," said Herodsfoot, tasting it.

Yorka had never before come across plates, spoons and forks, and found them highly amusing.

While they were eating, Dido asked her quietly, "Did you *know*, Yorka – about the baby being born in this house – when you sang your song?"

Yorka nodded, but said, "Hush! Too many ghosts about. Better they don't hear talk of baby."

The very minute they had finished eating, the elderly man said to Lord Herodsfoot, "Sir, you will now wish to go to rest. You and the boy-servant, follow me. Isabella the housekeeper will soon show the young girls where they may sleep."

And in a moment or two the grey-haired woman came back and sternly led Dido and Yorka in a different direction, along some more freezing stone passages, past dozens of closed doors, and up a spiral flight of stairs – up, and up, and up. I don't like this house one bit, Dido thought.

Dear knows what might be going on behind all those shut doors – prisoners, mad people who've been tied to their beds for twenty years, servants dying of sickness because nobody takes the trouble to care for them. And all these *stairs*! Our bedroom must be up at the top of a tower.

It was at the top of a tower. The door that Isabella opened led into a round room with three windows spaced at regular intervals in the wall. There were two small bamboo cots and two stools. A thin, black-haired woman was hurriedly throwing covers on to the cots.

"I will leave you now," snapped Isabella, and gave some instructions to the other woman in a low voice, addressing her as Katarina. As soon as she had left, Katarina ran to Dido, caught hold of her hands, and kissed them, calling down blessings on her head.

"You saved my daughter! Oh, thanks, thanks, meninha, a thousand thanks!"

"Saved your daughter?" Dido was completely astonished. "I don't reckon as how I saved anybody's daughter—"

Then she thought of Yorka and the snake. But Yorka's mother was dead... and this woman was not a Forest Person. She was an Angrian.

"Yes, yes, you did, you did! In the town. The Guard were after her – because she was in the street without a hood over her head – some boys stole it – but you let her into the hospital—"

"Great sakes!" said Dido, remembering. "Would they really have arrested her – just for not having a hood—?"

"Arrested her? They would have hung her up from a tree – as they do so many – if you had not helped her—"

With a shiver, Dido remembered the scene by the roadside before Tylo and she had reached the prison.

"Where is your daughter now?"

"Oh, she is safe. The nurses helped her – she hides –

never mind where! But I thank you, meninha, I bless you
– always, always—"

Kissing Dido's hand again, Katarina left. As she did so
she murmured conspiratorially, "Isabella ordered me to
lock the door. Don Enrique and Dona Esperanza trust
nobody. But I shall not lock the door. And if you should
need anything in the night – only call to me. I sleep at the
foot of the stair."

"How is it going with the poor girl who is having the
baby?" Dido murmured.

"Slowly. Not well. And the poor father – not here—"

After the door had closed, Yorka said, "I do not like to
sleep in bed. On floor is best."

"Suit yourself! Sleep where you like," Dido said cheerfully. "But you better wrap yourself in that quilt. It's
powerful cold up here. My word, though! We can think
ourselves lucky we don't live in Regina town. What a place
– where you get hanged for not wearing a titfer on your
noddle. Swelp me!"

She went to the nearest window and looked out. The
storm was still raging, gusts of wind made the tower quiver,
and flashes of lightning displayed the stable-buildings and
paddocks a long way below, the plantations farther off,
and the true forest rising raggedly behind them.

"We're awful high up. Even higher than a djeela tree!"
Dido chuckled. "At least djeela trees don't have ghosts in
'em – even if they do have snakes. Are there *so* many ghosts
in this house, Yorka?"

"Some – many," said Yorka. "All walk around this place,
hoping they grab that baby soon coming—"

"Well, you better make a good magic and stop them."

"I try."

And Yorka sat herself thoughtfully, cross-legged, with her
quilt round her shoulders.

Dido opened the window.

"Even one of them climbing snakes could hardly slither his way up here," she said.

Something did, though, later in the night. Dido had fallen asleep as soon as she lay down. The unaccustomed luxury of a real bed – even a hard narrow cot and scanty cover – flung her into slumber at once. But after a couple of hours she suddenly woke, aware that some sound had roused her. She looked up at the window nearest her bed. The storm had blown itself out, a bright moon shone. The window was clearly outlined in brilliant white moonshine. Dido saw a hand slip over the sill – then another hand – then a head and shoulders rose up, outlined against the pearly night sky.

Yorka was instantly awake too. "Who that climb in?" she whispered.

Talisman's voice answered. "Don't be afraid! Dido? Are you there? I've come to share your sleeping-quarters!"

"Doc Tally! Saints save us! Am I glad to see *you* again!"

The doctor swung her feet neatly over the sill and settled cross-legged on the floor. A sweet powerful scent, something like that of cloves, coming from her, immediately filled the room.

Yorka said at once – "You been with Auntie Tala'aa – you Shaki Doctor? You got sticky string, mend glasses?"

"Whose glasses?"

"These here, Mylord Oklosh."

Moving to the patch of moonlight where the doctor sat, Yorka produced the broken spectacles from her little pouch and displayed them.

"Oh yes, I can easily mend those with a bit of sticking-plaster," Talisman said. She had brought her bag of medical equipment, slung on her back. She delved into it and found the plaster. "You are Yorka, are you not? I met your aunt last night."

"Doc Tally," said Dido, as the repair was being swiftly and neatly executed, "how in the name of *wonder* did you climb up to that window?"

Talisman chuckled quietly.

"Well – you see – while I was doing my medical training – I spent a couple of months in the mountains of Transylvania with a kind of Senior Lady Magician—"

"A witch?" suggested Dido.

"I suppose you might call her that. Certainly she was a healer and a seer – and she taught me various ways of getting into houses where there is a sick person – sometimes, you know, there may be nobody around to let in the doctor. Or they may not *want* the doctor to get in. In this house I think there is somebody who is in bad pain – isn't that so?"

"On the nob, Doc," said Dido. "There's a poor gal somewhere downstairs having a baby – least ways she may have had it by now—"

"No, she has not," said the doctor. "I would know that. I had better go down directly and see to her."

"You may have a mite of trouble *getting* to her," Dido warned. "There's some fierce old hags in this house—"

"I daresay they will be glad enough to let me by," said Talisman drily. She picked up her bag. Out of it rolled something hard and round. Yorka let out a squeak of astonishment.

"One headbone! From Kulara, the Place of Stones!"

She picked up the object and held it in the moonlight. It was a human skull – small, dark in colour, and plainly very old indeed. "Where you get?" she demanded.

"No, no, my love, I know what you think, but indeed I didn't steal it from the Place of Stones," Talisman said soothingly. "I plan to take it *back* there. Later. I will tell you. Now I must go and look after that poor girl."

"Can we help, Doc?" said Dido.

"If I need you I will call. There's probably a whole troop of people in there already. Yorka will hear if I call – won't you, Yorka?"

"I hear," said Yorka.

"While I'm down there you think helpful thoughts."

After Talisman's light step had died away down the stair, Dido said, "How did she know your name was Yorka? I never told her that."

"She just been with my mother's sister Tala'aa," said Yorka. "Last night. Aunt Tala'aa probable help her out of jail."

"How do you know that?"

"Scent. Aunt Tala'aa, she every day pick melanthus curd, make ointment. No one else do like that."

"I see. I wonder how Talisman got in touch with your aunt."

"Aunt Tala'aa know many a thing. Sisingana know she help Doctor, from the drums."

"Can *you* hear the drums, Yorka? Do you know what they say?"

"No," said Yorka sadly. "Hear, yes, but not know what they say. Nor Tylo can. We learn speak other tongue, so drum noise slip away from ear."

"You mean, because you can speak to me in Shaki language, you can't understand drum language? What a blame shame," said Dido. "I bet you'd rather know what the drums are saying."

"Too late," said Yorka. "Too late now. Maybe, if Never Week come, hear drum again."

Never Week, Dido had learned from Tylo, was a time when everything that had gone wrong would be put right. Or the other way round.

Both girls felt too wide awake now to sleep again; instead they told each other stories. Meanwhile, Dido tried to think helpful thoughts.

Perhaps they did help.

Yorka said: "That girl down there. Now better. Girl-baby is come."

"Oh, I'm glad," said Dido. "The family won't be, though, will they? Angrians don't like girl-babies."

"No, can't inherit house, can't fight in battle. Girl-baby often put out in forest for wild pig to eat."

"*No!*" said Dido, horrified. "They don't *really* do that, do they? Those Angrians?"

"Golly-often. Often! But not this girl, maybe. Listen."

The two girls crouched in silence, listening, then Yorka said, "Baby find voice. Tell ghosts, go back where they came from."

"Where is that? Where *do* they come from?"

"Back-to-front land under ground. Under forest. Where sun rise in west, shadow go frontwards. Shadow land. Ghost people come from there."

The cry of a newborn, unnamed child, Yorka told Dido, contains terrific ghostly power. Giving a child a name, like putting a ring on its finger, ties down the spirit, reduces its force. But makes it safer, too, from the hungry spirits that cluster in search of prey whenever a baby is about to be born.

"Like tree-snake waiting for plum-bird chicks to hatch," Yorka said. "Ah! Now listen! Doctor calling us."

Dido could hear no call, but followed Yorka without hesitation. They ran down the winding stair and along another narrow damp passage to a kind of lobby where several maids were gathered outside a door. Isabella the housekeeper was there and sternly waved them back.

"Bad girls! How did you get out? Go away! Go to your room! This is no place for you."

But the door opened and Talisman's voice called from inside: "No! Let them come in. They are wanted. I need them here as witnesses."

Passing the group of servants, who unwillingly stood back to let them through, the girls went into a large untidy room, dimly lit by a dozen candles. Three or four maid-servants were running about with jugs and cloths and towels. The Senhora Esperanza Ereira stood, grim as a post, on the far side of the bed, which was the untidiest feature of the room, rumpled and crumpled, tangled with damp sheets and piled high at both ends with pillows.

Curled limply against the pillows and draped with a silk shawl was a skinny girl, utterly submerged in sleep. And, in a basket beside her on the bed, not sleeping at all, but looking alertly about, lay a tiny baby, wrapped in a shawl of djeela flowers.

Dr Talisman, standing by the bed, said: "Good. I need you two to witness the christening."

"This is not *right*. None of this is right," said the Senhora Esperanza sternly. "A christening should not be performed by a woman – even if she has trained as a doctor."

She swept Talisman with a disapproving glare. Is it because she's a doctor? wondered Dido, or because she is wearing men's clothes? It was plain that the senhora had not, for a single moment, been deceived by the men's clothes.

"Very well, senhora," said Talisman calmly. "Then let your husband, the Senhor Don Enrique Ereira, perform the ceremony."

"He will not. I mean," said the Senhora correcting herself, "he cannot. The Senhor is – is indisposed. He is unwell."

"In that case," suggested Dido, "how about Lord Herods-foot? He's a college-learned fellow, he'd oblige. I bet he'd do it for ye, all hunky-dory."

Despite the Senhora's look of even greater disapproval, Talisman said, "Is Lord Herodsfoot in the house? Yes, from all I hear of him, he would be an excellent choice. Let him be sent for." And putting her head out the door, she ordered, "Let the English milord be wakened and brought here directly."

"Senhora Medica," said Dona Esperanza crossly, "we must of *course* be obliged to you for saving my daughter's life – and the child—" (She don't sound a *mite* thankful, Dido thought.) "But now you go beyond what is needed or seemly."

"Oh, I don't think so," said Doctor Talisman cheerfully. "Not at all."

"You come here – a stranger to us, an outsider—"

"Not entirely, ma'am. I was born in this island twenty-five years ago."

"Indeed." This news seemed very unpleasing to the Senhora.

"And furthermore," Talisman went on, "I have, from one of my parents, the gift of knowing in advance – a very little – what fortune keeps in store for some of my patients. For instance—" she leaned down and touched one of the baby's fists with her finger; instantly the tiny hand grasped the finger and held it. Dr Talisman looked up, smiling, at the angry grandmother. "For instance, ma'am, just by this contact with your granddaughter's hand, I can tell you two things: one is that in the circle of people closely connected with her at this moment there is one who wishes her great harm. Safely christened, she will be in less danger from that. And, secondly, your granddaughter has an unusual future ahead of her. *If* – and it is only *if*, mark you – if she reaches the age of an adult, she may well become the ruler of this island. Of course that is only *one* chance among many – at every moment of our lives so many different choices face us, do they not—?

The Senhora did not seem particularly enchanted at the suggestion that her granddaughter might one day become Queen of Aratu. She began, "I do not at *all* under-

90

stand—" in an angry voice, but at this moment Lord Herodsfoot entered the room, tying his cravat with a hasty negligent hand, wearing the slightly blind, bemused, helpless look of a person who ordinarily wears glasses but has mislaid them. He was followed by Tylo, plainly anxious not to miss anything interesting that might be going on.

"You sent for me, ma'am? – Goodness gracious me," he added, peering about him at the disorderly, candle-lit room, "have I come to the right place?"

"Mylord Oklosh!" cried Yorka joyfully, "see, see, see! Shaki Talisman fix your glasses, very best!" And she ran forward, pulled Herodsfoot's hand so as to bring his head down to her level, and carefully, tenderly fitted the glasses on to his nose.

"My word! That *is* an improvement!" ejaculated Lord Herodsfoot, adjusting the spectacles with the palms of both hands. Then he looked straight ahead, and the first thing he saw was the face of Dr Talisman, studying him across the tumbled bed, wearing her usual expression of keen, alert attention.

"Dr Talisman, I believe?" He gave her his wide, friendly smile. "I cannot tell you, ma'am, how exceedingly happy I am to meet you, and how grateful I am for this work of rescue—" He touched the mended glasses. "I have been hearing so much about you, both from Miss Twite and from the boy Tylo here. But now, how can I be of use? – for I feel this is not a room where male guests are welcome for longer than is strictly needful." Now catching sight of the Senhora, grim and silent in the shadows, he made her a low bow, and said, "Ma'am: your most obedient servant . . ."

She slightly, silently inclined her head, but made no reply.

"We need this child christened," Talisman said briefly.

"And the Senhora here is of the opinion that the ceremony is best performed by a man. Sir, will you be so good . . .?"

It was plain that, during Lord Herodsfoot's extensive travels round the world, he had at various times been faced with unusual circumstances equal to these. He said: "Certainly; if you wish it, ma'am?" glancing from Talisman to the Senhora, who again very slightly inclined her veiled head.

"Would you have such a thing as a drop of holy water, or a thimbleful of djeela-nut oil?"

"Certainly not!" snapped the Senhora.

"Well, it is no matter. I have a thimbleful myself, which this boy's great-grandfather was so kind as to give me, in return for my reciting Shakespeare's sonnets to him." And he pulled a beautiful little spiral shell from his pocket. "Do you have a pin, my dear Doctor?"

Talisman produced a pin from her neck-cloth and Herodsfoot, with extreme care, removed a tiny plug of clay from the opening of the shell, and tipped a minute drop of oil on to his finger. Very quickly he replugged the shell with the speck of clay and returned it to his pocket. Meanwhile the overwhelming aromatic scent of concentrated djeela-juice filled the air of the whole chamber.

"Now," said Herodsfoot briskly, "where is this baby? Ah – there you are, my dear—" and he scooped the baby from its basket. She stared at him peacefully but made no sound.

"What name is she to be given, senhora?"

Grimly, the Senhora shook her head. "Her name is no affair of mine."

"Doctor Talisman? Do you know?"

"No, sir. I entered this house only in time to help with the confinement."

"Dear me! Shall we have to wake the mother? I would be most reluctant to do so."

92

"You would not be able to," said Talisman. "I gave her a draught which will keep her asleep till morning."

"Then we shall have to choose a name," said Herodsfoot, undaunted. "Senhora, what would you say to the name Vitorinha?"

But, as she was beginning a distasteful motion of her head, Yorka spoke up. "Baby's name be Miria."

"How do you know that?" inquired Talisman.

"My mother's sister Tala'aa tell me so."

"Good. Miria it shall be. Lord Herodsfoot—?"

He nodded, touched the baby's forehead with the finger anointed in djeela nut oil and said rapidly, "In the name of this island and its ancestral powers I pronounce this child's name to be Miria Francisca Ereira."

Then he popped her back into the basket, adding apologetically, "I always think it best for a child to have two names, in case it doesn't fancy the first one, so I gave her one of mine; I hope you don't think it a liberty, and that she will not object."

"Thank you sir," said the Senhora dourly. "At least Francisca is a more godly name than Miria – she should properly have been given her father's name also—"

"Oh, I do beg your pardon, ma'am – I had understood that in this land a child carries its mother's name?"

"That is so," the Senhora answered grimly, "but the father's name is customarily added as well."

"In that case let us add it by all means."

"Most unfortunately," said the Senhora, as if the words were being pulled out of her by pincers, "most unfortunately we do not know the father's name."

Dido noticed Doctor Talisman give a compassionate glance at the sleeping girl on the bed.

"Then," said Lord Herodsfoot, "I will write it down as I spoke it."

Pulling a notebook from his pocket he rapidly scribbled

a couple of lines, remarking "Doctor in attendance: shall I put Dr Talisman Van Linde?"

She nodded.

"And witnesses – Dido Twite and Yorka – can you sign there, my dears?"

Yorka could not write, but made her mark, a little flower-drawing. Dido wrote DIDO. Then Herodsfoot dripped a bit of wax on to the paper from a candle and pressed it with his seal-ring.

"There you are, ma'am, signed, sealed, and all in order: from this moment little miss is safe from all ghostly enemies."

He handed the paper to the Senhora, who looked far from pleased but received it with civility.

"Now we should all return to our chambers," she announced. "Doctor Talisman – I do not know which of my servants admitted you to my house—?"

Dido wondered very much what explanation Doctor Talisman would give for her presence in the mansion, but at this moment they were all startled by a clamour of shouts in another part of the building, and a thunderous banging on some distant door.

"Oh, heavens above, now what?" ejaculated the Senhora.

A footman came running in to announce: "Senhora, it is the Very Honourable Gerente Manoel – with a troop of Civil Guards – he asks admission—"

Dona Esperanza hurried away.

Chapter Six

"COME WITH ME!" WHISPERED A VOICE. "COME with me quickly, meninha – you and your friends!" It was the maid, Katarina. "You must not stay to meet the Gerente Manoel – they say he means you great harm!"

She led them along a passage to a large, damp library, its walls lined with shelves and shelves of musty, leather-bound books which looked as if nobody ever read them. A dying fire faintly warmed the air. In one of a pair of leather-covered armchairs a red-faced man snored, fathoms deep in slumber; a fumy odour of wine came from him, and half a dozen empty bottles lay on the floor by his chair. Dozens of candles in wall-sconces guttered and flickered towards their end.

"Dear me," said Herodsfoot. "Is that our host?"

"Senhor don Enrique," said Katarina. "But he will not stir till noon – he never does – he is full of wine. You will be safe in this room – nobody will think of looking for you here."

"But why should we hide? We have done nothing wrong."

Katarina looked impatient at Herodsfoot's simplicity.

"Not you perhaps, milord – but your friends. First, in the town hospital – the knife-work done on that Outros man – then, in the prison – one of the guards killed – they say the doctor did that—"

"One of the guards *killed?*" said Talisman, astounded. "But I never touched any of the guards – Yorka's aunt Tala'aa let me out while they were all playing Cows and Leopard—"

95

"However that may be, a guard *was* killed. And a page from the doctor's notebook was found on him—"

"Oh, croopus," said Dido, "I reckon it must have been one of the two guards that nabbed me. They were fighting each other – they were half-seas over and both had knives – one of them must have finished off his mate. And now they put the blame on Doc Tally. Well, but I could tell them how it really happened—"

"No," said Talisman. "That would not help. They will never believe you. They will not want to believe you. They will blame us both equally."

"You must at once leave this house," insisted Katarina. "All of you."

"Lord Herodsfoot's not accused of anything," objected Dido. "He could stop."

"And do you think I would stay behind," he said, "when the rest of you have to flee through the forest? I agree, it does seem the height of injustice when, by what I am told, Doctor Talisman has almost certainly just saved that poor girl's life – and brought her baby in to the world – but I fear these Angrian folk are not at all reasonable – especially when it comes to the treatment of women—"

"Hush!" entreated Katarina.

They could hear heavy footsteps and voices all over the house. Some passed the library door. They heard someone ask a question, and apparently receive a negative answer.

"So how are we to get away from here?" breathed Dido.

"I show you Don Enrique's private way to stable."

Katarina pulled back a section of shelves lined with sham books and opened a door. A flight of steps descended to a yard. Katarina led them round it, keeping in shadow, and so to the stables. She whispered something to a sleepy stable-hand who, without argument, brought out their horses. In another yard, not far away, they could hear the stamping, shouting, clatter, and whinnying of the Guards troop who had come in search of them; the noise drowned the sound of their own horses' hoofs as they moved away down the track.

"Katarina, thank you, *thank* you!" whispered Dido. "I hope you won't be in trouble from this—"

"No, no, meninha, why should they think of me? Now, make haste, make haste—"

The horses were rested (all except Talisman's mule, but it, luckily, had not had such a long journey on the previous day) and so they went quickly down the valley occupied by the Quinquilho ranch and into another one where the forest grew thick and untouched. By now the greenish light of dawn was beginning to flood the sky.

Lord Herodsfoot was still fretting about their unceremonious departure.

"No chance to say thanks to the old lady – not that she was very friendly – but after all she did give us dinner and beds—"

"I wonder if she is a friend of Manuel Roy?" said the doctor

Herodsfoot turned towards her eagerly. "Are you acquainted with that man? I believe I heard Dido say that you had met him in Europe?"

"Yes, my adopted father and I used to meet him here and there in gambling towns. And he often urged me to take a trip back to Aratu some time – suggested that I should return to visit the place where I was born—"

"Now I wonder why he did that?" mused Herodsfoot. "Do you think he can have had some private motive?"

"Why do you say that?"

"Old Asoun told me – when I was staying with him and we were discussing affairs in Aratu – he said Manoel is devouringly ambitious – he would like to succeed his brother as ruler of the island. Also, he hates his brother, who stopped supplying him with money to travel to

Europe. (Apparently there was some disgraceful episode – he cheated at cards, or killed a man in a duel – the Forest People, of course, know all these things.)"

"But why would Manoel want Doc Tally back here?" broke in Dido, who was riding, with Yorka perched on her saddle-bow, a few paces behind the others. "The island folk might like Tally better than him? If old John King's her father? If she's the heir? If she's the kid that got chucked in the sea?"

"My dear, do you think you are that child?" Herodsfoot asked Talisman.

She replied simply, "Yes, I do."

"Do you have any positive proof?"

"Yes, my medallion." she said. "With my name on it. Jane Kirlingshaw. King's name was Kirlingshaw before he changed it to King. Aunt Tala'aa said so."

"Yes," said Herodsfoot. "So I heard also from Asoun. That seems quite conclusive."

Wonder why he seems so glum about it, thought Dido.

"Do you have any ambition to become ruler of Aratu?"

"Oh, good heavens, no, none," Talisman said impatiently. "I want to be a doctor. A good one."

Lord Herodsfoot looked a trifle more cheerful. "A very proper ambition!" he congratulated her. "Now: does Manoel, do you think, know or suspect that you are his niece?"

"Oh, yes, I am sure he must," she answered. "I can remember his asking my adopted father all kinds of questions about how and when he found me. Yes – it does seem to hang together – he wanted me back on this island for reasons of his own. Perhaps to kill me, do you think? To eliminate me as a possible rival? That was what he intended when he threw me off the cliff perhaps—"

"Yes, what has happened up to now does suggest that. Or perhaps now he wants to have you under his control –

so that he can use the threat of imprisonment for these trumped-up crimes to get you to do what he wants."

He picked the wrong gal for that, thought Dido. "I don't see Doc Talisman doing what any cove wants, not unless Tally wants it too," she said.

Herodsfoot chuckled. "I quite agree with you there." He gave an admiring, respectful look at the doctor. "But Asoun was telling me about Manoel's plans. He has the support of the townspeople, because they are nearly all Angrians, with their strict, gloomy puritanical beliefs, and they let themselves be run by the Town Guard and lead very narrow lives."

"And treat females like toads," said Dido.

"Just so. But Manoel has little support from the Forest People, who live so differently. And the Forest People don't like him. Can you wonder? Their power lies in the Kanikke, the witches."

"But why do they accept the rule of John King? He's not a Forest Person."

"No; but he was married to one, and loved her very much, and adopted many of her ways. And he doesn't bother the Forest People and they don't bother him. The Forest People have no ambitions. Whereas the Town People want to cut down more forest and plant more plantations."

"More Forest People than Town People," put in Tylo.

"Yeah," said Dido, "but the Town People are active and pushy, so they get their way more than forest folk, who just want to sing Creation songs and eat bark bread when they are hungry."

"That's it," said Herodsfoot. "Exactly so. I think Manoel wants Doctor Talisman on his side because she would be acceptable to the Forest People. Is, already, one of them because of her mother. To them, she is a Kanikke."

"Yes, I am," said Talisman. "I began to know it almost as

99

soon as I came to Aratu." Dido thought of the scene in Manoel's courtyard. "And then Aunt Tala'aa told me so."

"Well," said Herodsfoot, "it certainly seems as if the most important thing just now is for you to get to see John King. Before somebody tries to throw you back into jail." He sounded depressed again. What a one he is for ups and downs, thought Dido.

Doctor Talisman evidently thought so too, for she said, "Enough of this conversation! Let us have a race. The forest is not so thick here. I will race you to the brook down there," she told Herodsfoot. "Are you ready – go!"

She kicked her mule into a canter and shot alongside of Herodsfoot, who, taken by surprise, needed a moment to get going, but soon overtook her, laughing and waving his hat, then drew ahead. Dido, with the extra weight (not that it was much) of Yorka on her pony, did not try to compete, but rode soberly on down towards the stream.

"He loves that Doc!" said Yorka. "From the minute he first see her."

"Do you think so? I do too," Dido said sadly.

"Why sad? Not bad to love!"

"Golly-good!" said Tylo cheerfully. "Better than hate, anyhow. That Manoel – he hate the whole *world*."

Dido could not explain the complicated pain she felt about Herodsfoot and Talisman. She was fond of them both. In fact, she thought, they were two of the nicest people she had ever come across. But she felt that the road ahead of them was a very slippery and twisty one, and that, however things worked out, the result might not be for the happiness of everybody.

"That girl back at the Quinquilho ranch," she said. "That girl Luisa. Why was the old lady so angry?"

"Because the father of that child a Forest Person," said Tylo. "My uncle's cousin's son Kaubre. Ereira family very angry about that."

100

"Oh, I see," said Dido. "Why isn't Luisa with him? In the forest?"

"He dead. Don Enrique shoot him."

Suddenly Dido had a strong feeling of homesickness for Battersea, London. Battersea was dirty and ugly, maybe, the people who lived there were poor and tough, they had to buy their food, it did not grow on trees, but there was no dark background to them, they all knew each other and did what was expected. Nor did they shoot each other. Or not much.

"There's too much blame mysteriousness about this island," she said.

At the stream, where there was a ford, Herodsfoot and Talisman were waiting for the others, resting their horses, letting them drink.

He was teasing her.

"I don't believe you are really a Kanikke. Or you wouldn't have let me beat you in the race."

Dido thought of telling Herodsfoot how Talisman had climbed up the tower. But she decided not to.

"Just the same, I am a Kanikke," Talisman retorted. "And, by and by – when I see fit – I shall prove it to you."

"Now I do remember you!" Herodsfoot suddenly exclaimed. "You were the little girl in a tartan dress who used to sit, sometimes, rather impatiently, on the steps of the Casino at Bad Szomberg, playing Tricotin in a tiny mother-of-pearl box, while the men were all inside playing Faro and Basset."

"And once you gave me a box of bonbons."

"Did I? I had forgotten that." They smiled at each other.

Tylo said, "Now we got climb up, very steep, to reach the Place of Stones. Got leave horses halfway up – too steep for them."

"You don't think Manoel and the Civil Guard will follow us here?"

"Can't follow through forest. And *nobody* go to Place of Stones. Too bad luck. Only Halmahi and Kanikke, people with strong soul. Most people too scared."

"*Somebody* went there," said Dido, "and pinched the skull that Doc Tally has. Where did you come across it, Doc?"

"My adopted father bought it for me – one time – when he was very rich, when he had won a huge amount of money at Four-Five-Six. He saw it in a curiosity shop in San Firmo, labelled 'Sacred skull from Aratu' and he knew that I wanted a skull anyway for my medical studies – so he bought it. He tried to find out who had sold it to the shop, and from the man's description he believed it was Manoel Roy. He knew that Manoel had lost heavily at the tables the day before – Manoel was always a wild gambler, lost more often than he won – and then, suddenly, he had plenty of money again."

"He had sold the skull? Must have brought it with him from the Place of Stones. It was quite brave of him to go and pinch it," remarked Dido. "If the place is supposed to be so spooky."

"He be sorry later, by golly," said Tylo. "He be sorry by and by."

The forest had thinned now, into patches of giant fern and wild clove trees, with grassy, shrubby stretches in between. It was mid morning, and growing very hot. Yorka showed Dido how to make a hat out of a huge ukka leaf, tied under the chin with grass.

The horses were left tethered in a shady grove when the track became too steep for them to manage, inside a ring of kandu nuts for protection against pearl-snakes, whose bite was just as deadly to horses as to humans. Talisman slung the skull round her neck in an ukka leaf.

The last part of the climb was extremely hard going. Here the ground was almost naked rock, silvery grey in colour, and thinly covered with pale dust, which made it slippery and treacherous underfoot.

"One thing – at least there's no snakes hereabouts," gasped Dido, when her feet had shot from under her for the sixth time, and she picked herself up, cross, bruised, and scraped. "Snakes have got more sense than climb this hill."

Instead of snakes there were birds – huge grey eagles floating almost motionless overhead, "Looking," Dido said, "as if for two ukka seeds they'd drop down and scrunch us up for their lunch—" and she sighed, for it seemed a long time since the meal they had eaten at the Quinquilho ranch the night before.

They were now up so high that a large part of the island was visible: behind them the forest like a rug of thick brilliant green fur; beyond, and all around, the celestial blue of the ocean. Ahead of them, slightly to the right, or west, rose the conical peak of Mount Fura, dark with trees up to half its height, then pale rock and scrub.

"It was once a volcano," said Lord Herodsfoot. "But extinct now, I am happy to say." From his saddle-bag he had taken a small telescope, and carried it with him up the mountain; through it, he studied the prospect ahead. "I think I can see a house, high on the mountainside; I suppose that is King's palace – Limbo Lodge – strange name to give it! It looks so close from here; hard to believe it is still a day's journey away."

Tylo took the glass from Herodsfoot and squinted through it. "Is so: that Limbo Lodge. But much far still; long golly-hour walking. Go down, then up."

"Yes, I see," said Dido, taking her turn with the glass. "There's a big gully in between us and that mountain, ain't there?"

Between the two greens – the green of the forest on this side, dark emerald in colour, and the paler, greyer green of the woods on Mount Fura – there could be seen a distant gap.

"Is there a river down there in that deep gorge?"

"Kai river," said Tylo nodding. "Very deep – fast river – probable must go down to cross beach – crocodiles too—"

"Don't they have a bridge?" asked Dido, who did not fancy the sound of crocodiles.

"Did have bridge, old Sovran John ordered smash. So I heard."

"*Why?*"

Tylo shrugged. "Don't want people see him too easy."

"But he's the ruler!" said Talisman. "It *should* be easy—"

"Do you think so?" said Herodsfoot. "Now, if I were the ruler – I should never wish to be bothered by subjects – I should sit in my study all day long, drinking Madeira wine and reading Latin poetry—"

"Oh!" She exploded with outrage, then saw that he was teasing her. "You should not say things like that – even in joke! It is a ruler's duty to listen to the needs of his people."

"But he's deaf, poor man – or so I understand – he simply can't hear what they ask him."

"Yes, that is true," put in Yorka. "He not hear any voice at all. People talk to him, they write word in book."

"Some say he lose hearing when skull taken from Place of Stones."

"Oh well," said Dido hopefully, "in that case, when Doc Tally puts the skull *back* in its hidey-hole, maybe the old cove will get back the use of his lug-holes. When do we get to this blessed Place of Stones, Tylo? My legs feel like banana peel."

A warm thick mist, damp and fresh, suddenly drifted down out of the sky as they climbed, and now hung close around them, blocking out the distant view.

"Keep go straight up hill," said Tylo. "Hold hands." He

took the hands of Dido and Yorka. Herodsfoot grasped the doctor's hand.

"This is like the mists in Ireland, where I come from," he said. "Have you ever been there, Talisman?"

"No, never."

"It's a beautiful country. I should like to take you there sometime."

Dido sighed.

They walked on cautiously through the thick whiteness.

"You ever been here before?" Dido whispered to Yorka. Somehow the denseness of the mist, the lack of visibility, made it natural to whisper.

Yorka shook her head.

"My auntie Tala'aa come here at Thunder Time. With other Kanikke. To talk to the Old Ones."

"Who are they?"

They, Dido learned, were the ancestors, who had put the stones in the Place of Stones at the beginning of things, long, long ago.

"Many, many treetimes."

"Don't this mist smell sweet? It's like breathing sugar and spice."

"Carry far sounds, too."

This was true. A faint, distant drumming could be heard, even by the non-forest people.

"I suppose old Asoun, or your Aunt Tala'aa, would know what those drums were saying?" Dido said to Yorka, and noticed a fleeting look of disquiet on Talisman's face.

Suddenly the steep slope flattened. Unexpectedly, they had come to the top of the rise, and stood on level ground, still in a close group, clasping each others' hands. And at the same moment they realised that they were among the Stones – three black monoliths reared up immediately around them, each one the height of a two-storey house.

105

And a fourth slab was perched horizontally across the tops of two of the others.

"*My word!*" cried out Herodsfoot with immense enthusiasm. "A cromlech! (Or, as the Bretons would have it, a dolmen.) And a very, very fine specimen!"

Peering about in the murk, they could see many more of the great stones close at hand; but all the others had fallen down. There were nine fallen ones, Dido reckoned, and a number of the flat slabs which must have rested on top, but many of those were shattered, so it was hard to decide how many there had been.

"Where d'you think your skull oughta go, Doc?" Dido murmured softly.

Of the three standing stones, one was bigger than the two others and stood apart from them. Talisman knelt down and examined its base.

"I'd been told that the skulls were buried under the upright stones, but they seem to be standing on solid rock," she whispered. "It is amazing that they have *stayed* standing for so long. They seem to be just balanced, not sunk into the ground—"

"No, look, Doc—" Dido had laid her cheek on the ground and was squinting closely at the base of another standing monolith. Then she went and studied one of the fallen stones. "This is really clever! See, they were pegged on to the ground. This one had a spur carved out on its underside that fitted into a slot in the rock below. A bit of the spur is busted off, but you can see how it was done – here's the hole in the rocky ground where it went, and there's a matching bit of the spur, still plugged in the hole. If I had a knife or a skewer I believe I could prise it out—"

Herodsfoot had a folding knife with an attachment for removing stones from horses' hoofs. This proved just right for delving the broken section of rock out of the hole.

"Now: I bet it fits on to the broken bit here, below the

big 'un, see—" said Dido proudly, and demonstrated. "Yes! It does! But how in the world did they hoist all them monster stones up this mountain – let alone fitting them like keys into keyholes—?"

Herodsfoot, meanwhile, was looking into the hole. "This goes deeper than the piece you took out, Dido," he said, and thrust in his arm, groping about in the cavity. "Yes, I thought so. See here!" and withdrawing his hand he triumphantly exhibited another skull, black, and coated with sand.

"Oh, put it back, *put it back*!" cried Yorka and Talisman, both together.

Lord Herodsfoot looked a little dismayed.

"Oh – yes – I suppose you are right—" he said sadly, gazing at the ebony-coloured skull. "I do covet it, I must confess! It is such a very perfect specimen – it *does* seem a pity—"

"No, no, quick, put it back," said Tylo, and Dido agreed. "Honest, mister – lord – Frankie – you better – listen!"

The sound of drumming had intensified. The throbbing in the air was like the hum of giant bees. Then, suddenly, to everyone's petrifaction, they heard voices. It was as if a window had opened, for a moment, into a room where people were talking. Some of the words spoken were in unknown languages, deep and guttural or sharp and bird-like. But some could be understood. A man's voice, loud and deep, said: "I will not have this!" Other, shriller voices could be heard begging, praying: "For mercy's sake, for mercy's sake!"

Yorka and Tylo clung to each other, white-faced. Dido and Herodsfoot looked around wildly. Talisman took two steps to Herodsfoot, removed the skull from his hands and speedily returned it to the hole from which he had taken it.

Then she said: "I think we should put something – a gift – to show we meant no harm—"

107

After a moment's frowning thought she took out her little notebook (which Dido had returned to her) and tucked it into the hole with the skull.

"Is well done," agreed Yorka, and added her necklace of nuts. Tylo put in a little knife made from a shell. Dido thought of her game-cloth – but it was too large to go into the hole, so she cut off a lock of her hair with Tylo's knife. Herodsfoot, visibly grieving, added his tiny shell of djeela-nut oil.

"You really think—?" he said. Their silent looks persuaded him.

As Talisman replugged the hole with the piece of rock that had been cut to fit, the drumming died down to a whispering throb.

Dido, looking sharply about, said, "Hey! I bet *this* is the hole where that so-and-so Manoel dug out the other skull – lookahere, Doc Tally!"

She pointed to a hole in the ground near the base of one of the fallen stones, with a lump of square-carved rock, evidently the plug which had come from it, lying nearby. Talisman probed the hole, but it contained no skull.

"I believe you are right, Dido." She slipped in the skull she had brought, and plugged up the hole with the piece of rock, which fitted exactly.

"There!" she said. "Now we have done all we could. I think we should leave this place at once."

Yorka and Tylo vehemently nodded their agreement.

"Oh!" pleaded Herodsfoot. "Can't we stay just a few minutes? This is such a unique, such a truly remarkable site. I would give anything to spend just a little more time here. Or to come back here again."

"Much, much good *not* come here," said Tylo, shivering.

"If it were not so misty!" lamented Herodsfoot. "If only I could make a drawing – I could write *such* an article for the *Journal of Natural Philosophy*—"

Talisman looked at him with sympathy. "Well – just for five minutes, then. Yorka – do you think—?"

She made a slight, sideways beckoning motion with her head; she and Yorka moved away towards the biggest standing stone. Herodsfoot, absorbed in his own activities, was measuring, pacing, scribbling notes about the arrangement of the rocks on the hilltop and making little drawings. "It is like Devil Among the Tailors," he was muttering, "or Dead Wall. The distances are similar, if I am not greatly mistaken."

Meanwhile Talisman and Yorka touched hands, blew on their fingers, and breathed a few words to each other in turn.

Tylo looked wholly disapproving.

"Not good, ask djingli of Old Ones," he muttered. "Not good, I think."

Djingli, Dido remembered, was a favour or tip.

Herodsfoot gave a cry of jubilation. For, all at once, the grey mist lifted, dispersed and was gone in a flash, the three great monoliths, slightly glittering with damp, stood up against a brilliantly blue sky; and a tremendous panorama was visible on every side of the hilltop.

"Oh, bless my soul, *what* a piece of luck," exulted Herodsfoot. "*What* good fortune, couldn't ask for better, upon my word, this is capital, capital—" and he hurried about even faster, pacing distances, reading his compass, taking bearings through his telescope.

"Lord Herodsfoot, we must go *now*," urged Talisman, after a few minutes of this. "We have a long distance to cover still – and we are very exposed, very visible here on this hilltop—" Talisman was extremely pale. Beads of sweat trickled down her brow.

"Oh, my dear girl, I know – but just a couple of minutes more—"

Now he was measuring the height of the monoliths.

Dido had moved out from among the stones – they gave her the cold colly-wobbles, as she muttered to Tylo – and was studying the southern tip of the island, through Herodsfoot's spyglass, which he had laid on a rock while he went to work with a tape-measure. Dido had a good look at John King's residence, two-thirds of the way up Mount Fura. It was a largeish white mansion, situated just at the edge of the tree-line. Its grounds and shrubberies were surrounded by high walls.

"And it's well guarded too," Dido said to Tylo. "I can see dozens of coves all around it. D'you think they will let us in, Tylo? It don't seem mighty likely to me – not if Manoel gets there first and tells his tale. He'll tell King that Doc Tally and I are a pair of murderers and that Cap Sanderson is a djeela-nut smuggler."

"Maybe so," said Tylo uncertainly. "Best we get on, hurry, get there first."

"Any chance you got a cousin there among the guard?"

He shook his head. "Not I know."

Dido turned the telescope eastwards. Here Mount Fura seemed to come to an abrupt stop – the gentle curve ended in a perpendicular line that ran straight down to the ocean.

"Blimey – is that the Cliff of Death?"

Tylo nodded.

"How high?"

"I no know. Cliff is sacred place – no one allowed there. Unless they go to jump. Maybe three-hundred-men high?"

Dido had not the least guess how high that might be. She thought, if the top of the cliff is a forbidden place, and Manoel went there to throw the baby over, that's another black mark he chalked up against himself with the Old 'Uns who set up the stones. I reckon he's in for big trouble, by and by. I only wisht it would come soon . . .

"*Please* Lord Herodsfoot – you *must* come away—"

"A moment – just let me get the dimensions of this big feller—"

Now, with his tape, he was measuring the circumference of the biggest monolith.

"Well I'll be blessed!" exclaimed Dido.

She had tracked the telescope down to the little harbour where the Kai river ran out into the ocean, at the eastern base of Mount Fura. Mount Fura was, in fact, a small steep island, separated from the rest of Aratu by the Kai ravine. And the harbour – Dido remembered it was called Manati, and there was a fishing village – was Aratu's only beach, all the rest of the coastline being craggy rock that fell straight into the sea.

"What you see?" inquired Tylo.

"There's the *Siwara*! In that little harbour; she's just tying up. Come and see, Doc Tally!" she called.

But Talisman was saying to Herodsfoot, "Listen, my friend, I lifted the mist for you – which was hard work. You have had time to do your drawings, now you really must be sensible and come—"

He burst out laughing. "*You* lifted that mist? Oh, my dear girl, come *on*! The mist going was just a happy accident – very sorry, but you can't take the credit for *that*!"

She gave him a very cool look. "Is that what you think?"

"My dear, it's what I *know*. Very sorry – but I'm not buying that one! Now – just one job more—" He placed his compass on the ground and made some calculations.

Doctor Talisman was angry. Two small red spots appeared on her cheekbones. She pressed her lips tightly together. Then she said: "You wish to return to this place?"

"Of course! Very, very much. If not on this visit to Aratu, then on some future visit."

"You don't really believe I am a Kanikke, do you?"

"My dear, I am quite sure that *you* believe it."

"Well, I will show you something."

111

Talisman picked up a small bone that was lying in the dust at the foot of the great monolith. Herodsfoot's eyes widened. He exclaimed, "Why, great heavens, I believe that is a man's finger-bone!"

"Never mind that. What is your full name?"

"My full name?" He was puzzled. "It is Algernon Francis Sebastian Fortinbras Carsluith, Baron Herodsfoot."

Using the bone, Talisman wrote these names on the smooth dusty rock.

"Now," she said. "That writing will remain there until your next visit."

He was very much amused. "That's a safe promise! When you know the chances against my coming back here are about a hundred to one – maybe five hundred to one!"

Chuckling, he packed away his writing tablet and prepared to descend the hill. "But it is a very, very kind gesture, my dear, and I am greatly obliged to you – I shall take the will for the deed."

Chapter Seven

A s THEY WALKED DOWN THE HILL, THE MIST rose again and swirled about them.

"How very lucky we were to have that interval of sunshine," said Herodsfoot happily.

He seemed unaware of any atmosphere, other than the mist. But Dido, walking between Yorka and Talisman, noticed Yorka give a quick, glancing look upwards at the doctor; Talisman's face remained completely blank.

"Yes; that was a piece of luck," she said after a moment.

"I suppose," Herodsfoot teased her, "now that my name is written up on that rockface in your handwriting, you'd say that put me in your power?"

"Would I say so?"

"Because of your being a Kanikke. And that being such a sacred place."

"Are you trying to make fun of the things the Forest People believe? I thought you sympathised with the Forest People? And understood their beliefs?"

"I do understand them. And I go halfway – well, one-third of the way – to sharing *some* of their beliefs. Isn't that enough? Nobody can share *all* of anybody else's beliefs. I know that one must be respectful; and on no account must one make fun of them. Isn't *that* enough?"

Suddenly his voice, his face had grown very anxious. "Dear Talisman, I'll believe in the fairy queen and Robin Goodfellow and – and King Oberon and the whole bag of tricks if only you won't be cross with me."

"It was never my intention to – *oh*," she cried out impatiently, "how I wish we had not been obliged to come here! The Forest People are quite right, it *is* a bad-luck place."

The mist had dispersed by the time they reached the grove where the horses had been tethered, and they saw there was a woman, one of the Forest People, waiting there. When she saw Talisman she made a deep bow and then fell on her knees beseechingly.

"Wise One, will you come to my wocho? It is my son – my little Oynat—" She spoke the Dilendi language; by now Dido understood enough to follow, and it seemed the doctor did too. "It is his eyes, Excellence. He sees nothing but devils. He is very much afraid. So are we all . . ."

"Yes, of course I will come." Talisman picked up her medical bag which she had left with the horses. "How far is it?"

"In the forest – two, perhaps three hours from here."

Herodsfoot began to protest. "But what about our plan to go to Limbo Lodge?"

"I *must* see what I can do for this woman's son," Talisman said patiently. "When I have done that, I will either join you this evening – where do you spend the night . . .?"

"It is at the house of a man called Ruiz – an Angrian, but he lives by himself in the forest," Herodsfoot said. "Tylo has been telling me about him."

"Well, if I can get there by midnight I will find somebody to guide me. Or I will come tomorrow morning."

Herodsfoot seemed wholly dissatisfied with this plan, but Talisman had already mounted her mule. "Yorka, will you come with me? In case there is anything I don't understand?" Yorka nodded. "We can all take it in turns to ride the mule."

The three set off at a rapid trot, going westwards.

"I don't know – I wish—" Herodsfoot began uneasily. "Was that woman telling a *true* tale?"

114

Tylo took no notice of this. "Best not hang-stand here, lordship," he urged. "Come quick off this hill."

It was plain that he regretted losing the company of Doctor Talisman; he looked after her sadly. He seemed to feel that her presence conferred some protection on the group.

Dido was sorry, too. Doctor Talisman was one of the most sensible people she had ever come across and – despite the fact that Tylo was a shrewd boy and knew his way all about the island – Dido felt that Lord Herodsfoot, though he had a kind heart and engaging manners, was like a loose cannon on a ship's deck: there was simply no knowing where he would roll off to next. It's lucky at least that most of the folk here seem to like him, she thought.

"So tell more about this Mario Ruiz feller," Dido asked Tylo as they jogged along a winding glade, hung about with dangling creepers and frilled with tree-ferns. "If he's an Angrian, why the dickens does he choose to live all on his lonesome in the forest? Does he have a spice plantation like the Ereiras?"

"No, no. He humble fellow. Not rich."

"What does he live on?"

"Hot spring near house. People sometime come, bathe, drink water."

"And pay him for that? I see. I wonder *why* he likes to live alone?"

"He wifie die. He a bit noddle-stricken." Tylo tapped his forehead.

"Bats in the belfry, you mean? I hope he's harmless."

"Now-and-now," said Tylo.

Dido reflected that people in Aratu whose wives died tended to grow peculiar. There was John King, shutting himself up in Limbo Lodge; and this Ruiz, choosing to settle in the jungle by a hot spring.

"Well, he sure fixed to live at the back of beyond."

115

Their way now led them up a deep narrow gorge with a watercourse beside the path, which was half hidden underneath juicy vegetation.

Lord Herodsfoot became very silent after Talisman left them, and rode for over two hours wrapped in thought.

Coming out of this meditation at last, he suddenly asked Dido: "Do you think she was angry with me?"

There could be no doubt who the *she* was that he referred to.

"Well yes – I reckon she was; a bit," said Dido bluntly.

"But why? Just for teasing her? Because she lays claim to magical powers? I mean, *really*!" said Herodsfoot. "I'm sure she's a good doctor and a clever girl – but one has to draw the line somewhere! Don't you think?"

"Mylord Oklosh," said Tylo very positively, "Doc Tally come-soon-been right-up Kanikke. She learn touch trouble-stone, write true question on black sand. She learn do all these things with Aunt Tala'aa. Own sister to Night Woman . . ."

"How can you be so sure?" Herodsfoot said sceptically. "Pray, when is all this supposed to have taken place?"

"When she see Aunt Tala'aa. Time with Aunt Tala'aa go—" Tylo made an expressive gesture, moving his hands back and forth.

"I don't see how all that *could* have happened – just in one night," argued Herodsfoot obstinately. "Really – surely – she is just an ordinary person – like you and me and Dido here. After all – she only arrived in this island two days ago. She *told* me so."

We ain't so blooming ordinary, Dido thought: I never before met *anybody* like Herodsfoot here – or Tylo, for that matter – and I guess *I'm* the only one on this island who comes from Battersea . . .

There was a loud crack of thunder overhead and a few heavy drops of rain began to splash down.

116

"I hope we ain't too far from the wocho of this Ruiz feller," Dido called to Tylo, who was riding about twenty yards ahead. "Sounds like dirty weather coming up—"

"Yes, must make haste—" he called back, and kicked his pony into a canter.

Ten seconds later a terrifying thing happened. The whole cliffside on their left, loosened perhaps by storms, suddenly became detached and roared down on to the trail with an ear-splitting booming rumble which reverberated up and down the narrow gully for several minutes after the first fall, as more and more fragments were dislodged from the rockface and followed the first landslide.

The horses of Dido and Herodsfoot screamed with terror and reared back from the huge pile of rock and earth which now blocked the way.

"Save us!" gasped Dido. "Tylo! TYLO! – Where are you?"

No answer came back from the monstrous heap of smoking rubble in front of them.

And at this moment the gathering storm broke in all its fury: rain lashed down in torrents, tremendous gusts of wind battered them, thunder cracked and pealed overhead, blue-white lightning made the scene stand out in nightmarish clarity.

"Oh my goodness *gracious* me!" lamented Herodsfoot. "That poor poor unfortunate boy! I fear he has indubitably perished under this shocking avalanche. There is no way in the world that we can rescue him! It is only by the mercy of providence that we ourselves did not likewise perish."

He seemed likely to go on in this vein for some time, but Dido said, "We'd best not stop here a-grieving and a-chewing it over, lordship. I'm as sorry as can be about Tylo, he was a right decent feller, but it ain't noways healthy here, we'd best go back. No *way* of going forward; and more of the cliff above us looks likely to come down. You can see the nags ain't happy—"

"I fear you are in the right," sighed Herodsfoot. "You do not think there is any chance that, if we called the boy's name, he might be able to respond?"

"Can try again, but I doubt it," Dido said. She yelled, "*Ty – lo!*" at the top of her lungs, so that her voice echoed between the sides of the ravine.

The only result was that some more pieces of rock and soil came clattering down on to the existing heap.

"No, mister, it ain't a bit of use. If he *is* there – on the far side of that devilish tip – he can't hear us, not with all the ruckus going on. All we can do is make tracks ourselves before we're pounded into mincemeat."

She turned her horse, and set off at a fast clip, trusting to the beast to find his own footing, for the rain in her face blinded her. Herodsfoot followed, letting out a stream of ejaculations and objurgations relating to the weather and the fate of Tylo and their own horrid plight.

"What shall we *do?*" he kept demanding. "What ever shall we do, Dido? Where shall we go now? What do you think is best to be done?"

"Well," said Dido, "we have to find the house of this Ruiz, for that's where Doc Tally said she'd meet us. And I remember Tylo saying earlier that there were two ways to get there and we'd take the quicker one – but he said there was another way over the top of the ridge. Best we go back and find that, if we can. There was a clump of nutmeg shrubs where he was telling me that; I remember those, just at the turn-off point. Trouble is, everything looks so different with the rain slamming down."

"You don't think we should endeavour to take shelter for a while from the elements?" suggested Lord Herodsfoot plaintively. The wind lashed them, the rain slapped them, huge branches, tossing, impeded their path.

"Nowhere *to* take shelter," returned Dido briefly. Rubbing her eyes against the rain, she peered ahead. "Ho!

I believe that's the nutmeg clump – now we have to go up over that rise, and then kinda bear right, so as to get back towards where he was heading before. It's too bad the nags ain't in better heart."

The horses were nervous and weary, upset by the storm. Arriving at a grove of tall, broad-leaved trees, Herodsfoot proposed again that they stop for a few minutes. "I believe the storm is abating," he pointed out hopefully. "A short respite may put new heart into our mounts."

It soon appeared that Lord Herodsfoot had a personal motive for wishing to halt at that particular spot. The sky was clearing and he had recognised, up above them, the unmistakable outline of the Place of Stones.

"Oh, I would give *worlds* – all the worlds I have to give – to pay another visit to that remarkable site."

At this, Dido was really shocked. The loss of Tylo – and their predicament – seemed to her incontestable reasons why they should keep going and cover as much ground as they possibly could before dusk fell, in order to reach their destination in daylight. But Herodsfoot had already dismounted and fastened his reins to a tree – she did not dare let him go off on his own, for heaven only knew how long he would stay up there, measuring, sketching, taking notes – and then he would very likely go down the wrong side of the hill and get himself lost . . .

So, reluctant, disapproving, and irate, Dido followed him up the hill. One circumstance, she noticed, made the climb easier than it had been on their previous visit – the heavy rain had rinsed off the dust which had formerly coated the rock surface. Although wet, it was not so slippery as it had been before, and the warm rock dried off quickly as soon as the rain ended.

"We mustn't stop there longer than *five* minutes!" Dido called, and wished with all her heart that Talisman were there to reinforce this command.

"Yes ... yes ... very well, very well," he muttered distractedly. "I cannot tell you how very significant the arrangement of these stones appears to me – how closely related the pattern is to – for instance – the game of Pong Hau K'i – or the game of Mulnello Quadruplo – (mind you, there is grave doubt as to whether that game was ever actually *played* – according to report, each player had five men, which were entered in alternate turns of play. When all five were in place, they had the power of moving in any direction to a contiguous point)—"

Herodsfoot's voice dried up. He came to a total stop.

Dido, just behind him, observed that he had turned chalk-white. He was staring at the ground as if he had seen a deadly snake.

Coming up alongside, Dido too stared at the ground, and found her own breathing suddenly blocked at a point somewhere between her chest and her throat. No air would go in, no air could come out.

She leaned forward, put her hands on her knees, and managed, with a gasp, to inhale.

On the dust, inscribed with a finger-bone just as Talisman had left them, were Herodsfoot's list of names: Algernon Francis Sebastian Fortinbras Carsluith, Baron Herodsfoot.

Everywhere else, on the slightly dome-shaped surface of the Place of Stones, the dust had been washed, blownswept, sluiced away by the storm. But just in this one spot the surface of the rock was quite dry; the letters remained in the dust exactly as Talisman had written them.

Dido picked up a great sodden ukka-leaf, which had blown up the hill, and swiftly wiped the words away, scrubbing the ground hard until there was nothing to be seen but some streaks of wet grit.

"Come along, my lord," she said briskly. "We must not waste any more time hereabouts. Dear knows how long it

120

will take us to get from this place to where Mario Ruiz lives."

She caught hold of Herodsfoot's hand and gave it a yank, obliging him to move away from the patch of ground where his name had been written.

"That's the dandy – come along – those nags will soon take a chill, so wet as they are, if they are left standing any longer. And *we* shall take a chill too—"

Gabbling out whatever random cautions and words of advice came into her head, she urged her companion back into the saddle, and untied his horse's tether. Once he made as if to push his spectacles off, by the earpiece, and she cried out sharply, "*Don't* do that, or you'll go and break them again—" and he gave her a startled look and desisted. Otherwise he seemed like a man in the grip of nightmare or paralysis; he sat his horse, staring straight ahead, and made no attempt to guide it, leaving it to follow where Dido led.

She found a kind of deer-track which crossed over a shrubby hillside and then led down to lower ground. Over to the right of this route, she hoped, was the gorge they had been threading when the fatal landslide occurred.

Did *she* make that happen? Dido wondered – Talisman? So he'd be *obliged* to go back to the stone circle and see his name? Did she lay out the whole business on purpose to teach him a lesson?

Somehow Dido could not believe this of Talisman. She might be impatient, yes, might lose her temper, yes; but to set a whole trap for the poor fellow – involving a storm, a landslide, and the loss of Tylo – no, no, surely not? Tally's a *good* person, Dido thought; so's he, for that matter, not an ounce of harm in the poor dear gentleman – it's too bad they got acrost each other.

Now the track ran down again into forest, thick, dark and green.

Dear only hope this is the right way, thought Dido apprehensively, for once we're in these trees you can't tell which way you're going, north, south, east or west – you might as well be in the main drain under Petticoat Lane. Don't I jist wish I had one o' those Memory Birds that the Forest People take around with them!

To her utter astonishment, no sooner had this thought framed itself than one of the little white, pink-headed birds fluttered down out of the branches above and settled on her horse's brow-band.

"Well – I'll – be jiggered!" gasped Dido. "Lord Herodsfoot – Frankie! look and see what's come!"

He gave her a lacklustre glance, hardly seeming to take in what she said, and rode on in silence. After a mile or two he said, "Did *you* see those words, Dido? Or did I dream them?"

"No, the words were there, mister, sure enough," said Dido. "I reckon there's a lot more in Doc Tally than meets the eye. I guess you just gotta put that in your kettle and boil it . . ."

Herodsfoot made a sound like a man who has just swallowed a raw egg, ice cold.

"Why? *Why*?" he cried out woefully. "Why can't she just be an ordinary person?"

"Well – you gotta face it, Frank – she *ain't* an ordinary person. And maybe if she were you wouldn't fancy her so much."

"I don't know – I just do not know," he said miserably. "I've travelled all over the globe – I possess a larger collection of Ancient and Interesting Games than anybody else in the Western Hemisphere – but I have never felt like this before, and I do not know what to do."

"Best thing you can do," said Dido practically, "is to collect all your games together and get yourself off this plaguey island and back to Lunnon Town and cheer up poor old King Jamie. That's summat you *can* do – and you're the only cove as can do it, seemingly. So that's what you must do. If we can get ahold of Cap Sanderson and the *Siwara*."

And she sighed.

Funny thing, she thought, when we were on the *Siwara* Doc Tally didn't seem anything out of the common. O' course then she was putting on an act, letting on to be a man – both Mr Mully and I twigged that, and very likely Cap Sanderson did too and thought it none of his affair – but then she was just like anybody else, seemingly, an ordinary enough young feller-me-lad. It was coming ashore on Aratu changed that. Doing that job on Mr Mully in the hospital – wonder how he's getting on? – and that game with the bowl of water in Manoel's yard – it was then I began to feel there was summat havey-cavey about her. No, not havey-cavey – but spookish. Maybe meeting Manoel again kinda twitched her. It must be a bit creepy to meet a feller that you are pretty sure once stuffed you in a clay pot and chucked you off the Cliff of Death. It'd sure make the cold slithers run down *my* back. And then the night she put in with Yorka's auntie, the old Kanikke lady. I guess that was what really changed her . . .

"Fancy, Frankie," she said. "I believe that's a house ahead of us! I reckon the Memory Bird brought us to Mr Ruiz' residence."

They were at the end of a long open glade. The customary fragrance of clove, cinnamon, djeela, ukka, and frangipani was now augmented by woodsmoke and the savour of broiling meat. Dido remembered – not for the first time – that she was ravenously hungry.

Mario Ruiz' house was perched against a slope of hill covered with tree ferns. It was neither in the wocho nor the Angrian style of architecture, being long and low, solidly built of logs, with a wooden shingled roof. The windows were screened and there was a stout door. An open stable or shed was built on to the end of the house. Patches of corn, okra, plantains, and coffee bushes grew in front of the building; fruit trees grew beyond it. All seemed orderly and peaceful. A man sat reading on a sawed-off log near the front door. He was a tall, skinny individual, an Angrian, with bushy, rusty grey hair and a deeply lined, gloomy face. He stood up, bowed as they approached him, and addressed himself to Lord Herodsfoot.

"Greetings, senhor! Salutations! You do much honour to my poor residence."

With a brief glance at Dido, Ruiz went on, "Tell your peon to stable the horses in that barn. Allow me to offer you a glass of wine."

This cove is supposed to be a bit off his rocker, Dido remembered; when I said that I hoped he was harmless, Tylo said – what *did* Tylo say? . . . Still the guy seems quiet and friendly enough – it sure is lucky how almost everybody *does* feel friendly to Frankie right off – I will say that for him.

—*But, oh, Tylo, where are you now?*

Reaching the stable Dido received a shock. For there was Tylo's pony, tied up, peacefully munching fodder, along with a mule and a few goats.

Dido's first impulse was to rush back to the house and find out if Tylo was there; her next was to see to the horses and look about her, before following the two men indoors. If Tylo *is* here, then, she thought, he's all hunky-dory; the nag seems well enough – and it never does harm, in a strange place, to check around, take a gander, count the exits and mark the loose floorboards. I wonder where the hot spring is that Tylo spoke of? Along there by the bank, maybe, where all those tall grasses and reeds are a-growing?

Remembering the hot spring made her feel thirsty; she thought, here's a well, anyhows, and a bucket on a rope. I'll take some water to the nags and drink a mouthful or two myself. Wouldn't trust the feller's wine. I jist hope Herodsfoot has the sense not to drink too much of it . . .

She was about to lower the pail into the well when, looking over the stone coping that encircled it, she received an even more atrocious shock: down below the rim she could see the head of Tylo, just above the level of the water.

"*Tylo!*" she gasped.

He heard her, but could not reply; a bandage was tied over his mouth.

"Here – haul yourself up!" whispered Dido, dropping the rope's end to him. But he shook his head and raised his hands; she could see that they were bound round and round, tightly together, with yards of cord.

"Croopus – I'll come down and get you."

This proved not at all easy. The well was narrow: Dido had to undo the bucket and go down head-first, binding herself to the well-rope by a travelling loop which – very fortunately – she had learned from a petty-officer on H.M.S. *Thrush* – then, hanging head-down, she had to undo Tylo's hands. The rope around his wrists was too tight, and by now soaked with water, for fingers to be of any use here; she had to work herself back up the rope, extract Herodsfoot's knife from his saddle-bag, then slither down again and saw through the strands round Tylo's wrists. All this had to be done very quietly; she was terrified that Ruiz might come out and discover what was going on.

Even after Tylo's wrists were free, his hands were at first too weak for him to be able to pull himself up, and Dido, hanging head-down, was not able to do more than support his weight and rub his wrists until, at last, by a few nods, he was able to assure her that now he thought he could climb out. Dido retreated up the rope, then lay flat on her stomach by the well and helped haul Tylo upwards. With a huge gulp of joy and relief she saw his bandaged head appear over the rim of the well, and dragged him out on to the grass. Then with the knife she cut off the gag over his mouth.

"Golly-heyo – Shaki-miss!" he gasped.

"*Oh, Tylo!*"

They hugged each other frantically. Tylo was slippery, coated in slime, since he had been sunk in the mud at the bottom of the well up to his neck.

"Think I sink much more too soon!" he said. "Think I sink over here."

He laid his hand across his eyes.

"But why did that man *do* it?"

"He noddle-stricken."

"You can say that again!"

"He think his mother send me."

"Why the pest should he think *that?* Or why should that put him in a pucker?"

"I bring him a bunch of toro fruit I see hang on vine."

Tylo explained that the mother of Ruiz had once tried to poison him with toro fruit (or so he had thought at the time) so it was a most unfortunate piece of bad luck that Tylo happened to arrive carrying the same gift. Ruiz had at once gone berserk and flown at Tylo. He was as strong as a gorilla.

"But maybe, by now, golly-likely, he forget all about me."

"Tell you what," said Dido, "put on one of Herodsfoot's shirts – I see he's got two spares in his saddle-bag – then you won't look the same and most likely the cove won't recognise you."

Tylo did this – laughing heartily and admiring himself; for the shirt was Lord Herodsfoot's best, with fine frilled cuffs – and then they went cautiously into the house.

All indoors appeared entirely peaceful and orderly. It was plain that the first thing Herodsfoot had spotted in Ruiz' living room was a game-board and a pack of cards. The two men were sitting at a small table, completely immersed in a game, which seemed very complicated, for it required cards, dice, ivory counters, as well as the board itself, which was marked out in squares. On each of these was a different emblem: hearts, anchors, crosses, horses' heads, bells, hammers, and swords. The men had glasses of wine beside them, but were so occupied with the game that neither player seemed to have taken more than a sip from his glass. A jug of wine stood on a shelf, a pail of water on the floor.

Dido stepped quietly around behind Lord Herodsfoot, picked up his glass, and emptied it back into the jug. Tylo, with a nod, performed the same service for Ruiz. Then, sniffing the jug, he took it outside and emptied it on to a plantain, before refilling it with water.

Dido began scanning the house for food. She found the meat that Ruiz had been cooking on a spit over the fire, but by now it was burned black, and inedible; he had forgotten all about it. But there were some plantains, which she sliced and fried, and a loaf of corn-bread, fruit, and a bowl of hard white goats' cheese.

She wondered whether to disturb the two men at their game by offering them a meal, but Tylo, in a whisper, dissuaded her. "We eat, Shaki-missie; let them play. Play game – very teryak." He used a Dilendi word that Dido had not heard before, but his gesture made its meaning quite plain: he smoothed his hands in curves in the air as if calming a stormy sea. And Dido could see for herself that absorption in the game was quelling some of Herodsfoot's miserable feelings about Talisman, about how in the world she had contrived to preserve his name, mockingly written in the dust, through a tempest that had torn up whole trees and tossed boulders like peppercorns. Ruiz, likewise, seemed commendably calm and even cheerful; every now and then he laughed with pleasure as some cunning move of his foiled one of Herodsfoot's gambits. It seemed he was the better player – not surprisingly, since he must spend most of his time playing this game against himself.

Dido and Tylo enjoyed a sustaining meal, then she persuaded him to lie down and sleep on Ruiz' bed – a straw-filled mattress on a wooden frame.

"I'll call you, right off, Tylo, if there's any trouble," she whispered, "but I reckon you're in the right of it, the longer those fellers play, the better it'll be for 'em. You sleep now, and I'll get a bit of kip later."

Tylo, who had suffered for at least five excruciating hours, standing in the well, slowly sinking, and not expecting to be rescued, was very glad of the chance to sleep, and nodded gratefully. Dido lit a teaberry candle, sat on a treestump stool, and peacefully watched the two men, wondering how many hours the game would last.

It lasted until dawn. Finally Ruiz shook his last dice, slapped down his last card, and swept all the counters off the board.

"I win, senhor! But, Mother of Light, what a game! The best I ever played! You are a champion player, my friend. I wish you might remain with me for a year."

"Alas!" said Herodsfoot. "There is nothing I would like better, my dear host, but I must return to my own land. The king there lies grievously sick, all for want of a game such as this, to raise his spirits and make the blood run more quickly through his veins."

"Then you must take him this one!" cried Ruiz enthusiastically, pushing cards, counters and dice into a leather bag. "Take it as my gift to the king of your land."

"No, no, I must not do that," said Herodsfoot, though he looked extremely tempted. "You are here alone in the forest, you need your game. I remember it, I will have a copy made."

At this, Ruiz seemed mortally offended. His weathered face darkened to a dusky plum colour.

"If you do not take my gift, senhor, I am dishonoured!"

Oh heavens, now what, Dido thought. Is Herodsfoot saying no to his offer going to knock the cove off his perch again? Surreptitiously she nudged Tylo and wished she was near enough to Herodsfoot to kick his ankle.

She caught his eye and mouthed the words; Take it!

Ruiz glanced angrily about him, all the good effects of the game apparently wiped from his mind. Dido tensed her knees under her, preparing to spring across the room and grab his arm if he suddenly assaulted Herodsfoot.

Then, just at that moment, there came a knock at the door and a voice – two voices – cried: "Hello, there! Is anybody at home?"

Chapter Eight

R UIZ, INSTANTLY DIVERTED FROM HIS ANGER, walked to the door and opened it. Outside, to Dido's huge joy and relief, were the three people that, out of all the world, she could most have wished to see: Talisman, Yorka, and Captain Sanderson.

"My stars! Are you a sight for sore eyes!" Dido whispered to Yorka, hugging her, while, with a deep bow, Ruiz ceremonially welcomed Captain Sanderson, assuring the new arrival that everything in the establishment was entirely at his disposal. Yorka and Talisman he appeared not to notice.

Tylo quietly led the two horses of the new visitors off to the stable. Then Ruiz turned to inspect Talisman and his eyes dilated.

The sun was hot by now, and Talisman had adopted the Angrian style of women's head-gear, wrapping a huge green ukka leaf over her hair and fastening it with a thong of grass. Despite her men's clothes, this made her look unmistakably female, and the sight of her did something drastic to Ruiz' fitful temperament: his eyes flashed, he flushed a dark angry red again, snatched up a sharp knife from a shelf, bounded with tigerish speed to where Talisman stood just inside the doorway, and hurled her to the ground. There he held her with one hand clamped around her throat, and the other, grasping the knife, less than half an inch from her left eye.

"*Now!*" he said, between heavy gasps of breath, "this woman – I can tell – is an accursed sorceress – as was my wife – as was my mother – I can see that, *very* plainly – so, give me one good reason why I should not kill her at once and rid the world of a pest?"

Talisman, perfectly calm, lay looking up into the face of the madman.

"Keep still," she said softly to Herodsfoot and Sanderson, who, transfixed with horror, stood out of reach on the other side of the room.

Then Talisman addressed Ruiz. "Tell me about your wife?" she inquired in an interested conversational manner. "Did she often play games with you? I see that you have many games in your house."

"Games? No, indeed she did not! Games are not for women! She cooked and cleaned and took care of my house. We lived in Regina, peaceably. Then one day a neighbour said to me, 'Thy wife is a witch.' I laughed at him. I did not believe him. 'I will prove it,' he said. 'Come with me at the next full moon.' I went with him at the full moon and saw my wife, with others, picking melanthus pods – which, *all* know, are mostly used by witches. When she came home I accused her and we had bitter words. She told me she picked the pods to make a cure for the ague. I told her she must never do so again. She said nothing. Next day I found a spider in my shoe. Its bite would have been my death. She had planned to kill me."

"So, what did you do?" Talisman asked.

"I threw her off the harbour wall," said Ruiz.

"The spider might have crawled into your shoe by accident."

Ruiz gave a short, wild laugh. "Do you not think I have asked myself that question a thousand thousand times? But no—" he gripped the knife more tightly – "my mother said I had acted rightly, my wife was a witch, and it was well that she should perish, as it would be well that all witches should be wiped out. They practise accursed arts. Their slaughter is a worthy deed."

"In our country," observed Herodsfoot, in an amiable, argumentative tone, "we have no witches."

Talisman grinned up at Herodsfoot encouragingly. Croopus, thought Dido, *she's* a well-plucked 'un.

"A fortunate country, yours!" said Ruiz in evident disbelief. "What afflictions have you, if not witchcraft?" He glanced up at Herodsfoot, and the knife-point moved away, fractionally, from Talisman's eye.

"Scientists," said Herodsfoot after a pause for thought. "We have scientists."

"What crimes do they commit?"

"They seek for knowledge – without stopping to consider what harmful purpose that knowledge may be put to. They make weapons to kill men at long range – instead of fighting hand-to-hand as men were intended to. They make medicines that will send men mad. They make carriages that are powered to run, using the heat of steam, faster than a horse can gallop – needless and dangerous."

"That *is* witchcraft!" said Ruiz triumphantly. "Witchcraft without doubt. Are not such people persecuted and burned?"

"On the contrary, they are highly acclaimed and paid much money," said Herodsfoot. "And now I beg you to let Doctor Talisman go. What harm has she done you? She is not – she is *not* a witch, but a healer, who takes care of sick people and cures illness—"

Ruiz reflected. Then he said, "Tell me more about your country. What other evils do you have?"

"Oh," said Herodsfoot rather desperately, "we have – we have people called lawyers who, for pay, aggravate other men's quarrels—"

"How can that be? Who would pay for such a service?"

"Oh, plenty do. You'd be surprised—"

"And nobody persecutes them, nobody burns them?"

"By no means. They are well paid and respected."

"What folly. *I* would not pay someone to make bad blood between me and a neighbour."

132

"No," said Herodsfoot, "but you believed a neighbour when he told you that your wife was a witch."

Ruiz meditated a while. "If he told me *again*, perhaps, the next time I would not believe him."

Quite casually he stood up, dropped the knife – it fell within three inches of Talisman's eye – and moved to put a pot of water on the fire. Happening to notice a bamboo flutelike instrument on a shelf among jars of dice and counters, he picked it up and asked, "Can you play music on this, senhor?"

Speechless, Herodsfoot shook his head. Tylo, who had returned from seeing to the horses, volunteered: "I play that, Shaki-lord. Very good."

"Play then," said Ruiz, who did not seem to remember Tylo at all.

Tylo began to play – a quick, monotonous tune on about five notes.

Talisman unobtrusively stood up and dusted herself off. Herodsfoot moved towards the door, giving her an inquiring look, but she shook her head.

"He will be better now," she said quietly.

Ruiz was busying himself making coffee in an earthenware pot. When it was ready he courteously handed cups to Herodsfoot and Sanderson, but ignored Talisman, Tylo, Yorka and Dido as if they did not exist.

"Let's go and take a gander at the hot spring," whispered Dido. "I wouldn't say no to a good wash."

"I know where," nodded Tylo. "You come."

"Where did you come up with Cap Sanderson?" Dido asked Talisman.

"His guide brought him to me."

Tylo led them past the fruit trees to the place Dido had noticed earlier where the long grasses grew. A muddy path led between these to a curious steamy grotto in the hillside, where a hot spring burst out of a cleft in the rock. If he has this, I wonder Ruiz bothered to sink a well, Dido thought, but guessed the answer immediately: the water had a disgusting smell, like bad fish; nobody would drink it if they could get anything better. Despite this, the hot water banished their aches like magic and had a soothing effect on cuts and bruises.

"But watch for snakes," warned Tylo. "Many come here for warm—" and indeed, Dido saw several.

"Holy fish, Tylo!" she said, as they dried themselves on their shirts, "isn't there a better place to stay in the forest than with that feller? He's as crazy as a sting-monkey – he nearly had Tally's eye out; and before that he was all set to fly at poor Lordy for not taking his game to King Jamie – and look what he did to *you* – I'd rather sleep in the Place of Stones than spend another night with him."

"Poor man," said Talisman, "little Oynat's mother told me about him. His mother, not his wife, was a witch – a woman called Modreda in Regina town – she hated the girl he married, and brought neighbours in to tell false tales about her; in the end Modreda so poisoned his mind that he killed his wife and then he went mad... The mother, they say, is out of her wits also as a result, and wanders all over the town looking for him . . ."

Dido remembered the woman they had met as the stretcher-bearers climbed the hill to the hospital.

"There's a heap of trouble in this island," she said.

"It is all the result of the curse the Forest People put on the Angrians."

"There *must* be a better way of dealing with folk than by putting curses on them," Dido argued.

Now Herodsfoot and Sanderson came out of the house, saying polite farewells to their host. He, yawning profoundly, was obviously about to throw himself on his bed for a long sleep.

Sanderson noticed the rest of the party drying themselves and combing hair with fingers.

"By George!" he said. "I wouldna say no to a good wash and brush-up. Wait just another five minutes – if you please – fetch out the ponies – I'll not keep ye more than that—" and he strode off towards the hot spring, and vanished among the waving grasses. They heard the sound of splashing, then a sudden yell.

"Oh, confound it! One of those skellums has bitten me!"

"Oh, no!" exclaimed Talisman in dismay.

She raced towards the grass-clump, pulling a tiny flask from her pocket as she ran, and encountered the Captain, staggering towards her, shirtless, shaking his right fist, from which dangled a pearl-snake.

"Got his perditioned fangs sunk right in my finger!" he roared.

"*Don't pull,* Captain-Shaki!" cried Tylo, but it was too late – Sanderson had dragged the snake loose from its grip on his finger, thrown it to the ground and stamped on it. "That's done for *him,* at all events," he panted.

"Yes, but now he has left his venom-fang in you," said Talisman, "and I shall be obliged to cut it out. It will be very painful – I shall have to do it directly – Yorka!" she called. "Can you bring my bag here as fast as you can run?"

Yorka came running with the doctor's bag, from which Talisman snatched out a surgical blade.

"Turn your eyes away – don't look," she ordered the Captain. "I shall have to cut off quite a slice of your finger,"

"Oh, deuce take it, ma'am, I have seen worse things than that in sea-battles!"

He bore her surgery without wincing, but did let out a loud gasp when she poured liquid on to the cut from her little flask.

"It is kandu oil – very concentrated. Counters the effect of the snake venom. Aunt Tala'aa gave it to me. Nonethe-

135

less I am afraid that for a day you are going to be a very sick man, Captain. We shall have to leave you here – you will not be able to ride."

"May the devil fly away with me if I submit to stay here in the company of that blankety-blank madman!" the Captain swore – but he was forced to give in to the doctor's edict, for in ten minutes his arm was swollen to the size of a bolster and he was half delirious.

"*Now* what are we to do?" pondered the doctor, half to herself.

Ruiz, as they had expected, was fast asleep on his cot. But they found a spare palliasse for Sanderson and placed it on a chest; and Talisman rendered him almost insensible by a powerful dose of poppy syrup. "That should keep him quiet for a number of hours," she said. "But who is going to tend him when he wakes?"

"I better," said Yorka.

"You, little one? Can you manage him?"

"Often do so." Yorka described how she had looked after her grandfather and grandmother when they were bitten by snakes, and both had recovered.

"But how about the man Ruiz? Won't you be scared of him?"

Ruiz would not see her, Yorka said. She went into a quick, low-voiced explanation, which Talisman listened to, nodding.

"Yes. I see. Just so. Very well – excellent. I shall come here, tomorrow, if I can. Before that, if the Captain is well enough to ride, I think you should take him straight back to the town. Yes, I know he wants to go down to his ship in the harbour, but by then the ship will probably have sailed, it would be a wasted journey. If I cannot come I will send a message to you. Goodbye, my dear!"

Talisman touched her palms to Yorka's cheeks for a

moment, in the Forest salutation, then the party left, and trotted off along the glade.

Herodsfoot, however, was deeply troubled about leaving Yorka to tend a sick man in the company of crazy Ruiz.

"Is it right? *Can* it be right?"

"No, no, do not fret yourself, she will do very well," said the doctor absently. "Yorka is very capable. She will look after Sanderson just as she ought, and when Ruiz wakes – which he may not do for at least a day, perhaps two – she will make herself taku."

"Taku? What is that?" asked Herodsfoot.

"Well – has it never occurred to you to wonder – here we are, travelling through the forest, hour after hour – yet we see little or nothing of the people who live here – although there may be many of them, all around us? Yorka has explained that to me. They have a gift of making themselves invisible, or nearly so. Inconspicuous. Ruiz simply will not notice Yorka. She will be taku."

"Oh, come now—" began Herodsfoot. Then he appeared to have second thoughts and rode along in dejected silence.

Dido asked Talisman if she had managed to cure the little boy whose mother had come to them near the Place of Stones. "He saw devils, didn't he? What ailed him?"

"Little Oynat? Oh, it was very simple." Talisman laughed "He had eaten a whole bagful of those toadstools – the purple-and-white ones. His mother had told him not to, so he went right away and did it. Forest children are not often so disobedient. They can't afford to be, or they would all be dead."

"Could you cure him?"

"I gave him a great dose of khajri and water. It is like mustard. It made him vomit. Now he is very sorry for himself, but he is not seeing any devils."

Dido asked the doctor about Ruiz

137

"Couldn't you cure him of his crazy ways?"

Talisman sighed. "It would be difficult. He has this poisoned view of witches so deep in his mind . . . it would be a long and toilsome task."

Herodsfoot rode for a long way in silence, then said to Talisman in a low voice, "You have learned so much about this island in so short a time. I have been here longer than you, yet I seem to know so much less."

"Well," Talisman pointed out, "you must remember that I was born here and lived here until the age of five. Things that I had wholly forgotten now begin to come back to me more and more − snatches of language, facts I learned then, songs, stories, scents, tastes − it is all returning, like a tide. You know how last night's dream suddenly flashes back to you, just before you fall asleep? − sometimes it seems to me that all our dreams are joined together in one continuous chain. It is the daytime life that is a queer, interrupted illusion."

"Oh, *yes!*" cried Dido excitedly. "I've had that feeling − often! Sometimes you look about and think: Am I really here? In Aratu? Where is *here?* Who is Dido? And then the feeling goes away again − till next time."

Herodsfoot looked at them both − first one, then the other − and shook his head in a kind of despair.

"Where are we going?" he asked after a while.

"We are going to Limbo Lodge, John King's house, which we hope to reach tomorrow. But as we have been told that the bridge over the gorge of the Kai river has been demolished, we are going first to Manati harbour, down below, where the Kai river runs across the beach into the sea, because Captain Sanderson's ship is there and he wants to know about it − who borrowed it, and why, and when they will return it to Regina port and what compensation they will pay him. And there *is* a way to Limbo

Lodge up from Manati beach, but I am told that it is very steep."

"I see," was all Herodsfoot had to say.

"Doc Tally," said Dido after a while, "where did you meet Captain Sanderson?"

"He was making for Manati harbour, but he and his guide had been obliged to leave their path because of the landslide."

"Like us," said Dido. "Croopus, that time I thought Tylo'd had it for sure. And then——" She remembered the horror of the moment when she saw his head down in the well, and fell silent. Was Yorka really going to be safe in that snaky place, with that noddle-stricken unreliable Ruiz? For that matter, was Captain Sanderson? He was a short-tempered man, Dido had seen him explode with rage on the *Siwara* when one of the crew did something stupid – suppose he played some board game with Ruiz – and won? Would Ruiz take it badly? Or, if Ruiz won, would Sanderson be annoyed?

Games, thought Dido; they sure cause a lot of trouble.

"Where's Manoel all this time?" she asked Talisman. "Where do you think he went, after he didn't catch us at the Ereira place?"

"Sanderson's guide Trinki told us Manoel went on towards Limbo Lodge. He may be there ahead of us. In which case we shall have to use guile."

Dido had not the least notion how to use guile. But she had a lot of confidence in Talisman.

"Where did Trinki go?"

"He had a message that his father was dying on the other side of the island," said Talisman. "So he asked if he might leave us. He knew Yorka would be able to lead us to Ruiz' house."

Their path now ran quite steeply downhill and Dido supposed that the sea lay right at the bottom, though the

139

forest was still so thick and the trees so tall that nothing could be seen ahead but leaves and ferns and creepers. There was a change in the fauna though: more crabs and fewer lizards, more seagulls and frigate-birds, not so many parrots.

A distant bellowing could be heard down below them.

"What the blazes can that be?" said Dido. "Sounds like whales."

Soon they came out into a little bay, steep on the right-hand side, where a massive cliff rose and a river ran out, in swift-flowing sandy runlets across the beach. On the left, or eastward side of the bay, there was a low headland and swampy shallows with palm trees and dangling creepers.

The horses threw up their heads and whinnied at the sudden blaze of light, and the space and fresh salt breeze; their riders were more concerned by the distant sight that met their eyes: the *Siwara*, half a mile offshore, briskly heading out to sea with all sails set. A feathery white wake curved gracefully behind her, like the flourish after a signature.

"Oh dear me. *What* a pity," remarked Lord Herodsfoot. "Really it is just as well that Captain Sanderson was *not* with us; he might have been very greatly provoked at missing his ship by such a short margin."

"I don't get it," said Dido. "Who fetched the *Siwara* down here to this nook-shotten spot? And why? And where's she going now?"

"Back to Regina," said Talisman. "With the cargo she picked up here. Manoel seized her – or some of his Town Guard did – to grab the opportunity of a load that was waiting here at Manati. The ship that was due to take the load on board here had been wrecked in a storm."

"How in the world do you know all this?" demanded Herodsfoot.

Talisman looked at him rather apologetically. "You will

140

not like it – my reason for knowing – perhaps you won't believe me."

"Oh, spare me any more supernatural doings!" he muttered.

"No, it is not supernatural. It is the drumming. The drum messages," Talisman explained. "I am beginning to understand them – well, some of them, the simpler ones. For instance the *Siwara* – according to the drums – is now on her way to Regina to meet a trading schooner who will receive her cargo and carry it to Valparaiso. Of course it is an act of piracy. The cargo properly belongs to John King. Manoel has grabbed the chance of stealing it in order to finance an uprising against King."

"So? What is this blessed cargo? Djeela nuts?"

"No, even more precious. Look—"

In the little harbour there was not a soul to be seen. The waves washed gently on the sandy beach. To the west side, beyond the river, a rocky platform had been cut out of the cliff so that ships with a fairly deep draught could anchor alongside of it. A sloping ramp led up to this wharf. The horses had splashed through the shallow river and up the ramp. The quay was deserted and bare; a few discarded warps lay tangled about a bollard; they were the only evidence of human activity. No, not quite: Dido, looking down as her feet crunched on grit, noticed that handfuls of small pearls lay all over the rock, in hollows and crannies, like drifts of fallen leaves in a rutted road; most of the tiny gleaming things were no larger than peppercorns, but a few were as big as peas.

"Stone the crows!" Dido picked up a handful and trickled them through her fingers. "Pearls! Where do they come from then, Doc?"

Talisman pointed south. "Coral reefs – about halfway between Aratu and Mount Ximboë, the submerged volcano. Ximboë keeps the water warm and the pearl

141

oysters thrive on it. The pearls are not so handsome as those from the Persian Gulf or the gulf of Manaar. But they have their value . . ."

"Good heavens!" Herodsfoot picked up a fistful of the shining things and studied them. "Pearls! (I understand they are ninety per cent calcium carbonate, and the rest is water and organic matter; possibly caused by parasitic worms . . .) It is queer that humans should be so attracted by them . . ."

"Who fishes 'em up?" asked Dido.

"There is a village on the other side of that point. The villagers go out in their grass dhows two or three times a year and dive for them."

"Are they Forest People? Or Angrians?"

"Neither. They are a tribe who has always been there. Or at least," said Talisman, "as long as the memory of the ancestors goes back. They do not want the pearls for themselves, but exchange them for fish-hooks and tea."

"Kw'ul," said Tylo nodding. "Forest People rather have nuts. Shaki-misses like kw'ul round neck. No other use. Can't eat kw'ul."

"We had better leave this place," said Talisman. "There is no reason now to remain here. And quite a number of excellent reasons for going."

She pointed down to the sandy beach. Beyond its curve a number of objects which Dido had taken for logs of driftwood, trunks of trees washed up on the shore, were now in motion. They were making a slow but purposeful way towards the quay. Not so slow, in fact; some of them commanded quite a turn of speed.

"Crocodiles."

"*Estuarian* crocodiles!" Herodsfoot's tone was as fervent as if he had come across a living specimen of some species believed for centuries to be extinct. "And what superb specimens! Look at their size! Why, I believe some of them may be as much as thirty feet long. And only look at their girth! Only hear them bellow!"

The crocodiles were a muddy green-brown in colour, and covered with lumps and wrinkles. Their eyes, red and staring, stood out from their heads like doorknobs.

"Crumbs! Let's get away from here," said Dido. "We better nip across the beach smartish, before they come round to this side. There's some in the sea, too."

She strode off the quay, leading her horse, who was equally keen to leave.

"If one of them should get close to you," advised Talisman, "move sideways. Their bodies are not very well articulated; they can go straight ahead, but are not capable of a quick turn to either side."

The party did not wait to test the truth of this; a hasty retreat was beaten. The horses, sweating and crying out with fright, could only just be kept under control as the nearest crocodile came within fifteen feet of Herodsfoot, who declared wistfully that they were quite the most superior specimens he had ever come across; he would dearly have liked to study them at closer range.

He insisted on stopping for a few minutes when the party was safely established, well above the beach on a shelf of rock which the crocodiles apparently did not consider it worth their while to climb.

"Hark at 'em bellow, though!" said Dido, awestruck. "And look at the way they jump out of the water! They beat grasshoppers all to pieces!"

On the far side of the cove, where trees overhung the water, several crocodiles, having lost interest in the humans, were after a group of monkeys who were gobbling fruit from low-growing branches. Dido saw a fifteen-foot monster leap clear out of the water and snatch a monkey from the boughs.

"Blister me! I shan't half have bad dreams tonight!"

143

"I believe they may live to an age of twenty years or more," sighed Herodsfoot. "Yet when they are born they are no bigger than a man's hand."

"Too bad they don't stay that size."

"Now, here I am going to leave you," suddenly announced Talisman.

She was greeted by a silence of shock; then cries of protest.

"*Leave* us? Pray, what can you mean?"

"No, no, Doc; don't you go for to do that!"

"Much, much good not, Shaki-doc!"

"How do you mean, *leave* us?" repeated Herodsfoot shakily. "Where will you go? And how are we to go on without you?"

Talisman sighed, and explained. "You will go up that track – you can see it from here, very steep, in the trees – which follows the course of the Kai river on its north side, and in due course reaches the bridge."

"But I thought – I had understood – did we not hear that the bridge had been destroyed?"

"I now have reason to believe that a temporary bridge may have been thrown across."

"But Tally – Doc dear – where are *you* going?"

"I am going up here," said Talisman. She nodded backwards at the cliff, which rose black and sheer above the quay on the western side of the cove.

"Up *there?* Have you taken leave of your senses?"

"Up the Cliff of Death?"

"*Is* that the Cliff of Death?" inquired Dido. "Is that where you got chucked off?"

Talisman nodded. "Seeing the place made me remember. I was snatched out of my cot at night and shut inside a clay pot." A slight quiver passed over her face. "The lid came off as he threw me down. That is one reason

144

why I am going back the same way. It is a thing I have to do."

Herodsfoot exploded. "I never heard anything so outrageously nonsensical in the whole of my life. Climb up that? A professional mountaineer couldn't do it."

"Could he not?" Talisman smiled. "Well, I think I shall be able to do it."

"What's up at the top?" Dido asked.

"King's house. His palace. Limbo Lodge. They will be surprised to see me there." Talisman smiled again.

"You just bet they will!" Dido could see that the plan had its advantages. "So what should *we* do?"

"Go up the river. Cross the bridge – if there is one. If not . . . you will have to improvise. Then, ask to see King. Tell him – if I have not been able to reach him already – about the theft of the *Siwara* . . . Ask for compensation for Sanderson's cargo of tea and sugar."

"Suppose they throw us into jail for killing that guard?"

"Suppose no bridge?"

"You will have to do what seems best. But if I get to Limbo Lodge before you I may be able to take care of that."

Herodsfoot had paid no heed to any of this. "I never heard such an idiotic, hare-brained scheme! You must be out of your mind."

"No. I am not. And I am going." She turned calmly away from them, then turned back to say, "Tylo, will you lead my mule up, please. We don't want the poor beast eaten by crocodiles."

"Yes, Shaki-missie."

"Talisman, you cannot, really, seriously, entertain the notion of climbing up that rockface – suppose you fall?"

"Then I shall make a fine tasty meal for the crocodiles."

"I beg you – I entreat you—"

"Now, Francis, please do not demean yourself and

145

embarrass me and these children by such folly. Just go, now."

She walked briskly away, back along the rock jetty, and past a buttress of the cliff, out of sight. Dido looked up at the rockface respectfully. It was breathtakingly high, three or four times at least the height of the Ereiras' tower, and sheer, smooth black rock, like a wall. But still, if Talisman thought she had the skill to climb it, Dido presumed that her confidence was justified.

There's more to her than meets the eye, Dido thought, and she said to Herodsfoot, who was in a terrible state, white as a fish, his face crumpled, beads of sweat rolling down his brow – "Honest, Frankie, you shouldn't put yourself in such a pelter about her. Doc Tally knows what she's about. She's a real dab at climbing. And I'm a climber too – I know! Just you come along with us and you'll see – it'll all work out."

She put a bit more confidence into her voice than she really felt, and tugged at the poor man's hand to get him away from the cove, since the crocodiles had not entirely given up hope of a meal of human flesh and were scrabbling eagerly at the base of the rock shelf, while bellowing in a dismal and deafening chorus.

"Come along – let's get away from those brutes."

The track up from Manati cove towards King's residence was wider and had a better surface than the one on which they had come down to the harbour; evidently it was used more; but it was so extremely steep that they made no attempt to ride the horses, for it would have been almost impossible not to slide backwards over their tails. The path zigzagged upwards in a series of short, sharp bends, and seemed to climb up and up for ever. To their left, beyond a bank and a hedge of thorns, the ground dropped away sharply. At first they could see the Kai river, trickling over the beach in its network of shallow tea-coloured rivulets, and the disappointed crocodiles snapping their huge jaws; then, as they mounted higher, the river was lost from view, but they could hear its voice: first a brisk chatter as it splashed among small rocks, then a loud roar as the gorge narrowed and a large mass of water had to force its way through a narrow passage.

On their right, thick forest rose almost vertically to form what must have been the flank of Mount Fura before the southern tip of the island of Aratu split off in some prehistoric upheaval. Here the rock showed through the trees in strange columns, arches, and folds, created over centuries by falling water from the hillside above. Sometimes there were cave entrances, half hidden by trailing creepers.

Poor Herodsfoot was sunk in a silence of misery. Dido felt truly sorry for him. She could follow his thoughts tolerably well: if Talisman fell from the cliff and was killed, he had lost her for ever; if she managed to climb it, he had lost her just as finally, for that would make plainer still the huge mysterious gulf that divided them.

To distract her own mind, and, she hoped, Herodsfoot's too, she talked to Tylo. "Tylo, don't the Forest People want those pearls at all?"

"Kw'ul? No, Shaki-Dido. What use? Can't eat. No good for medicine. If Outros people want, let them have."

"But the Forest People can sell them for money."

"Who want money?"

Thinking it over, Dido could see that there was really nothing that the Forest People could do with money. They had all they needed – food, clothes, medicine, shelter; for entertainment, the long creation-songs that the men, the Hamahi, sang each day; for news, the drum messages, echoing softly through the forest; for company, each other.

"You could travel to other lands . . ."

"Who want that? When forest so kaetik?"

147

Kaetik, Dido knew, meant both beautiful and satisfactory. There seemed no answer to that.

"But sometimes people must be lonely in the forest?"

"No, why? Forest is enough."

And if, Tylo explained, a Forest Person wished for the company of another Forest Person, there was always likely to be one, within a couple of miles – "one culoh-flower's walk". A culoh flower, Dido knew, lasted exactly an hour from blooming to dropping; they were quite useful, in the rare event that some process needed to be timed.

And, when they met each other, what a pleasure! They gossiped, they laughed, they had jokes. Forest People, Dido had already noticed, from observing Tylo and Yorka, simply adored jokes, and could generally find something to chuckle over, even in the direst situation.

"Do you think the Angrians will ever go away and leave Aratu for good?"

It did seem a shame, Dido thought, that this glum race had ever come to inhabit the happy island. No doubt they had been made yet gloomier by the curse of homesickness and dissatisfaction that the Forest People had laid on them – that was unfortunate – but you'd think that would make them even more anxious to leave. But then, where could they go? It was hundreds of years since their forefathers came here from Angria – and who else in the world would welcome such a dismal tribe? They would probably not be welcome even in Angria. She said something of this to Tylo. He was more optimistic. "They maybe not so sad in other land."

"But other lands already have their own people living there. No room for a new lot. Specially such dismal ones."

"Maybe they all drown in sea. Maybe ship get wreck," Tylo said hopefully.

Dido did not feel this was a practical solution.

Tylo's other idea seemed likelier, though no more cheerful.

"Maybe all Outros people kill each other."

She asked him about the dispute between the Angrians. It was simply, he said, that Manoel wanted to take over from his brother as ruler of the island. "He always jealous of old Sovran John."

Long ago Manoel too, Dido learned, had loved Erato, the woman John King had brought up and then married. "He angry about that. Deep angry."

"I see. So when Erato died, he threw her kid off the cliff. Thinking he'd inherit from his brother by and by. But that time was long in coming. And when he found the kid was still alive, he fixed to bring her back. But why do that? Seems crazy."

No, not crazy, Tylo said, because either he could get rid of her, once and for all, or, if she turned out to be useful, being half a Forest Person, he could use her on his side.

"Only it didn't work out like that. So now what's happening?"

The Angrians were divided, Tylo said. The ones in Regina town were for Manoel, because they knew him, and he promised to reduce taxes and make it legal for anybody to grow djeela trees (which at present were King's monopoly) and he had plans to cut down more and more of the forest and increase the pearl fisheries and grow more spice plantations.

"So who don't want that among the Angrians? What do the others want?"

Some old-fashioned Angrians, living in the forest, like the Ereiras, said Tylo, had not come down yet on one side or the other; and John King's own bodyguard, living up at Limbo Lodge, were devoted to King, despite his deafness and short temper, and wanted no changes.

"How many of those?"

149

Tylo spread out his two hands ten times.

"About a hundred. And how many in Regina town?"

Maybe five times that number, Tylo guessed.

"Doesn't look like King stands much of a chance, then."

But Tylo was hopeful. Everybody knew, he said, that Aratu was the centre of the universe. "Ritari-ga'ar!" – the central axis on which the whole globe and the skies revolved. Some day, everybody in the world would die, and then they would all go to the great forest in the Underworld, where everything grew upside-down and revolved in the other direction; but that time would not come until the last three of the great stones up on the hilltop had fallen and crumbled away. Much would happen before then. And he personally thought, and so did many of the Forest People, that, since matters were so satisfactory – on the whole – now, in Aratu, so kaetik, the gods would not allow any great change to take place.

"I do hope that's so," said Dido thoughtfully. "But I guess the Outros folk don't think everything's so kaetik—"

"So maybe all kill each other," Tylo cheerfully repeated. They went on climbing.

"Bless us and save us," sighed Dido after what seemed like several hours. "Is this mountain ever going to end? My knees feel as if they'd been used for swabbing the deck . . ."

Tylo peered ahead. "Mist come again. Better leave horses in cave. If Guard up top, may need to dodge and hide—"

"Yus. I'm right with you there," said Dido. "Horses would be nothing but a nuisance. Are we near the top, do you think?"

Not far, Tylo guessed. So, as they were passing a capacious cave, with twisted stalactites round its entrance, making it easy to recognise, they left the horses inside, with an armful of keedo-grass and sprinkle of kandu nuts to protect them from snakes. Tylo also laced a tendril of opoë vine across the cave mouth.

150

"What's that for?"

"Smell bad. Stop horse from stray, stop wild beast get in."

Herodsfoot had remained silent all this time, wound up totally in his own woe.

As they climbed on, the mist became ever thicker. Presently Tylo sniffed, and said, "I smell meat, bread, cook on hilltop. Better we stop here, hide in cave till mist lift. Guard up yonder."

The lip of the gorge, Dido gathered, where the bridge to Limbo Lodge (if it was still there) spanned the ravine, was quite a dangerous spot. There was a sheer drop to the rapids of the Kai river, hundreds of feet below. Easy enough, in a thick fog, to step over the brink into eternity.

"I wonder folk took the trouble to go over the bridge to the Cliff of Death."

Well, but that was a holy place, Tylo explained. People went there if the gods commanded them to.

"Do the gods ever command it?"

Oh yes, Tylo said. Every now and then, if the Forest People grew too many for the island to support them in a kaetik manner, the gods would recommend that a hundred or so should go and throw themselves off the Cliff of Death.

"And folk don't mind doing that?"

Of course not, if it was for the good of all, said Tylo patiently. It was an honour. There were always enough volunteers. They knew they would only be moving on to the next great forest in the other world. They took with them their favourite songs, their favourite games, a pocket full of bark bread or djeela fruit and the best jokes they had heard lately to tell the ancestors, the dwellers in the upside-down groves that awaited them there.

"Hush, now! I hear voices!" Tylo's acute hearing, like his sense of smell, was way ahead of Herodsfoot's or Dido's. "Go in cave here, wait!" he breathed, touched Dido's hand,

and beckoned her sideways off the track. She, likewise, caught Herodsfoot's hand, pulling him after her.

The cave Tylo had entered was dripping with stalactites and lined with glow-worms which made it possible to see that it was a long, narrow crevice leading backwards into the hillside. Dido could not help wondering what unfriendly creatures might inhabit this dark passage, as well as the glow-worms; however, they saw nothing by the faint glimmering light, but heard a great many bats, faintly squeaking and flittering overhead. Dido thought of snakes and crocodiles and sting-monkeys and devoutly hoped they were all elsewhere. Crocodiles, she told herself firmly, would never climb as high up the mountain as this, and sting-monkeys lived in trees, not caves.

"Now wait here," whispered Tylo, "while I go-see."

Dido found a ledge of rock for herself and another for Herodsfoot to sit on. While they waited, she thought of Talisman. How long would it take to climb that lofty cliff? An hour? Two hours? Three hours? It would not be long now, till the end of the day. If Talisman had not reached the top before dark fell, she would be done for – had she thought of that, when she began her climb? And the mist, too, would make the climb infinitely more difficult and dangerous, because she would not be able to see far enough ahead to plan her route.

Oh, Doc Tally, thought Dido fervently, I sure do hope you've made it to the top by this time.

She heard a faint groan come from Herodsfoot; his thoughts must run parallel to hers.

And then suddenly Tylo was back with them, pressing his fingers against their lips in urgent caution.

"What's up?" Dido was beginning to whisper, when she heard the cause of his alarm – voices and footsteps of men inside the cave.

Dido's first impulse was to slip farther back along the

152

narrow passage. But Tylo's hand now warned her to keep still, and she could see this made sense; Herodsfoot would not be able to move quietly enough to retreat without discovery. The men – there seemed to be three of them – had not come into the cave hunting for them, but apparently to have a private conversation. They stood just inside the entrance and talked in low voices.

"You have guards posted at each end of the bridge?"

"Certainly, Gerente."

Ha, so the bridge is still there, thought Dido, and poked Tylo in the ribs. She could feel his nod in reply.

Is one of those men Manoel? Dido wondered. Is he the only Gerente, or are there others? She could not be sure if the voice was his. But when he spoke again, she decided that it was Manoel.

"You have brought me one of the fire-trimmers?"

"Yes, Gerente, I have brought Zmora. He nine-treetime Halmahi, know much about forest fire."

Dido heard Tylo beside her suck in his breath – with horror, with grief, with astonishment? His grip on her hand tightened.

"Good," said Manoel's voice – Dido felt more and more certain that it *was* Manoel – his voice had a nasal arrogant twang about it which she had taken a strong dislike to when having breakfast at his house. "Now then, you, Zmora, it seems you are the man we want."

"For what can you want me, I wonder, Shaki-sir?" inquired a polite, elderly voice.

"You know much about the forest. And you know about fires, how they start and how they can be stopped again."

"One branch-length I know about such things. A whole tree-length, not so."

"What does the fellow mean?" said Manoel impatiently. "Does he know or does he not?"

"What you wish to find out, Gerente?"

153

"Listen, you, Zmora. You fellows have the knack of setting fire to the forest, isn't that so, when you choose to do so. With that glowing fungus of yours? And then, you can put the fire out again when you choose, can't you?"

"*Small* fire, Shaki, golly-likely. Big fire, not so." Here Zmora went into a complicated explanation, partly in the Dilendi language, from which Dido gathered that putting forest fires out depended mainly on the weather.

"If I want to light a fire now, a big fire, burn half the forest on the island, could you put it out?"

Zmora burst out laughing. Quite plainly this suggestion, this crazy notion, was the best joke he had heard in months. "Oh-ho-ho-ho-ho-ho-ho! Shaki-sir! You make great fun with old Zmora! No one, *no one*, but the greatest fool in the world would, at this time, burn half the forest on the island! And if you so much as burn half, you could *never* put fire out again. You would burn whole island. Aratu would be dead, finish. Like Pati island, Shaki-sir!"

"So you won't, or can't, make a fire for us, eh?"

Zmora's reply was in the Dilendi language, and Dido could not follow it all, but she gathered that he was saying a very firm no.

Manoel gave some order, in an undertone, to the third man, who said,

"Shall it be done now, Gerente?"

"Yes, certainly now! We do not want him going back and talking about this to any of his mates. Over the cliff with him—"

There followed a brief scuffle, and a low cry from Zmora, as he was hustled out of the cave by the two other men; another cry, part grunt, part gasp, and then Manoel came back into the cave, remarking, "That will prevent him from telling tales, at all events! But it is a cursed nuisance that he could not be any use to us. Tiresome old fool! Find me Capitan Ereira, will you, and bring him here. I must think."

154

"Yes, Gerente."

The second man's footsteps died away up the path, and a small red glow near the mouth of the cave suggested that Manoel had lit a cigar. The warm scent of tobacco floated back along the passage, and Dido could feel Herodsfoot make a sharp movement, which was instantly and firmly suppressed by Tylo. She herself was in a state of shock. Something dreadful, *horrible*, had happened, under cover of the dark, recorded by nothing more than a couple of brief cries: a man had been killed, thrown over the cliff, simply because he would not agree to light a fire which might destroy the whole forest.

I always reckoned that Manoel was a wrong 'un, Dido thought. I wonder if his brother's as bad? If so it's a poor look-out for Doc Tally, even if she gets to Limbo Lodge; shame these poor Forest Folk have such a scaly pair ruling the roost round here. If it weren't for them – and the Angrians – Aratu wouldn't be a bad place to live . . .

More footsteps. The second voice announced respectfully: "Here is Capitan Ereira, Gerente."

"Good. You may leave us now."

When the steps had gone again, Manoel said: "Mateo. Is there any news of your sister?"

"No, Gerente."

"Where do you think she has gone?"

"I think she may have been making for the Cliff of Death. I fear she might have got there before the guard was set on the bridge."

"That was a wretched piece of bungling stupidity!" said Manoel angrily. "The bridge ought to have been guarded all along – certainly as soon as the news came that she was gone from your parents' home—"

"I know, I know, Gerente," said Mateo's voice apologetically. "But I myself did not receive the information until half an hour ago—"

"Is there any further news of the party with the English lord and Irmala?"

"Some of them spent the night with the madman, Ruiz. But not Irmala. She was with a woman of the forest."

"Where are they now?"

"They were last spotted going in the direction of Manati beach."

"In that case they may not be far from here now. Order your guards to be extra vigilant."

"Yes, Gerente. I have already done so."

"That woman is a great danger to us."

"Which, sir? Irmala – or my sister?"

"Both, both! If Irmala gets to Limbo – or if your sister comes into contact with any of the Forest People – if only they would stay in one place, instead of shifting about as they keep doing – it is so devilish difficult even to judge how many there are—"

"A good forest blaze would wipe out most of them, sir—"

"Yes, yes, no doubt! But the ones who escaped would be exceedingly ill-disposed."

"They might not guess who began the fire."

"Oh, they would. They would! There is no deceiving them in such matters. And they have such unexpected powers—"

"What is your plan regarding the d – regarding Irmala?"

There was a long pause. Then Manoel said: "*If* she is to remain alive—" he hesitated – "*if* she is to live, she must marry. She is dangerously wilful and wayward. Her marriage is essential. She escaped from the House of Correction – she must have had help to do that. From whom? We don't know. She has spent nights in the forest with the Dilendi people. Already it seems they trust her. She is a capable doctor – she was able to heal that young sailor's head injury. News of that has spread across the island. It seems she already has standing as a Kanikke and a witch."

"We *need* a doctor – there has not been one on the island since O Medico died."

"Yes, but we cannot allow her to go running around loose. She would take the part of the Forest People against the Angrians. She would impede all our plans. Would *you* marry her, Mateo?" Manoel suddenly asked.

"*I?*" There was another long pause. "I – I have no mind to marry, Gerente. And – and I do not think that would work – not from what I hear of her."

"I suppose *I* could marry her," Manoel said thoughtfully.

"You? But you are her uncle!"

"And who is to know that?"

"Does she know it?"

"I am not certain. She knows some of her history – that she came from here. It is the greatest misfortune that she should have survived," Manoel said gloomily. "When I heard of the child being picked up by the Dutch freighter, I could hardly believe that ill-luck had targeted me yet again."

"You and I, Gerente, are both sons of the Night-Woman. Do you remember what that crazy witch said when you had her put in the stocks for not wearing a headdress – she said that women of our families would bring us great trouble."

"I had forgotten," Manoel said slowly. "Yes, I had forgotten that. This island is *plagued* by women! Without them, we should do better. If my brother had never married – if that child had never been born – if your sister Luisa had never met that hot-headed young poet Kaubre—"

"What about the Englishman? Do you think that he might marry Irmala?"

"What's-his-name? – Herodsfoot? Oh no. He is of no account," Manoel said. "He travels about collecting games and butterflies – for some trifling purpose. Irmala would never marry him, I am certain of that. He is a poor creature – a no-account fellow. No, I think that Irmala had better die. The island must do without a doctor. Order your men to maintain an active search for her, and, as soon as she is found, she had better follow Zmora over the cliff."

"What about the rest of the party – Herodsfoot and the English girl, and the sailor who suffered the head injury? There is also the captain of the ship."

"Too many to die by snake-bite," Manoel said thoughtfully. "We do need that fire. Somehow it must be contrived. I feel sure the old fool was wrong. The Dilendi are superstitious about fires. But come, it grows late. We should go back to camp. What was that noise?"

"What noise, Gerente?"

"For a moment – just then – I thought I caught the sound of a baby crying—"

"Heaven forbid!" said Mateo, shivering.

The two men left the cave and walked away up the cliff path.

Chapter Nine

THERE WAS A HORRIFIED SILENCE FOR A NUMBER of minutes after Manoel and Mateo had left the cave. Then Tylo whispered: "Us go more back far in . . ."

They did so. When they had gone what Tylo considered a safe distance along the windings of the passage, he blew on a piece of fire-fungus, which gave off a glow not much brighter than that of the glow-worms, but was sufficient to show them each other's shocked faces.

"That Manoel!" breathed Dido. "That Manoel is a real hellion. Fancy *murdering* that poor old fellow, that Zmora, just because he wouldn't set a fire for them—"

"Zmora," said Tylo mournfully. "Zmora my father's cousin's aunt's tree-uncle. Very wise man. Very tree-old."

Herodsfoot came out of his long silence. He said, "Am I right in thinking they killed that man? I was never so shocked – never so scandalised! It is the most monstrous thing! If there were a British Resident in this island, I would record the strongest possible protest – I would demand proper retribution—"

"But there ain't a British whatshisname," Dido pointed out. "So any retribution we gotta do ourselves – though I don't quite see how—"

"What is that wretched man up to?" demanded Herodsfoot. "What is his aim?"

"Why do they want somebody to marry Doc Tally?" Dido wanted to know.

"Is that who they mean when they say Irmala – why do they call her that?"

"Forest name for her," explained Tylo. "When she burn,

nurse-woman in King's house Asgard – her ma die when she born, but nurse Kanikke called her Irmala."

"How do you know that?"

"Aunt Tala'aa tell me."

"Aunt Tala'aa seems to know everything – What a lot of names Tally's got – Jane – Talisman – Irmala—"

Herodsfoot heaved a great sigh.

Poor Frankie, Dido thought. She did not say it aloud. It was a bit hard on him though, she thought, hearing that scaly Manoel say all those nasty things about him – that he was a no-account, a trifling fellow, a poor thing. And it ain't true, besides. Frankie is a bit slow, and a mite careless with his glasses, but he's as decent a fellow as ever walked down the pike . . .

"What is Manoel up to?" Herodsfoot asked again.

"He want to push out his brother Sovran John. He got Town Guard camped up by bridge, ready attack Limbo Lodge."

"His own brother? – Now I remember," muttered Herodsfoot, mostly to himself. "In Bad Szomberg, I remember there was some scandal attached to Manoel Roy – after cheating at cards he had waylaid a person who threatened to expose him and stabbed the man – but nothing was proved—"

"Why doesn't his brother *stop* him? If he has his own guards over there in the palace?"

Tylo pondered: "Sovran John maybe not know. And we Forest Folk not like fight," he presently offered.

"But John King ain't a Forest Person. He came from Norfolk," Dido said.

"But he old now, he learn Forest notions."

"That's true; and he had them from his wife, too, didn't he? But do you reckon he really doesn't know what Manoel is up to?"

"Golly-maybe," said Tylo doubtfully. "Or maybe he hope,

still, whispering leaves, sand-voices, knot in grass blow across Manoel path, trip him—"

He had lost Dido. She did not understand these references.

"What we gotta do, Tylo?" she said. "We can't go and call on John King if his brother Manoel is camped in front of the bridge with his Guards. There's no other way across the gorge. We're in a bit of a fix. And, from what Manoel said to that other cove, he plans to do us all in. Who *was* the other guy, the one Manoel called Mateo? Is he kin to those folk where we stayed?"

"He that gal's brother."

"But he said his sister had gone off to the Cliff of Death—"

"Hush!" whispered Tylo. "Listen!"

Far back in the cave where they now were, the silence was very complete: the massive rock above and around them seemed to banish all noise, save an occasional faint drip of water.

No, not quite all noise. Tiny, in the distance, far, far away, came the smallest possible cry – not more than the thinnest spider-web of sound.

"Where's it coming from?" breathed Dido.

"Maybe more frontways? In side cave? You stay here, Shaki-Dido," said Tylo softly. "Stay here with Milord Oklosh. I go look."

"S'pose you don't come back?"

"I come, I come. You see. If I no come, you go back to horses, go back to my Sisingana."

"Could I ever find the way?"

"I think you find it, Shaki-Dido. You got good baraat," Tylo told her encouragingly. Dido did not know exactly what baraat was – common-sense, maybe – but his tone cheered her.

161

Tylo broke off a morsel of fire-fungus, passed it to her, and slipped off along the passage.

"Where's the boy gone?" asked Herodsfoot after a while.

"There was a noise – sounded like a baby crying."

"A *baby*? In a place like this? Who in the world . . .? Oh, dear me," sighed Herodsfoot. "I feel so useless. If only . . . if only Talisman were here . . . How happy we should be to see her."

You never said a truer word, Frankie, thought Dido.

Then she thought she caught the sound of soft pattering footsteps. In a moment she was sure of it. Tylo was returning.

He came rather slowly. Dido was puzzled, momentarily, as he seemed to have balanced the fire-fungus on his head, on a flat flake of stone, while he carried a bundle in his arms. It was too dark to see what he held until he came up to Dido and passed her the bundle, which felt like an outsize grass birdsnest with something warm and solid in the middle. As Tylo handed the bundle to Dido, it let out a faint chirrup and waved a fist.

"Save us! A baby!"

"Paper tell who," said Tylo.

Having handed Dido the baby, he removed the fire-fungus from his head and pulled a folded paper from his waistband. Holding the fungus beside the paper, he raised it near enough to Dido's face so that she was able to read the few lines written on it.

"I have gone to jump off the Cliff of Death and rejoin my beloved Kaubre who was killed by my brother and father. I will not take my baby, for if the tree-fathers of Aratu wish her to live, she will be found and cared for. Whoever finds this paper, please, if she is still living, take my baby to a tree-mother. Luisa Ereira."

What a shame, thought Dido. Doc Talisman goes to all the trouble of keeping that gal from dying, helping her baby be born, and then she has to go and jump off the Cliff of Death.

Now what's to be done?

"Where's the nearest tree-mother?" she murmured to Tylo.

He seemed a bit nonplussed. "Best we go down to horse-cave."

"Yeah, that would be farther away from those coves and their camp. In case the baby lets out a yip and they hear her. And you got some djeela-juice in one o' the saddle-bags, haven't you? Maybe she'd take a drop of that."

So they moved, with the utmost care and caution, out of the cave and back down the cliff path. The mist was still very thick, the night still black-dark and the going, down the narrow, slippery, twisting path, was slow, unpleasant, and very often terrifying. Dido, holding the bundle of baby, was glad that Tylo walked ahead of her, sometimes reaching back a friendly hand to steady her on the sharper turns. Herodsfoot came behind Dido, every now and then letting out little subdued grunts of anxiety. Dido could sense, as if by telepathy, each time he felt an impulse to take off his glasses and wipe them.

"*Don't* take those glasses off, Frankie! – wiping them won't make a mite of difference in this tarnal fog."

(So far the plaster that Talisman wrapped round the earpiece had held firm, but it was becoming very grubby and frayed.)

They could tell when they drew near to the lower cave because of the warm smell of horse that came drifting up the cliff path. Stepping slowly down, carrying the grass-wrapped baby (who was quite heavy – she must weigh as much as a Michaelmas goose) – Dido became possessed by an unreasonable fear. Suppose those massive crocodiles had decided to clamber all the way up the cliff path and devour the horses? But when they reached the lower cave, all

163

seemed orderly and quiet, the horses peaceably munching on their fodder and no rapacious reptiles to be seen.

The baby was so tranquil and well behaved that Dido wondered if her mother had given her a dose of some calming herb juice to quiet her when they escaped from the Quinquilho ranch. But when offered a sip of djeela juice she sucked it willingly enough, then went back to sleep in her cocoon of grass and leaves.

"What'll us do now?" Dido whispered to Tylo, and he whispered back, "Wait till day come."

This seemed a sensible plan, as they were all exhausted after the day's trek through the forest, the parting from Talisman at the cliff foot, and the long struggle up and down the cliff path. They piled themselves beds of keedograss and opoë vine, sprinkled kandu nuts, and gratefully lay down to sleep. Outside they could hear the distant roar of the Kai river, far below still, and sometimes the cry of a night bird.

It should have been easy to sink into slumber, but Dido lay wakeful and worried.

We are in a right dicey pickle, she thought, with those Angrian coves up above, a-planning to do in old John King, and Doc Tally lord knows where, and Cap Sanderson laid up with snake-bite in that crazy-feller's hut – and the *Siwara* loaded with pearls on its way to Valparaiso leaving us marooned in Aratu – I reckon Cap'n Hughes back on the *Thrush* will be wondering where the devil we've got to – and poor old Multiple in that creepy hospital being cared for by a passel of witches – all because we came hunting for Frankie Herodsfoot and his precious games. Those games just better cure old King Jamie of his megrims, if we ever do get back to London, that's all . . .

At last she slept.

And woke to a thin silver blade of sunlight slicing in from the cave's upper left-hand corner, piercing between the bulbous stalactites; and Yorka's small hard hands urgently tugging her awake.

"*Yorka!*"

"Shaki-Dido! You wake quick! I bring news and breakfast!"

"We got news too," said Dido, "We found a baby."

"O-o-o-o!" Yorka exclaimed mournfully as Dido told the baby's history. "Well, well, that poor Outros girl she now with her Kaubre in under-forest, better than stay in dark cold unkind house. But we best take the baby to Aunt Tala'aa pretty quick—"

"Where *is* Aunt Tala'aa?"

"Breakfast first, we feed baby, then now-and-now I find out."

Yorka had brought tikkol fruit, which had firm juicy pink flesh under a thin brittle rind. The baby accepted some of its juice, trickled into her mouth, and then slept again. Yorka showed Dido how to wrap her snugly in one of the huge green ukka leaves.

"What about Cap Sanderson, where did you leave him?" asked Dido.

Yorka said she had fetched back the guide, Trinki, who had taken care of Sanderson before, when he was making for Manati harbour. "Take him back to Regina town. Snakebite better. Ruiz still sleep."

"I thought Trinki's father was dying."

"Father die, go to underforest, Trinki glad come back."

"I just hope Sanderson won't get into trouble in Regina town. He was so angry about his ship—"

Herodsfoot, who had been munching tikkol fruit in gloomy silence (it seemed as if, on top of everything else, he was suffering from a homesick longing for bacon, eggs, toast, and marmalade), now said, "And what are *we* proposing to do?"

"First find Aunt Tala'aa," said Yorka.

Dido had been wondering how Yorka had been able to summon Trinki to conduct Captain Sanderson back to the town. Now she watched with interest as Yorka stepped outside the cave, climbed a short way up the sloping cliff-face to a knob of rock, and stood on this, tilting her head as far back as it would go. She looked as if she were staring intently at the sky, but her eyes were shut. So she stood, absolutely still, for about five minutes. Once Herodsfoot began to say something, but Tylo hushed him with a gesture. Dido, listening intently, caught the faint sound of drums in the far distance; also – more disquieting and closer at hand – a sharp crackle, now and then, which might be rifle-fire.

Now Yorka came down from her rock. "Aunt Tala'aa not far. On Mount Fura."

"But that's where Limbo Lodge is – ain't it?" said Dido. "Across the gorge?"

Tylo said: "Maybe Aunt Tala'aa go visit old Sovran John. Be golly-good she do that."

"So what do *we* do? Is there a bridge? Can we get across?"

"I go see," said Tylo. "You-all wait here." And he flitted away up the steep cliff path.

"I hope he'll be careful," said Dido anxiously. "Seems to me I heard gunfire up there."

"He go taku," said Yorka.

Then Yorka related an item of news which she had been politely withholding until the party's plans had been discussed. While at the foot of the cliff path, by the crocodile beach, she had seen a strange sight. A large number of men – "five times fingers and toes" – climbed, quite easily it seemed, down the Cliff of Death – "like some person before made foot-places in rock."

"Stairs?" said Dido. "Steps? Like when we went to bed in the Ereira house, high up in the tower?"

166

"Yes. Stair path on cliff, men coming down, many, many Outros men."

"That's mighty queer. D'you think John King was one of them; escaping from Limbo Lodge by the back door?"

"Old Sovran King much old climb cliff," said Yorka firmly.

"What did the men do when they got to the bottom? How did they get past all those crocodiles?"

They had dropped rafts into the sea, Yorka said, big light rafts made of sliced-up clove-wood; they climbed down on to the rafts and floated away up the west side of the island.

"Where will they get to?"

"Regina town."

Yorka explained that every few months, when the volcano south of the island was due to erupt, a warm ocean current set in, flowing northwards, which would, in about three days, carry the rafts directly to the north tip of the island.

"Do you think they were going for help? Help to fight Manoel?"

Yorka thought this unlikely. "Who would help?"

"The Forest People?"

But the Forest People would *never* fight, Yorka said. Their task was to sing and listen and heal; what useful result did fighting ever produce?

Now Tylo came back. His report was discouraging. Manoel Roy, with a large troop of Angrian Town Guard, was encamped on the brink of the gorge by the bridge over the Kai ravine. The bridge could not be crossed.

Guards with muskets patrolled it every few minutes. And the troop, from time to time, fired their muskets into the forest which surrounded Limbo Lodge.

"Maybe Manoel plans to starve King out," said Herodsfoot. "What a way to use your own brother! *Disgraceful!* When I return to London I shall tell His Majesty King

James that we must immediately cancel our treaty of trade and defence with Aratu."

"Before that, though," said Dido, "how are we going to get to *see* John King? Had us better climb up those steps in the cliff?"

She did not sound at all eager. Herodsfoot turned pale at the very suggestion, and both Tylo and Yorka were opposed to it.

"Cliff of Death holy place, for jumping off, not climbing up."

"Talisman did."

"Well . . ."

Talisman had her own good reasons and was special, their silence conveyed.

"So – what, then?"

Yorka had a plan. It would not be too hard, she said, to make another bridge. They would do it farther down the gorge, around several bends, where Manoel and his men could not see what they were up to.

"But the gorge is wider down there. And how in the *world*, may I ask, can you build a bridge?" asked Herodsfoot in disbelief. He did not sound any happier about this idea than he had at the notion of climbing home-made steps up a thousand-foot cliff.

But Yorka sent Tylo off to the fishing-village on the other side of the headland with a gift of some djeela-pods, which she had by her, and a request for shark-rope.

"What is shark-rope, Yorka?"

"Rope made from human hair, very strong, easy catch shark."

While Tylo was gone, Yorka strolled down the cliff path, looking across the gorge, until she found what she considered a suitable place for a bridge. And she set Dido to collecting spider-webs. These were plentiful, all up and down the cliff path, spread over the thorny, heather shrubs

168

which grew on the lip of the cliff and at the edge of the trees. The large grey-black-and-yellow spiders who spun the webs were not at all pleased at having their handiwork taken away, and shook their legs furiously at Dido, who did not greatly care for the task of despoiling them.

"Will they bite me?" she asked Yorka, who said, "Not if you don't let them."

Herodsfoot was no use at this job as his short sight prevented him from seeing where the webs were, and he broke the stem of his glasses again trying to help.

"Lucky spider-web good for mending glasses," Yorka said, and did an emergency repair while Dido went on with the web-collecting. In the end they had a substantial heap, which Yorka skilfully twisted into a thin line, only just visible in the sunshine. Then Yorka's memory-bird was sent across the gorge at the selected spot with instructions to fly round a chosen tree and come back again with the end of the cord. A thicker strand was now attached and pulled across.

At this point Tylo returned from his trip to the fishing-village with two huge hanks of human hair-cord and a gift of shark steaks. When he saw the slender strand stretched across the ravine he beamed approval.

"Golly-good! Soon now we make bridge."

Herodsfoot had been watching these activities with incredulous disapproval. "We cross *that?* Who, pray, will carry the baby? And what about the horses?"

"I fetch Trinki, he take horses back to Regina," said Yorka.

Meanwhile Dido cooked the shark steaks, and Tylo passed a third strand, then a fourth, across the width of the gorge. Next a length of rope was pulled across; and another. Then Tylo went across himself, holding the upper rope, sliding his feet along the lower; Dido found it imposs-ible to watch him, she gulped, and had to close her eyes, thinking of the roaring white water forcing its way between

169

rocks so very far down below, but he did it without the least concern, and skipped ashore on the far side to fasten the ropes more securely and clear out a foothold on the top of the cliff. The forest grew right down to the cliff edge on that side, but Yorka had chosen her site well; there were two large smooth tikkol trees which provided a strong reliable support for the bridge. By the time the shark steaks were cooked, Tylo and Yorka had constructed a trustworthy-looking rope bridge with two strands of rope on each side, an upper and a lower, and a network of cord zigzagging between, forming a floor, or footing.

Tylo and Yorka had both been across the gorge several times, during the construction of the bridge; now Yorka said, "You go this time, Dido, take baby; time you go," as if she were conferring a big privilege, and Tylo, returning from a scouting trip up the cliff path, said, "Best us all go, pretty-golly quick. Outros guards coming down path for look-about."

With a lump in her gullet the size of a cricket-ball, Dido picked up the baby and moved towards the bridge.

"No, no, baby on back," said Yorka, and, with a swift whipping of opoë vine, fastened the bundle of baby and ukka-leaf on to Dido's shoulders. "Now you got two hand for hold."

Dido found it best not to look at the foamy water crashing and thundering among the rocks such a long way below those frail-seeming strands of rope that supported her feet. She kept her eyes steadily fixed straight ahead, on the dark tree-covered slope in front, and tried to ignore sounds from behind – the rattle of musket-fire, and then, more ominously, men's shouts from higher up the hill on her right. She knew the bridge was not strong enough to support more than one person at a time; she tried to accelerate her pace, but it made the rope structure swing about in a terrifying way, and she dared not go any faster.

170

"Come along, Shaki-Dido – you do good!" shouted Tylo encouragingly from the far bank. She plunged on desperately. The baby woke and let out a thin wail. Muskets cracked from the hillside behind her right shoulder, and she saw a chip fly off one of the tikkol trunks. Then Tylo's hand was grasping hers, pulling her up on to the cliff edge.

"Good now you Shaki-Dido lie down behind tree," urged Tylo, and she was glad to do so, but could not help peering out to see Yorka, nimble as a sting-monkey, flit across the bridge, hardly more visible than a gust of wind among branches. Last came Herodsfoot, and Dido grew sick with fright as she watched his gangling, awkward progress. Now the men with their muskets were not more than three or four turns of the cliff path from the bushes above Yorka's bridge – Dido could see the flashes and the puffs of smoke as they discharged their weapons. It seemed impossible that they should miss him. But luckily their aim was poor, and Herodsfoot's own clumsiness stood him in good stead – the bridge swung about so wildly that he was never in the same spot for two consecutive seconds. But just as Tylo had caught one of his hands to pull him to safety, a bullet did catch him in the shoulder and he jerked uncontrollably and cried out.

"Come, quick come!" cried Yorka, and grabbed his arm; he was dragged on to the bank and hustled down out of view. Tylo without wasting a moment cut through the support-cords of the bridge and jerked on a rope which attached it by a slip-knot on the opposite side. The whole flimsy structure dropped into the gorge and was gone.

"What a shame!" said Dido. "After all that trouble to make it! But let's look at poor Frankie. Is he hurt bad?"

"Not too bad, I think!" gasped Herodsfoot, who was being alternately scolded and comforted by Yorka.

"Did the bullet lodge in you?"

171

"No, it scraped my collar-bone and passed on. I was lucky."

"Golly-lucky!" agreed Tylo. "Come on now, best we get out of here."

With Tylo and Yorka taking an arm apiece, Herodsfoot was bundled back among the trees, and Dido followed with the baby as fast as she could. The forest was much thicker here on the north-facing side of the gorge, so that in a very few minutes they were completely masked by trees and could not be seen by the musketeers; but still these men kept up their fire for a long time, peppering the whole hillside, and sometimes by pure chance a shot came dangerously close.

"Too bad now they know it's us, and that we are here," said Dido.

"Won't know that longtime," said Tylo, and he laid a course diagonally upward through the trees, whistling to his memory-bird and listening to its twittered answers, then slightly changing direction, all the time edging and twisting his way through close-growing vegetation, lianas, creeper, tree-fern, palm boles and opoë vine. Not so much spice at this end of the island, Dido noticed, maybe it's not so hot here.

The forest smelt juicy, rather than spicy.

It was just as well that Tylo and the memory-bird between them seemed to know where they were heading, for dusk now fell fast; making the rope bridge had taken up a lot of the day.

The marksmen finally gave up their fire, perhaps thinking it a waste of ammunition. But it was plain that the gorge must be very narrow here, and the edge of it not far off, for Dido could sometimes smell camp-fires and meat cooking, and catch the sound, now and then, of men's voices; Tylo must be leading his party parallel with the gorge rather than turning south towards King's residence, which Dido recalled as being about half-way up Mount Fura, nestled snugly in a lap of the forest between two spurs of hillside.

"Where are you taking us, Tylo?" she asked, when they paused for a rest in a small clearing where for once it was possible to see the sky above, all clustered with stars.

Tylo said: "Not good fetch up Sovran's house in dark night."

"Guards might shoot at us?"

"Can be so. Also, come Sovran Island, good first stop Ghost House."

"*What* is the *Ghost House*, Tylo?"

Yorka here chipped in. "House Sovran John build his wifie. After she die."

"Her tomb?"

Dido did not know the Dilendi word for *tomb*, so she used the English one. But neither Tylo nor Yorka were familiar with this word.

"Where she was buried?" Dido offered instead.

"Buried? No, *no*!"

Only Angrians buried their dead, Dido learned. The Forest People thought this a disgusting practice; they burned the bodies of their dead relations and then threw them off the Cliff of Death in clay pots. Dido wondered a little where the skulls had come from that were buried under the monoliths at the Place of Stones, but was too polite to ask. Perhaps the skulls were from some long-earlier time when habits were different.

"Ghost House," said Tylo, after about half an hour's climb.

They had reached a small clearing, what seemed like a hollow in the hillside, perhaps the site of an old quarry. The ground here was flat and seemed mossy under foot. Dido noticed two things: first that the place was chilly, which surprised her very much. She could not remember

feeling so cold since the *Thrush* had left the Straits of
Magellan. Secondly, despite its chill, the air was heavy with
the fragrance of spices – musk, aloe, amber-gris, pepper,
civet, bezoar. Her nose prickled, she wanted to sneeze.
Looking up she saw, through the opening in the trees, that
a hazy pale moon was floating overhead, half veiled by
wisps of cloud.

"Where does all the scent come from?" she whispered
to Yorka, who whispered back: "Gifts to Ghost House. Many
people bring."

"Not now they won't. Not with Manoel's guards loosing
off their barkers at anybody who steps this way," said Dido.
"What's the gifts for?"

Yorka made a vague answer. "People sorry King wifie die.
Sorry her baby die. Hope some day they come back."

Tylo said: "Mylord Oklosh some poorly. Best stop here.
Yorka you wrap him in cobweb."

Poor Herodsfoot was indeed weak from pain and loss of
blood; it was high time they halted. Dido was surprised
that Yorka and Tylo seemed quite prepared to use the
Ghost House as a night camping site.

It was a queer little building. Built of pale rock, it was
quite visible in the dull moonlight. To Dido it seemed most
unpractical. It consisted of twelve pillars, set in a square,
approached by steps and standing on a stone platform. A
flat roof did not entirely cover the space enclosed by the
pillars; a double spiral of steps led up through a large
opening in the roof. On the roof could be seen the statue
of a woman, holding a child. Both woman and child were
veiled and only partly visible.

Yorka had lowered Herodsfoot on to the steps leading
up to the pillars, and was binding up his wound with a
handful of cobwebs gathered on the way, and strips of
ukka-leaf.

174

Dido was glad to sit and rest beside them, moving the baby from her shoulder to her lap.

"Is that John King's wife?" she whispered to Tylo, pointing to the statue. He nodded.

The Outros people, he told her, regarded this as a very haunted place, and disliked coming here after dark. So although they were not very far, now, from the bridge and the Guards' camp, no one would be coming that way before daylight.

"Forest People ain't afraid of ghosts?" inquired Dido.

"Not golly-likely." Tylo chuckled. Ghosts, after all, were only Auntie Naewa or Uncle Tobure – what harm could they do? The poor things were only trying to tell you something useful, or feeling a bit lonely, not having found their way, yet, to the other forest; there was no harm in ghosts. Not in forest. Only in houses were ghosts harmful.

"You stay here," Tylo said, "I go find us supper from camp."

"*Tylo! No!* You don't mean you are going to swipe some vittles from the Guards?"

But that was what he did mean to do.

"How will you cross the bridge?"

"I go taku, they never see me. Go under bridge hand-wise. And hear what they talk about."

He slung a leaf-bag on his back and slipped away among the trees.

There was an old wocho behind the Ghost House, in very poor repair. Perhaps it was left over from the time when the little monument had been constructed, had been used to house the builders or their tools. Dido and Yorka, deciding that it would make a good sleeping-place, carried in armfuls of dried moss and creeper to make beds for the party.

This'll be my fifth night in Aratu, thought Dido; it seems more like five months.

175

"What makes it so cold just here?" she asked Yorka.

Yorka said: "The ghost."

"John King's wife?"

"Dead wife feel cold till husband come. King wifie feel extra cold; she die of poison."

"Croopus," said Dido, "I bet *my* mum wouldn't feel cold if my dad weren't about. She'd be dancing in the street. There! That'll be more comfortable for Frankie and the baby than lying on the cold stone floor."

Tylo came back from his raid on the camp looking much more serious than when he had set out, despite the fact that he brought a pot of hot stew and a bag of fruit.

Manoel had got hold of old Ta'asbuie, he said, which was a very bad and worrying thing.

"Old Ta'asbuie do anything for drink."

The Forest People hardly ever touched strong drink, wine or spirits; and small wonder; in order to keep alive and undamaged in the forest you needed eyes alert and your wits about you. But Ta'asbuie, found orphaned as a baby and brought up by an Angrian schoolteacher, had acquired a passion for palm toddy and would do almost anything for a couple of drinks.

"Is pity, for he number one fire-shooter."

"What's that?"

Tylo explained. If the Forest People wanted – as they occasionally did – to burn out a small patch of forest, they first soaked the surrounding area with pails of water.

"Or make rain, but not all Kanikke can do that."

When the surrounding forest was thoroughly wet, the fire-shooter, from a safe distance, shot a flaming arrow into the middle of the section that was to be burned.

"Why not just light it with a bit of fire-fungus?"

Because, said Tylo, the forest, and the forest earth were so very combustible that the whole patch would explode, unless the greatest care was taken. That was why cooking-fires were always contained in stone caskets and why, mostly, the Forest People ate their food raw.

"So what's Manoel want with this Ta'asbuie?"

"Wants him shoot fire arrow on to Mount Fura. Burn out John King."

"Oh, murder," said Dido, and Herodsfoot, who had been silently listening, exclaimed, "But that is monstrous! A crime! A crime of the blackest kind! Firstly, a fire on Mount Fura would mean the death of John King – his household – not to mention ourselves; not only that, but it would destroy all the animal life on this portion of the island. And – if the wind should change and blow northwards over the gorge – the whole island might go up in flames. It is the most wickedly irresponsible plan! It is not to be thought of!"

"*Better* be thought of," said Tylo, frowning. "We go early, before sun-up, warn Sovran John."

"Then we had best all go to sleep directly," said Herodsfoot.

The stew eaten, everybody went to rest in the wocho. The baby, peacefully replete with fruit-juice, was already in a deep slumber.

But Dido could not sleep. Hearing everyone else's quiet breathing only made her more wakeful; she slipped out of the wocho and went to sit on the steps of the monument. Now it seemed to her – strangely enough – that she could hear a voice singing: not very loud, the kind of untroubled, quiet song that a person might sing, almost under their breath, while doing a job of work, picking berries, or ironing, or hemming a shirt. The song – now and then Dido could just about catch the words – was all about how we came, once, from our old grandmother the sea, and were due to end up, bleached and desiccated, with our old grandfather the desert – and a long, strange journey it was between the two extremes . . .

"O-o-o, from swim to fly, from wet to dry,
From fly to blow, blow in the wind, o-o-o . . ."

It was a queer song, rather like the ones Yorka sang, thought Dido, but who could be the singer? Might it be Aunt Tala'aa, didn't Yorka say that she was to be found in this part of the island?

The song was interrupted by an angry voice. And this voice was perfectly familiar to Dido – she had heard it quite recently and could not mistake. It was that of Manoel; harsh, nasal, and arrogant.

"Will you stop that caterwauling and pay me some heed?"

"O-o-o, why should I, why should I?"

"Because I love you!"

"And a strange way you had of showing your love!"

"Oh, Erato, don't torment me! Say one kind thing to me!"

"You found a witch to poison me," she sang,
"You threw my daughter into the sea,
You plan ill luck for my poor old King
Why should I say you one kind thing?"

"You never loved John!"

"I never loved either of you. But he was my husband, brought me up and was kind to me. *You* never raised me a monument! You were far away, playing with dice and dominoes in Europe. Games! If you had the choice between me, alive, and a pair of never-lose dice, which would you take? Don't trouble to answer, I know!"

"I love you!" he shouted angrily.

"Easy words. Now my daughter has come back – do you plan to throw her into the sea a second time? Or what is your plan?"

"I have no plan. Where is she? Do you know where she is? I have no plan!"

"Oh, come! You first put the notion of coming back to Aratu into her head so that she could be useful to you – or you could dispose of her; you had her hustled into jail on a lame charge so that she would have to be obliged to you – but she got out, the clever thing; your trail is all over the landscape like a snail's slime, you cannot conceal it."

"I hate this island! I wish it were under the sea."

"If it were under the sea, you would not be able to come and scold me. Scolding a ghost! What a dismal hobby!"

"I love you! I love you!"

"Oh, my dear Paul! Enough! You had best find another watchword, for that one won't help you, and soon you are going to fall over the edge . . ."

"What do you *mean? Edge?* What edge?"

But there came no answer to that. The other voice began singing again:

> "From wet to dry, from swim to fly,
> O,o,o, the wind does blow . . ."

Ghosts talking, thought Dido, I didn't reckon, when I came to Aratu, that I'd be hearing *ghosts talking.*

At least – *one* of them was a ghost . . . Where was Manoel?

Stretched on the steps of the monument, Dido fell asleep.

Chapter Ten

DIDO WOKE WITH A START, FROM A DREAM OF having burned the toast and being scolded by her mother. What had woken her was the smell of smoke.

She sprang to her feet in a fright.

The sight that met her eyes then did not at all diminish her fright. Now, in broad daylight, it was easy to see that the little stone-built Ghost House was within a bowshot-length of the gorge. A wide sloping path led down from the building to a wooden footbridge which spanned the ravine, here at its deepest. On the farther side of the bridge, tents were visible among the trees, and men with muskets, patrolling.

But what riveted Dido's attention was the sight of Manoel, with two other men, standing not much more than a hundred yards away on this side of the ravine, close to the bridge. One of the men was an Angrian in officer's uniform, the other a Forest Person who seemed the worse for liquor; he kept giggling foolishly, waving his hands, and looking about him in a vacant manner, as if he wondered what he was doing there. He held a bow.

Manoel noticed Dido when she stood up and addressed her in a scornful, indifferent tone.

"Oh – so you are there? I suppose Herodsfoot is somewhere about? Well, you won't be there for long. Capitan Ereira," he ordered the uniformed officer, "tell the man, Ta-asbuie, to shoot a couple more arrows. And to waste no time about it."

His voice, which was not particularly loud, travelled clearly up the slope. Must be thrown by some kind of echo from the other bank, Dido guessed. And that's how it must have worked last night when he was a-chatting to the ghost.

But there was no time to lose in idle thoughts. Without troubling to answer Manoel, Dido scooted round to the wocho at the rear. Here she found Tylo and Yorka frantically trying to rouse Herodsfoot, who was flushed, wild-eyed and rambling, evidently in a fever from his bullet-wound, not at all in prime condition.

"Shaki-sir, *must* get up! Must climb hill to Sovran house!"

"I could as soon climb Mount Everest," mumbled Herodsfoot. "Could as soon climb Mount Kanchenjunga. Could as soon—"

Tylo and Yorka exchanged despairing glances.

Dido turned and looked behind her. Manoel's two companions had retired to the far side of the bridge. They had a brazier from which came smoke and flame.

Tylo said: "Yorka, can you make rain?"

"Never yet." Yorka pressed her hands tight against her chest. "But I try," she said.

"Is all we can hope for," said Tylo.

Dido, looking around, saw that this was probably true. The drunken Forest Man, Ta'asbuie, reeling from one side to another in fits of hysterical laughter, was dipping arrows into the brazier and loosing them off as soon as they began to flame. His aim was fairly wild; quite a few of the arrows fell in the river. One lodged on the bridge, which began to burn; Manoel, with a quick, furious order, summoned a soldier to extinguish it. But several arrows had already fallen among the trees surrounding the Ghost House; a fierce crackling could be heard; billows of smoke went spiralling up into the sky from different parts of the forest.

Dido caught Captain Ereira's voice from the bridge saying anxiously, "Sir, sir, do you think this is really wise? Suppose the wind changes – suppose it should blow from the south?—" Manoel made no reply.

"Save us!" muttered Dido. "I reckon this is the tightest corner yet."

She picked up the baby, wondering which way to run. There were fires among the trees, both to right and left.

"No-no-*no*!" said Yorka. "You help me, Dido! Miria help too! Wake her. Now: you both help make rain. Like this. Think of water. Think big water. Think *hard*. Then put the water up in the sky."

Yorka herself then seemed to go into a trance. She stood – as she had when divining the whereabouts of Aunt Tala'aa – with her face turned up to the sky and eyes closed. Her hands were clenched. She wore a frowning expression of terrific concentration, and was murmuring a Dilendi phrase over and over, but Dido could not hear what she said, her voice was too soft.

Dido herself, obeying instructions, thought about water. She thought of oceans, rivers, waterfalls, jugs full, mugs full, cups full, bowls full. She thought of fountains, brooks, ponds, gutters. She thought of the spittle in her mouth, the tears in her eyes (these were quite copious, with smoke now drifting thickly about the Ghost House). She thought of the blood running in her veins. She thought of the baby she held in her arms. "Our bodies are like cucumbers," she remembered Herodsfoot saying, a day or two ago, as they munched their lunch. "Ninety per cent water."

This baby is just like a sponge full of water, thought Dido. The baby, as if catching her thought, woke up and began to cry with terrific vigour. She yelled with all her heart. Perhaps the smoke had got into her eyes also.

Rain, thought Dido. Let it rain. Let it stream, pelt, pour, thunder, lighten. I am putting all those ponds and lakes up in the sky. I am putting oceans there. I am putting the River Thames. I am putting djeela juice, tea, coffee, milk, lemonade, up into the sky. I am lifting the whole Pacific Ocean and wrapping it round the sun . . .

A drop fell on her right hand.

She looked up, startled.

The sky had been its usual brilliant blue, with not a cloud in sight. But now two things were happening. The birds – parrots, frigate-birds, parakeets, owls, gulls, memory-birds – were all flying about in confusion, and crying and squawking. And across the sky, skeins of haze were floating like spider-webs, joining and tangling, weaving together to form a fabric of cloud – and from this fabric, drops were beginning to fall . . .

"Rain!" gasped Tylo. "*Ashtaa* Yorka – you did it! You really made the rain come." And he made her a deep bow, pressing his hands together.

Yorka opened her eyes. The raindrops were now falling quite plentifully and a gust of wind, fanning up from the south, suddenly whipped across the gorge, carrying with it a hunk of flame, which completely enwrapped Captain Ereira and Ta'asbuie, reduced the bridge to a shrivelled wisp, and then swept on into the middle of the Angrian camp. There were shouts and screams of terror, and some violent explosions; after that the drumming of almost solid rain and a tremendous crack of thunder drowned all other noises.

"Into the Ghost House!" ordered Tylo – his words were inaudible, but his gesture was plain. Dido hastily tucked the baby into a sheltered corner and then helped Tylo with Herodsfoot who was too weak to move himself; they half-led, half-carried him under the overhang of the roof.

Yorka still stood outside in the downpour with her skinny arms upraised, apparently encouraging it to keep on raining and not stop.

"Bless my soul!" muttered Herodsfoot. "The fish will be rising. How I wish that I had brought my rod and tackle . . ."

Dido was peering down across the gorge, trying to see through solid sheets of water. She caught a glimpse of Captain Ereira and Ta'asbuie being carried into the camp;

she could not decide whether they were dead or just badly burned. And where was Manoel? She could not see him.

Yorka now came into the Ghost House with a look of calm achievement on her face. "Rain come," she said.

"Croopus, Yorka," said Dido, giving Yorka a tremendous hug. "I'll justabout say it *did* come. You're a skinny little critter, Yorka, but I'll tell you – you are real Grade A champion class when it comes to making rain!"

This remark was endorsed by a voice from behind them. A lady who came walking between the pillars of the ghost-house said approvingly: "Excellently managed, Yorka! I could have done it no better myself!"

Yorka's face became brilliant. "Aunt Tala'aa!"

She made a deep bow, and the traditional greeting of child to adult in the Forest, placing her hands, palm inwards, on the lady's cheeks.

"Now, my dear child – as the rain has served its purpose for the moment – it would make it easier for us to hear each other speak if you turned it off again."

Yorka nodded and, leaving the Ghost House, went back into the deluge and made some signals to the sky, which soon began to take effect. The thunder stopped pealing. The torrent of water from the bank of heavy cloud gradu-ally eased, slowed down, and finally came to a stop. All that could be heard now was a musical drip-drip from the overweighted branches. The sky began to clear and clouds of steam rose from the ground.

But Yorka herself, Dido noticed, turned extremely pale, staggered slightly, and sat down on a rock as if, for a moment, she had lost her sense of balance. A thin trickle of blood ran from each nostril.

"You been taken queer, duck?" Dido asked anxiously.

Yorka shook her head.

"Cloud-rain pull out blood," she whispered, dabbing it away with a leaf. "Not bad – soon better."

184

But Dido noticed that she moved slowly and with caution for half an hour. Dido herself felt stiff and tired as if she had run in a race.

Meanwhile Aunt Tala'aa looked keenly about her at the other occupants of the ghost-house, and Dido studied the newcomer with deep interest.

Aunt Tala'aa was plainly a Forest Person, honey-coloured in complexion, and curly-haired (though at present her short, pure white hair hung draggled with rain); she was rather taller than most Forest People, about the same height as Lord Herodsfoot.

Her clothes were black, like those of the Angrian women, but she wore them very differently. Angrian women's clothes were always dusty and shapeless, intended to be inconspicuous, looking old and worn even if they were not. Aunt Tala'aa's clothes though black, and at the moment drenched with rain, were severely elegant, a long narrow skirt under a cape with a dark plum-coloured lining and floating white bands at the neck. She had a flat triangular black cap on her head.

Dido had once seen a bishop, who also happened to be a Professor of Law, riding through the streets of London in a carriage. He had impressed Dido very much – looked so shrewd and learned, but also *good* at the same time; this old girl reminded Dido of that bishop. It'd take a really downy 'un to put anything across Auntie Tala'aa, thought Dido.

It seemed as if their thoughts collided, for the old lady turned and subjected Dido to a piercing scrutiny.

"You are Dido Twite," she said.

"Yes, ma'am," agreed Dido, thinking, How does she know that?

"Talisman told me about you – about you all," said Aunt Tala'aa. "We shall be friends. But first I see that our friend here – you must be Lord Herodsfoot, are you not? – needs some medical attention for his hurt shoulder."

She stepped outside, was gone, perhaps, a couple of minutes, and returned with two leaves. One she placed on Herodsfoot's shoulder, and covered it with a new poultice of cobweb; the other she instructed him to hold on his tongue for three minutes, then swallow.

When he had done so – and almost at once he began to look a little better – he murmured faintly, "Madam – did I hear you correctly just now when you addressed Dido – did I hear you say that *Talisman* had spoken to you of us?"

"Indeed she has. She has given me very good descriptions of you all."

"Then she is alive? She is safe? She survived that dreadful climb?"

"She did – she is at Limbo Lodge – and, as soon as you are able to walk, I think that we should make our way there."

"Oh, *yes!*" said Herodsfoot fervently.

In ten minutes – so efficacious was the power of the herb he had swallowed – Herodsfoot declared that he was quite able to undertake the walk to Limbo Lodge. He looked transformed – pale still, but hopeful, happy, and alert. Aunt Tala'aa said that the walk would take no more than twenty minutes. And it was much easier going than any of the tracks they had followed up to now, being wide and well trodden – plainly the way from John King's house to the bridge had been much used.

As they climbed the hill Dido overheard snatches of conversation between Herodsfoot and Aunt Tala'aa. "You speak remarkably good English, ma'am – but, pray, how should I properly address you?"

She laughed. "Well, you could call me Aunt Tala'aa as most people do – or you could call me Professor Limisoë

– I learned my English at the University of Cambridge and my French at the Sorbonne in Paris, where I studied for my Master's Degree in Occult Philosophy."

Herodsfoot was enraptured. "Aha! then you must know a great deal about the Tarot – and the Eight Immortals – and the thong games that the Arctic Folk may play only when the sun is above the horizon in their brief summer—"

In no time the two of them were chatting away like old friends, and he was addressing her as Auntie Tala'aa.

Limbo Lodge, seen from closer to, appeared large, low, and rambling. It was sited at the edge of the forest line, among clumps of clove and djeela trees, in a kind of wild garden. Over to the eastern boundary of this, the ground seemed to come to an abrupt stop: here, Dido guessed, was the Cliff of Death. It seemed to her a very odd thing to build one's house within so short a distance of such an awesome spot.

Not a soul seemed to be stirring anywhere.

None of the group were aware of the dark figure that shadowed them among the trees.

A veranda skirted two sides of the house. Aunt Tala'aa led the way up a flight of steps on to the veranda. Looking in windows as they passed outside, Dido saw a games-room with a billiard table, punchball, dartsboard, and smaller tables marked for chess or chequers. Next door was a library lined with books, a lamp burning on a table, but this, like the games room, was silent and unoccupied.

Then, out of a door farther along, came Talisman, running, joyful, her face blazing with delight and triumph.

"Oh, I am so happy that you got here safely!" she cried. "Come in! come in! Have you had breakfast? No? Then come to the kitchen – my father will see you all later . . ."

Her brilliant smile embraced them all equally. She turned and led them along a wide passage to a room on the other side of the house whose large windows looked up the mountain to its craggy summit. This room was amazingly untidy, as if it had been occupied by a great number of people who had all left in a hurry without troubling to take anything with them Plates, bowls, baskets of fruit, loaves of bread lay about mixed with tennis rackets, footballs, fencing foils and hockey-sticks. There were also a great many notebooks: dozens and dozens of them, all sizes.

Talisman was putting a pot of water on the stove to make coffee, finding clean plates, chattering away.

"Would you believe it – my father knew me *at once*! It was so wonderful! After I climbed the cliff—"

Dido, filled with curiosity, peered inside some of the notebooks. Why keep notebooks in the kitchen? Why keep so many? She found they were all filled with handwriting and each one contained a curious one-sided dialogue. Each book had a name on it: 'Jorge', 'Enrique', 'Tomas', 'Pepe'. Dido leafed through several of them. Then the solution came to her. Of course – John King was stone deaf. Each person who had any dealings with him carried a book and wrote down what he wanted to say.

Poor old cove, thought Dido, staring down at these one-sided conversations, each in a different handwriting, no wonder he went a bit queer in the attic and shut himself up in Limbo Lodge. Must have been like living inside of a barrel.

Dinner is served, Excellency. The deputation of fishermen is here with a sample of pearls. The barber is waiting to trim your beard. Do you wish to see the accused men? The tailor with a coat for a fitting. Senhor Manoel is here . . . Would your Excellency prefer guava or melon?

Then Dido picked up a book labelled Manoel. This one was different. Looking here and there, turning pages at random, Dido found Manoel's side in a series of furious arguments, scribbled so violently that the writing sometimes dug into the paper: I cannot stand life here any longer. *Please* let me go to Europe again. *Please* let me go. I promise that I will not play for high stakes. I swear it! I think you are mad. A mad, bigoted tyrant! I am your own brother, I am worth more than this. *Why* do you not let me go away from here?

"Breakfast is served!" said Talisman. She had swept all the hugger-mugger of objects off a large table into a basket that looked as if it had held firewood, and had set out plates, bowls of fruit, loaves, and cups of coffee. They were all glad to pull up stools and sit down. Herodsfoot ate little (though he seemed to have recovered remarkably fast from his bullet wound); he could not take his eyes off Talisman. But the others were ravenous.

"Where have you *been*, Aunt Tala'aa?" asked Talisman, putting a bowl of tikkol fruit in front of the old lady. "When I saw the smoke come up the hillside near the Ghost House, then – for the first time – I was afraid. Really afraid. I could not find you in my mind. Where were you? Did you make that rain?"

"I was in ekarin. No, I did not make the rain."

"What is ekarin?" murmured Dido to Yorka, who was sitting beside her, trying to feed the baby with goats' milk, of which there was a supply in Limbo Lodge. Miria did not fancy goats' milk at all and was demonstrating, with yells, that she would prefer djeela juice.

"Ekarin. That is when somebody goes away from this world for a time. The sun does it. He sets. The moon also. Gods do it. And Kanikke must do it too. They need to, to keep up their strength and knowledge and baraat."

"I see."

"No. The rain," Aunt Tala'aa said, with the pride of a teacher whose pupil has done superlatively well, "the rain was made by Yorka here, who should grow up to be one of the most notable Kanikke that our island has ever produced. Indeed, she is one already."

Yorka hung her head bashfully and stared at her plate.

"Dido helped me," she muttered. "And so did Miria. It was her loud shrieks that really opened the sky."

"We must find a first-class foster-mother for that baby," said Aunt Tala'aa, smiling at Talisman, who looked as if she thought that would be an easy task.

"Talisman?" said Dido. "Tell us about your meeting with your old man. Was he surprised to see you?"

"It took what seemed like an eternity to climb the cliff," said Talisman. "I cut steps as I went, with a knife that Aunt Tala'aa had given me. For I thought I might need to go back down that way if – if my father did not accept me. When I reached the top I was so tired that I crawled into a hollow among the bushes and went to sleep. Two of the guards found me there. They wanted to throw me over the cliff, but I – but I persuaded them not to . . . I said they should bring me to see John King, and, in the end, they did. When I was brought to him, I was going to show him my medallion, but there was no need. He said 'Erato!' and, and embraced me—" she dashed a tear from her eye, "and then he said, 'Before your mother died, she and I were playing a game of chess. Now we can finish that game, you and I.'"

"But why," said Dido, "did all his guards go off, climbing down the cliff?"

"That was my father's idea. He said, 'If Manoel chooses to come and besiege Limbo Lodge in this spiteful, stupid way, I shall play a trick on him. I shall send my guard round by sea to Regina. There I hope they can persuade the townspeople – the ones that are left – to a different way of thinking. I daresay the numbers will be about equal!"

"But what does your father plan to do himself? He can hardly stay here without food or servants," said Herodsfoot.

190

"Oh, he has some plans," said Talisman. The radiant smile came back to her face. She went on: "The wonderful, the amazing thing is that his deafness is getting better. I am being able to cure it. A tincture made from the venom of pearl-snakes – is not that strange? – Aunt Tala'aa and I had talked of it, and I decided to try it on him – and, as a result, his hearing is coming back. Is not that wonderful? Often before I have felt satisfaction at a cure because my guess had been proved right – but I have *never* felt happiness like this before. If I can do this for him, what more can I not do to help him, what can we not achieve together? It can be the beginning of a better time for Aratu."

Poor Frankie, thought Dido, looking at Herodsfoot's face, I don't reckon there's much of a chance for you in among all that . . .

"But now," said Talisman, "let me take you to meet my father. He is not strong enough, yet, to speak to you all; but I will introduce Lord Herodsfoot. And you three just step inside the door and greet him—"

Accordingly Dido, Tylo, and Yorka stayed in the rear of the group as Talisman led them along the wide passage to the door of a room that faced up towards the mountain crest.

Aunt Tala'aa remained in the kitchen feeding the baby. No doubt she was acquainted with John King already.

Talisman walked through the open door, with Herodsfoot behind her, and motioned to the others to stay where they were and come no farther.

They saw a large, spacious room, wildly cluttered, like the kitchen, with a collection of miscellaneous articles – astrolabes, carpenters' tools, orreries, telescopes, musical instruments, chess sets, piles of books, tubes of paint and palettes. Halfway between the door and the large French window stood a great gold-and-silver four-poster bed. In

191

this reclined an old man – a magnificent old man, wrapped in a black wool robe like that of a monk.

Croopus, thought Dido, he sure looks more like a real king than poor old King Jamie does. (She had seen King James III of England once, at a military display in St James's Park and thought but poorly of him). John King's bush of hair and beard were white, his eyes were deep-set and gleaming, a craggy brow was offset by a jaw like the bulwark of a galleon. It was the face of a clever and powerful man, yet not a cruel or mean one, thought Dido; he knows his own mind, that's all. But how much heed does he pay to other folks' minds?

He certainly loved and heeded his daughter Talisman: the look he gave her was pure devotion, and he stretched out his hand as if she had been away from his bedside for ten hours, instead of ten minutes.

"Father!" she said loudly and clearly. "You know I told you of Lord Herodsfoot, who has been visiting Aratu in search of ancient games – here he is—"

Her introduction was never finished, for at this moment her words were violently interrupted. The glass of the window shattered, splinters from it hurtled all over the room and a man burst through the gaping hole that had been made.

It was Manoel – but a very different Manoel from the calm, scornful man they had met in Regina town. This Manoel was blackened with soot from head to foot, his clothes were singed and tattered, his face, shoulder and side were disfigured by a great angry red burn mark.

He held pistols in both hands.

"This is your finish, John King!" he said loudly. "And your daughter too. Time's up! From now on, *I* give orders here—"

As he spoke he took aim, and now fired directly at the man on the bed. But also while he spoke two things had been happening: Herodsfoot, who had moved to the end of the bed, threw himself at the intruder, ducking low, and managed to knock his feet from under him; and little Yorka, quick as a flash, darted at the man on the bed and pulled him out of the line of fire.

Both pistols exploded; one shot hit the canopy of the bed and brought it down in a tangle of massive, gold-embroidered folds; the other shot took Yorka full in the chest and killed her instantly.

Herodsfoot and Manoel rolled over and over, kicking and struggling, until Talisman, who had snatched up one of the pistols dropped by Manoel, managed to deal him a fierce blow on the head with the butt of it, and knocked him senseless.

"Father?" she cried urgently, "are you all right? Father? You were not hit?"

"No, no, I am well enough," said King. "But this child – I fear she is done for."

He pulled back the gold canopy and revealed Yorka lying in a pool of blood.

"*Oh, no!*" cried Talisman. "Yorka! *Not Yorka!*"

And Tylo, from his place by the door, let out a long, heartbroken wail.

Herodsfoot, disentangling himself from Manoel, stood up. His face was white with shock.

"*Not* poor little Yorka?" he stammered. "Not *dead?* I am so grieved – so horrified—"

Dido could not speak at all. Her throat was tight with anguish.

Tylo, running to the bed, clasped Yorka's hand, as if in hopes there might still be some sign of life in her, some chance to bring her back. But there was not. His head sank down, he stood silent, with tears running down his cheeks. Then he turned and made for the door.

"I go fetch Aunt Tala'aa," he said.

But Aunt Tala'aa herself appeared at that moment, carrying Miria.

"What is all this commotion?" she demanded.

But she took in the scene immediately: Manoel sprawled on the floor, Yorka's body on the bed, John King in his black serge robe looking shaken and appalled by the suddenness of these happenings.

Aunt Tala'aa was frozen by a passion of rage and grief.

It was a silent passion. She looked steadily at Yorka, drew a deep, careful breath, and said, "Our island has lost something irreplaceable. That child was the best – could have been the best – since your wife, since Erato," she told John King. "But now she is gone. For always. We can't bring her back. And this – this human *rat*—" she looked down at the prone body of Manoel " – *he* had to wipe her out. Like the fool who sets fire to the forest because he wants to fry an egg for his supper. Well, he has done enough harm for this lifetime. He shall do no more. His time has come." She addressed Manoel sharply.

"Wake up, you! Get up!"

To Dido's astonishment Manoel, who had seemed deeply unconscious, gradually came out of his faint and hoisted himself to his feet. He looked blearily round the room, his face tightened with disgust as he saw the various people in it, and finally his mouth twisted in aversion at the sight of Aunt Tala'aa and the baby.

"So you've come back, you old hag," he muttered.

"I have come back," said Aunt Tala'aa. "Not before time. And you are about to leave."

"Much obliged!"

"For years your wish has been to travel from this island. And now it is going to be granted. Today you have cost me one of my best students."

She gestured to the body of Yorka, among the fold of the gold canopy.

"*Her?*" Manoel seemed baffled. "That child? If she got killed it was her own fault. She shouldn't have got in the way. I never meant to kill *her.*"

"Do you think that makes it any better? You kill without regard. A human life is no more to you than an empty bottle you toss away. You killed my Erato because she laughed at you and refused your offers. You have hated all women since then. You did your best to kill Erato's daughter. Now you are going away to a black hole where you will be cold and bored for the rest of eternity. There will be no games to play there: no dice, no cards, no tally-sticks, no counters. You may stay there until your mother turns into a hyena and comes to pounce on you. And you may remember, if you choose to do so, that you were sent into the dark by a woman. And by a baby. A baby whose name you have cause to remember. Look at me!"

She stood facing Manoel, one palm raised in the air, the other arm holding the baby. Manoel gazed at her vacantly, with his jaw fallen, mouth open, prominent eyes staring. Gradually his expression became fixed, a curious whining gasp issued from his mouth, and he sank, first to his knees, then in total collapse on the floor.

"*Ashtaa*, Tala'aa-kanikke!" murmured Tylo. "You make an end of that poison-man. Is good."

"Merciful heavens!" exclaimed Herodsfoot. "Is the man dead? Just like that?"

"He is dead, and will trouble us no more," said Aunt Tala'aa. "We will not think of him again."

Tylo said, "I take him away."

He left the room and reappeared in a few moments with a wheeled basket-chair, presumably kept for the use of John King. Tylo and Herodsfoot between them lifted the body of Manoel into the chair.

"Good," said Aunt Tala'aa. "Now you can tip him over

the Cliff of Death. The hungry mouths down below can make an end of him."

"What about Yorka?" said Dido sadly.

"Little Yorka. We shall burn her on a fire of sandalwood and djeela-bark. And let the wind carry her ashes away. But you, in the meantime, my friend," Aunt Tala'aa said to John King, "I think you had better return to bed."

"Not in *this* room," he said in dismay. "Too many bad things have happened here."

"No, no, we shall find some other. Rooms in plenty in this house."

When another chamber had been chosen, and John King settled in it, with Talisman beside him, playing the hyena game on a beautiful spiral board made of nutmeg wood, Aunt Tala'aa, Tylo, Dido, and Lord Herodsfoot walked slowly out on to the veranda of Limbo Lodge. They were all dejected and silent. The sight of the woods below, with burnt patches still steaming from Yorka's rain, did nothing to cheer them.

But Aunt Tala'aa said, trying to be brisk about it: "We should not grieve for *her*. Only for ourselves. She is now receiving a Kanikke's welcome in the Other Forest."

Tylo said: "And Manoel sent to Black Hole. That one very good thing."

"What shall we do now?" said Dido. "We can't cross the bridge, it's burnt. Manoel must have been on this side when that happened. And those fellows over there in the camp won't know that he is dead. Do you think we should tell them? In case they start shooting again?"

"No," said Aunt Tala'aa. "As they do not know what has happened they will wait and wait for Manoel to reappear, and then gradually they will drift away home. So, that way, probably when we go to Regina, only some, not all of those men will have returned."

"But – but how *can* we get to Regina? The bridge is

burned—" Dido swallowed, remembering how Tylo and Yorka wove their own bridge of rope. Would she be able to help Tylo make another?

"We go by ship."

"You don't mean – climb down the cliff to Manati harbour?" Herodsfoot came out of his gloomy reverie to inquire.

"No, no. Let us go and look at the ship. That will take our minds off sad things."

Aunt Tala'aa led the way down the steps off the veranda and across the stretch of short grass to the cliff top. A low building stood near the southern tip of the promontory. In front of this, a small ship was perched upon chocks: a solid, stubby, clinker-built sloop, Bermuda-rigged, with an enclosed cabin. Her name was painted on the side: *The Lass of Cley.*

"Dear me," said Herodsfoot. "That seems a stout, seaworthy little craft – but how in the world to get it down to the water?"

Here they were, perhaps a bowshot length from the edge of the cliff; a thousand feet above the Pacific Ocean, which they could see, black, blue, silvery, and crinkled, away to the south.

Aunt Tala'aa smiled. "No problem. In a few days the undersea volcano Mount Ximboč will erupt. The eruption is always preceded by earthquakes in this region. Part of the cliff we are standing on will fall."

She began to walk about near the cliff edge, pacing to and fro, counting the paces. She had taken a forked rod from the boat-yard and held it with both hands, her thumbs pointing upwards and backwards along the forks. When it quivered, as it did now and then, she stuck a sliver of bamboo into the ground.

"See," she said, "that defines the area of the rock-fall. Now it only remains to shift the boat to this spot."

197

"On rollers?" suggested Herodsfoot doubtfully. "But how shall we pull it? And then—" his words absolutely dried up in his throat as he contemplated the scheme which Aunt Tala'aa seemed to be proposing.

"You mean," he said hoarsely, "we put the boat here and then wait for it to fall into the sea?"

"Ah, the sea will not be so far down then," Aunt Tala'aa said, laughing at his dismay. "You will see! After Mount Ximboë erupts, a great wave races northwards past this island. They call it the onda. All we have to do is choose our moment when the wave approaches – we shall see it coming, here, for a long time before it arrives – then launch off at the moment when it is nearest."

"Just so," muttered Herodsfoot in a hollow voice.

But Tylo was enthusiastic. "Like ride a dolphin."

This, he had told Dido, was a favourite sport of the island boys, when dolphins were in a co-operative humour.

"Well, I reckon it's the best way to get to Regina town," Dido remarked. "How long does it take a boat on that onda, Auntie Tala'aa?"

"Not more than nine or ten hours. The most difficult part is steering *out* of the onda when we reach the north tip of the island."

"Oh yes – I remember that was why Doc Tally never got back to her dad after Manoel threw her in the sea and the Dutch boat picked her up, 'cos the current took the ship right up to the Moluccas."

"Just so. John King used to be a skilful sailor – but whether he will be equal to the task at this time remains to be seen," Aunt Tala'aa said equably.

Herodsfoot croaked out: "Er – sailing used to be quite a little hobby of mine – before I began collecting games."

"Then you are just the man we need," said Aunt Tala'aa, giving him a kindly look.

Chapter Eleven

THEY SPENT TWO DAYS AND TWO NIGHTS AT Limbo Lodge. Most of this time was passed by Dido, Herodsfoot, and Tylo in playing games, of which they found a huge selection about the place. Dido's favourite was Hyena, a board game somewhat akin to Ludo, using a spiral track on which players moved their counters according to throws of dice. The counter was the player's mother, going to the well for water. If she managed to escape all the hazards on the way, and returned with a jug of water, she turned into a hyena and could pounce on all the other contestants. This tickled Dido greatly.

"Coo! Don't I just wish *my* ma would turn into a hyena! She couldn't be any meaner than she is already."

Dido's own parents were so disagreeable that she could not help envying the happy relationship that had sprung up between John King and his daughter Talisman.

He got up from his bed on the morning after they had arrived, declaring that he was entirely better, and spent most of his time in an armchair by a window facing out to the southern sea. Sometimes Herodsfoot spent time with him, and played a game of Go, or Hnefatafl, or Four Field Kono, but in general it was Talisman who sat beside him, holding his hand, looking lovingly into his face, and discussing, endlessly, what should be done for the welfare of the island of Aratu. Sometimes Aunt Tala'aa joined them and shared these discussions, but Aunt Tala'aa was a true Forest Person; she could hardly endure to be in one place for more than six or seven hours, and would often vanish away on her own concerns.

"Where do you *go*, Aunt Tala'aa?" Dido asked her.

199

"Oh ... here and there! Up and down. To and fro. Sometimes to the camp, to see how they go on there. Many were killed by that fire. The others – poor things – they are in great confusion, some deserting. Other times I take a look at the madman Ruiz – or those sad Ereiras—"

"But, Aunt Tala'aa – how do you get across the gorge? How do you get about?"

Aunt Tala'aa smiled. "Oh, comme-ci, comme-ca! One way or another. Lo'ongoh ..." She used a Dilendi phrase that Dido had not heard before.

"Aunt Tala'aa – what did you mean by that thing you said to Manoel about the baby?"

Aunt Tala'aa said, "Once – long ago – Manoel (in those days he was still known as Paul, Paul Kirlingshaw) he played a game of Mancala with a Forest Man. Manoel cheated – he moved his piece when the other man had left the board to fetch his baby who was crying. But a memory-bird saw what Manoel did and told its master when he came back. And the man's wife, who was a Kanikke, held up the baby and said, 'Angrian man! The next time you see a baby with the same name as our daughter, your wits will leave you for ever and they will never return. From then, you will be as good as dead.' So always, after that, Manoel hated the company of women and small children and would avoid them whenever he could."

"What was the baby's name?"

"Miria. It is a name often used by the Forest People. It means Daughter of the Sun."

"Is it so terrible – to cheat in a game?"

Aunt Tala'aa looked at Dido seriously. "It is the first step towards annihilation of the spirit."

"I see. So it was quite kind of you to knock Manoel off, after he had seen Miria. Otherwise he'd have been ninepence in the shilling for the rest of his life."

200

"All I did was remind him. After that, sheer terror finished him off."

Dido gazed at Aunt Tala'aa with respect.

"Did you know that Manoel had pinched a skull from the Place of Stones?"

"Yes, a memory-bird told me that. If he had ever gone back to that place, one of the stones would have fallen and crushed him."

"No wonder he didn't care for Aratu."

"He was a poor, despicable wretch," Aunt Tala'aa dismissed Manoel with a wave of the hand. "The urge to gamble is a disease – like the craving for opium, or rum-toddy." Dido nodded. She knew all about that. "Some might say – leave such poor fools alone, to wreak their own destruction. But the danger is that they do harm to others – they steal, they lie, they commit crimes to pay for their habit. And they infect their companions."

"Yes. That's so," said Dido sadly.

"We will think of him no more. He did great harm to Aratu. But matters will mend now."

Tylo came to summon them to Yorka's death-rites.

On the stone floor of the little Ghost House, he and Dido had built a pyre of musk, aloes, ambergris, djeela-bark, sandalwood, pepper, bezoar and nutmeg leaves. Yorka's body was tucked into this, wrapped in the gold brocade from King's four-poster. Aunt Tala'aa had removed the wooden ring from her finger.

"Even a wooden ring may tie down her spirit." Tala'aa gave it to Dido. Then, with a piece of fire-fungus she touched the djeela-bark and blew on it gently. At once a clear green flame shot up. In five minutes the little fragrant pile was totally burned, without smoke or sound. Dido wondered that no wind stirred the flame, for, outside the ghost-house, she could see that a strong southerly breeze was bending the branches of the clove-trees; then she noticed that both Tala'aa and Talisman wore expressions of deep concentration, focused on the flame; she remembered Yorka making the rain, and, before that, Yorka and Talisman at the Place of Stones, dispersing the mist.

It'd be great to be able to do that, Dido thought, and noticed, as the last spark died away, Tala'aa's eye fixed measuringly upon her.

"Teirale haseem – go with light feet, Yorka," called Tylo loudly, and the others echoed him; and Dido heard another voice take up the message from above, a voice that she recognised, which then went on to sing:

"O-o-o, from swim to fly, from wet to dry
from fly to blow, blow in the wind, o-o-o . . ."

Dido looked around, startled. Nobody else seemed to have heard the ghost song. But again, she noticed the eye of Aunt Tala'aa fixed on her measuringly.

When they returned to Limbo Lodge, Tala'aa pointed to the sky in the south. "It will not be long now till the onda. We had better provision the boat."

They ran back and forth to the *Lass of Cley* with food, fruit, water, and warm waterproof clothes.

Herodsfoot caused some dispute by his urgent request to bring a dozen games, wholly unfamiliar to him, which he had found about the house. In the end he was persuaded that there really was no room for them, and, despite his arguments, he was obliged to reduce the number to three, when he pointed out that John King might need some entertainment during the trip.

Dido felt extremely sorry for Herodsfoot; she suspected that he was terrified of what was going to happen next and was making use of this distraction to keep himself from thinking about it, and from the ever-widening gulf between him and Talisman. His eyes were fixed on her piteously whenever she came near him.

Dido heard John King ask his daughter: "Should I bring some notebooks to Regina? In case – in case I can't hear what people say to me?" and Talisman's reply: "No, Father! You can hear very well now – as well as anybody. And, if you are in any doubt about what somebody has said, you can always ask me. I shall always be there."

Always, Dido thought.

"Now we must move the boat to the cliff edge," Talisman said. "Look at the sky."

It was early morning on their third day. The sun had risen behind a huge, inflamed angry cloud. A high rustling wind whined briefly over the cliff-top and was gone. When it had fallen, the air became intensely sultry and humid. Talisman decreed that they must all put on cork jackets; Dido, stifling in hers, felt sweat trickling between her shoulderblades.

"How are we *ever* going to get that boat to the cliff edge?" demanded Herodsfoot.

"I have a certain skill at carrying weights," Talisman quietly reminded him. "If you, my father, will go to the starboard quarter, you, Francis, and Tylo to the port, Dido at the prow—" she placed them all well forward and then went with Tala'aa to the stern. "Are you all ready? When I give the word, *lift!*"

And somehow, astonishingly, the boat was in the air, its entire weight apparently born by Talisman and Tala'aa at the stern, while the bearers at the front did no more than keep it steady and balanced. They moved out of the boat-yard at a slow but regular pace and covered the short distance to the area marked by bamboo wands in three minutes. Lowering was anxious: first the two women knelt, carrying the weight on their shoulders; then, with cracking muscles, the other three let down the bows. The *Lass of*

Cley lay on her side, leaning away from the red and angry ocean at the foot of the cliff, which seemed hungry to receive her.

This is a pretty hare-brained business, thought Dido. Suppose the boat gets smashed in the landslide? Or is swamped by rocks falling on it? Or turns turtle and fills up when it hits the water? And us? How can we fall as far as that without getting knocked about?

Oh well, can't make an omelette without breaking eggs.

"Now we must go on board," said Talisman.

They did so, King helped by Herodsfoot and his daughter. Dido noticed that he never even turned back to look at the house where he had lived for so long.

"The craft has three whaleskin flotation tanks below its deck," he said encouragingly to his passengers. "If it should capsize, it will still float on its side, or upside down, and we may make shift to paddle round to Regina."

Oh, thanks a handful, mister, thought Dido, and what about the sharks? But King seems to think the whole thing is a big junket.

Indeed King was calm and smiling and seemed entirely pleased by the adventure. Well, thought Dido, it must make a change for him after all those years at Limbo Lodge.

They stuffed themselves into the cabin and shut the door. There were four small portholes. Dido looked through one and saw an odd, copper-coloured cloud take shape over the southern horizon and come hastening towards them. In a moment the sky was darkened by a choking, coppery haze, the cliff-top outside turned rust-colour, and the *Lass of Cley* was turned to a ship of copper.

"It is dust," said Tala'aa, "from the volcano."

The dust came filtering into the closed cabin. They all began to gag and choke, and hurriedly tied cloths over their mouths and noses.

Talisman was holding a straw between her two palms and

204

watching it intently. It quivered once. "There!" she said. "That was it. Listen!"

They listened, straining their ears in the muffling silence which had fallen with the dust. A dozen times Dido thought she heard a sound which turned out to be no sound at all. When at last it did begin it was so tiny that she thought she had imagined it. But it grew from a rustle to a whisper, from a whisper to a murmur, from a murmur to a sigh, from a sigh to a high continuous note, which went on as long as it takes to peel an apple – and then suddenly the bottom seemed to fall out of the world, the blood creaked and stammered in their ears, and the red dust that was everywhere in the cabin flew up and dashed against the ceiling.

There was no time for speech as they hurtled down. Herodsfoot started to say "What—?" and then with a bone-wrenching crash they hit the water and furrowed their way into a green hill of sea. Dido saw the dark green shoot across her port-hole, and thought, I never expected to die this way. I shan't see Blackfriars Bridge again, (why she picked out Blackfriars Bridge she could not have said) and then the green gave place to a bright grey, the boat righted itself with a long shuddering heave, and Talisman, fighting her way upright, cried, "Quick! We must get a sail on her or we shall be thrown against the rocks!"

They flung themselves out of the cabin into the cockpit. The well was half full of water. Tylo seized a gourd and began bailing furiously.

John King took the tiller.

"We shall do, now," he said. "When she gets a bit of way on her."

Talisman had scrambled out of the cockpit and was busy on the cabin roof with the jib sheet, Herodsfoot helping her. In a moment the canvas unrolled and the ship began to slide through hillocks of water, running southwards towards that ominous gleam of steel-coloured light in the southern sky. The wind whistled in the shrouds.

"What about the mainsail?" shouted Herodsfoot, gesturing overhead.

"Not yet," said King. "This wind will strengthen."

Dido found another gourd and helped Tylo bale.

"The planks are dry," King told them. "You'll have to keep doing that until they swell up."

"Why are we steering south?" Herodsfoot wanted to know.

The high black mass of cliff was slipping away from them, and presently they could see Manati harbour and its anchorage.

"We want to catch the onda from Mount Ximboë," King said. "We need to get clear of the island." He passed the tiller to his daughter and said, "Keep her steady with the wind on your left cheek."

Talisman smiled at Herodsfoot. Her face was brilliant with happiness.

"You never expected it would be such a lark as this, did you?" she said, through the black hair that was blowing about her face.

The *Lass of Cley* was slipping through short, hurrying seas, each one trailing a white mass of bubbles, while the wind poured their crests sideways. The waves came from the south, they were becoming larger and uglier, but King looked at them with approval.

"Soon we shall see the onda," he said. "Many's the time I've watched it from Limbo Lodge. We want to stay well to eastwards till the front of it has passed us."

There was now not more than an inch of water in the cockpit. Tylo went to the cabin and brought out some food; dried bananas and ukka cakes. He and Dido took turns to eat and bale.

"Ah," said Aunt Tala'aa. "Look." She pointed south.

They seemed to be staring up an immense hillside of water – a hillside composed of innumerable smaller hillocks, all moving steadily towards them. The whole ocean was tilted. At the top of the slope was a single, vast heap of sea, a single wave larger than Mount Fura itself, weighing heaven only knew how many thousands of tons, rolling in terror and majesty, driving the smaller seas before it like a flock of hurrying sheep.

"There's the onda," said King comfortably. "We are very well placed for it."

To Dido it seemed that they were placed exactly where that hastening mountain of water would descend on them and demolish them. Her mouth went dry, her skin crept.

"*Very* well placed," King repeated placidly. "Has the cockpit stopped taking water? Good. Dido and Tylo, be ready to help haul up the mainsail when the onda has passed us. The wind drops, when it has passed. But the seas will be dangerous. Talisman, find a couple of oil barrels and spike them."

"It will be a speedy end," Talisman said cheerfully to Herodsfoot as they balanced on the cabin roof, watching the approach of the onda. Then, noticing his expression, she added, "It won't pass within three miles of us. My father knows what he is about."

Up went the mainsail, and, as it did so, a huge flock of birds suddenly passed over the boat with a disconcerting whistle of wings, audible even above the sound of the water. One moment they were there, the next, helped on their way by the wind, they were specks over the water to the north, hastening to take shelter in Aratu. King went back to the tiller.

And, after all, when the onda passed them nothing terrible happened, only the distracted sea took a new direction and began to pull at them instead of pushing. The sail was fully hoisted. The boat was bucketing wildly in a shifting tumble of broken foam; snarling, worrying breakers bit and clawed at them and King had to use all his strength, which was considerable, to keep the *Lass of Cley* heading the way she should go.

Tylo and Herodsfoot ladled oil over the side; it seemed impossible that should do any good, but they felt the benefit at once. The torn, hurrying water round them smoothed out and gentled; instead of slapping over the sides the waves rubbed silkily along the bulwarks like fawning cats.

King held on a westward course for another half hour, then changed direction and let wind and current drive the boat north like a feather in a gale.

During three hours they sailed, and saw nothing, for mountainous seas hid the coastline of Aratu from them.

As soon as they were steady on their course, King declared, "Now I must sleep. Do not call me unless there is any cause for disquiet." He gave the tiller to Talisman, said to Herodsfoot, "Stay with her and help her," then rolled into the cabin and lay down on one of the two bunks. In a moment he was fast asleep.

"Where is Aunt Tala'aa?" Dido asked Tylo, suddenly anxious. "Is she asleep on the other bunk?"

He shook his head. "Aunt Tala'aa travel on ahead."

"How could she? You mean, she has left the ship?"

"She think we hunky-dory now." (That was a phrase he had caught from Dido.)

"But – *how* did she go?"

Tylo shrugged. "With Aunt Tala'aa, you never see. One moment she here, next she gone."

Dusk came early that day.

"Always early dark after Mount Ximboë throw up," Tylo said. Dido supposed it was the dust in the atmosphere. A few stars, only the brightest, shone out in the sky.

There was a lighthouse on the northernmost tip of

Aratu. Far ahead, now, they could see the loom of its beam wheel across the horizon.

"We better wake Sovran King," Tylo said, but King came out just then of his own accord, sniffed the air, studied the stars, and said, "Now it is time to alter course to the north-east. Give me the tiller and you all be ready to get the sail across."

Getting the sail across was a fierce struggle, and at one point the swinging boom knocked Dido into the sea. Herodsfoot, without the least hesitation, looped a line over his arm and dived in after her; he grabbed her and had her back on board before she had time to remember that she could not swim, or only a few strokes; the last time swimming had been required was when she had been cast away off a ship called the *Dark Dew* in the English North Sea.

"Thanks, Frankie!" she gulped as he dumped her over the rail.

"That was deedily done, Francis," Talisman said, and John King scolded Dido. "Be more careful, child, another time!"

"Croopus, mister, I jist hope there *ain't* another time," Dido protested.

"If Lord Herodsfoot had not pulled you out, that current would have taken you up to Amboina!"

"Well, that's where we aim to go – supposing Cap Sanderson has got his ship back."

Meanwhile, thanks to John King's skilful steering, they had slipped eastward, out of the onda current, and were now rounding the northerly tip of Aratu. Ahead of them lay the long harbour, with a few distant lights twinkling. Dido remembered how they had sailed in on the *Siwara*, and how a careless sailor had dropped a copper weight, his wedhoe, on to Mr Multiple's head. Now it occurred to her to wonder – had the man done it on purpose? To oblige the *Siwara* to stay in harbour for several days? Could

Manoel somehow have got hold of the man and bribed him beforehand?

Well, I'll never know about that, thought Dido, but anyway Manoel is under hatches, and that is a right good thing.

Now they were sailing down the long harbour, and as they did so a miscellaneous flotilla of tiny little crazily rigged boats came out and passed them.

"Fishermen," explained Tylo. "Always the fishers go out soon after onda pass by – much, much fish then."

The little ships wanted information about the *Lass of Cley* – who sailed in her? – and Tylo, leaning over the side, supplied it. When he told who was on board a wild burst of ragged cheering broke out, and several of the craft turned round to accompany them into port.

The drumming, which had been noticeable as soon as they rounded the lighthouse point, became louder and louder. More lights flashed out, all across the town and the harbour front.

"I guess word has got about," Dido said to Tylo. "Do you think that is good or bad?"

He reflected. "I think it is good. Aunt Tala'aa will have spread news."

John King was gazing ahead at the lights of Regina as a man studies a long-lost treasure, rediscovered after many years.

"Why," cried Dido, as they rounded the harbour bar, "look, there's the *Siwara!*"

Wearing a somewhat haphazard and dishevelled appearance, the old tramp lay in her previous berth. There was just enough breeze in the harbour for John King to steer in neatly and bring to between the *Siwara* and the pier. A man stood keeping guard on the *Siwara's* foredeck.

"Who is your master?" King called up to him, as the *Lass of Cley* lost way and came gently to a stop.

"Senhor Manoel." Then the man suddenly realised who he was talking to, and gasped. "Senhor King! Your Excellency!"

At this moment hubbub broke out on the harbour front. A respectful, interested crowd had been gathering at the top of the stone landing-steps that led down from the quayside. Now at the sight of King standing on the cabin roof, his eyes gleaming in the lamplight, and his hair shining bright silver, murmurs of astonishment changed to joyful shouts of welcome, which rose up to a burst of cheering.

Dido, Tylo, and Herodsfoot quietly set about mooring the *Lass of Cley* while King and Talisman climbed the harbour steps.

Reaching the top of the steps, King addressed the crowd.

He said: "My friends, after my long illness I have come back to you. I am well – strong – restored – happy to look after you and live among you as I did before. There will be no more strife and dispute. All shall be done with justice and reason. Better – I have with me my dear daughter Talisman, child of my beloved wife Erato, whom you all remember. Talisman will be my eyes and ears, and your best friend. She is also a Kanikke and will heal you when you are sick."

There was another burst of cheering. Just one or two voices could be heard asking, "And Manoel? Where is Manoel?"

King said: "My brother – is no longer with us. There was a curse on him from long ago – it caught up with him. He is dead. Aunt Tala'aa will tell you the whole story. Now – I and my friends – who have come up from Limbo Lodge riding on the onda – we are weary and need a house to sleep in. Can such a house be found?"

But easily, fifty voices told him. The town was half empty. There was a fine house right here on the front which had

211

once been a hostel for pilgrims coming to visit the Place of Stones. It was his to command.

It was called the Maison Dieu.

Before the crew of the *Lass of Cley* had finished mooring, furling the sails, coiling ropes, fastening ties, tidying the cabin, making all fit to be left, the crowd had spread a pathway for John King across the harbour front to his temporary home. At first Dido thought it was made from white petals of flowers, scattered across the stone paving, but as she followed behind King and Talisman, she saw that the pale shapes were playing-cards with all kinds of emblems on them: bulls, leaves, clubs, swords, hearts, pikes, paving-tiles and trefoil.

It's the fortune-telling pack, Dido remembered. That my aunt Tinty Kirlingshaw used to fetch out when she told folks' futures. And the trump card in that was called the Maison Dieu, with a picture of a tumbledown tower. I wonder why?

The Maison Dieu in Regina town was not precisely tumbledown, but plainly it had not been used for some time; the courtyard was full of old nets, oars, fishing tackle, and coils of rotten rope. However, sheets, beds, chairs and furnishings were soon brought by the welcoming crowd, lamps were lit, and a festive meal provided.

Talisman thanked the hospitable crowd, and politely asked them to leave.

"My father is only just recovered from a long illness, he is tired, and has had a hard, dangerous trip from Mount Fura. Tomorrow he will be glad to welcome all who wish to see him, and he particularly wishes to see the Town Fathers of Regina, the leaders of the Civil Guard, and any Forest People who care to come. Now he bids you goodnight."

The crew of the *Lass of Cley* were glad to retire early. It had been a long and strenuous day.

But Dido, for some reason, found herself reluctant to settle to sleep in any of the rooms of the old Maison Dieu. It smelt dank and musty, it reminded her too much of Quinquilho ranch. She made herself a bed from unravelled ropes, frayed nets, and scraps of canvas, in a sheltered corner of the arcaded courtyard.

First thing in the morning, she thought, I go looking for Cap Sanderson and Mr Mully. Maybe they'll know up at the hospital. And she fell deeply asleep.

She was destined to wake before day, though. In the small hours the moon came glinting down into the courtyard, making the shadows blacker and the patches of light sharper, waking Dido with its brilliance. And into the middle of this black-and-white scene stole a frail, thin black figure.

For a moment, Dido's heart was in her mouth. Then, with a gulp, she summoned her wits and self-confidence.

"Who are you?" she whispered. "What do you want here?"

The hooded head turned towards her. Through the black veil she could see the glitter of eyes.

"My son! I am seeking for my son! Did you bring him here? Did you bring him with you?"

Now Dido recognised the piteous voice. She had heard it before. A long time ago, it seemed. She said quietly,

"No, Modreda. Your son Ruiz is not here. He is far away in the forest."

"He is truly not here? You would not lie to me?"

"Certainly not! Not on my mother's head!" For what that's worth, Dido thought.

Then Dido was overtaken by a sudden, extraordinary impulse. Afterwards she thought: What in the wide world came over me? Where did it come from?

She said to Modreda: "Listen to me. You have served your sentence. You have been to the well, and brought your

213

water home. You lied to your son about his poor wife, yes, you did; but now you have paid that debt. It is your turn to be free. Quit this town and go into the forest."

"Do you give me leave?"

"It ain't for me to give you leave," Dido said. "But summat tells me you got your ticket. So go on! Shove off! Up sticks with you and skedaddle. Leave this doleful town. And a good journey to you . . ."

The hooded figure turned, bowed deeply to Dido – but then, did not stand erect again. She seemed to glide out of the courtyard on all fours.

Croopus, thought Dido: *she's turned into a hyena*.

And went back to sleep.

Chapter Twelve

IN THE MORNING, DIDO THOUGHT THAT PERHAPS it had been a dream about Modreda. It seemed too improbable to be real. But sometime, she thought, I'll ask Auntie Tala'aa about it. And then realised with a sad jolt that, if she did find Captain Sanderson and Mr Multiple – if it was possible to set sail on the *Siwara* – they would not be seeing Aunt Tala'aa again; no, nor Tylo, nor Talisman, nor John King.

I'll miss them. I'll miss them a whole lot.

She had no need to go searching for Captain Sanderson and Mr Multiple: they turned up at breakfast time, having heard the news of King's arrival. Sanderson was bristling with indignation, ready to denounce the brigands who had hijacked his ship; but had the wind completely taken out of his sails by King's amiable agreement with every word he said.

"Indeed, my dear sir, you are entirely right. It was a most disgraceful act of brigandage. Piracy! The ship is yours, of course, to take whenever you wish to leave, and any reparation that it is in my power to make shall at once be yours."

"The ship had a *full cargo*," stated Captain Sanderson. "The cargo was thrown out on the quayside and is now lost, either stolen or destroyed by weather—"

"What was the cargo?"

"*Tea*, sir, the very best Hyson tea, and Barbados sugar."

"I fear, sir, that we are quite unable to replace those commodities—" King said in a mild conciliating tone.

"Man, it is downright disgraceful. I knew – I kenned well how it wad be—"

215

"But can I not persuade you to accept the existing cargo instead?"

"And whit wad that be?" demanded Sanderson suspiciously.

"A load of pearls from the Odome reef."

"*Pearls?* I'll thank ye not to make game of me, sir!"

It took Sanderson a visit to the ship and the evidence of his own eyes to convince him that King was speaking the truth; and then he would accept only half the load, insisting that the value of what remained would, even so, be worth ten times what he had lost.

The rest of the pearls would be deposited in the Aratu national treasury.

"Instead," said Talisman to Herodsfoot, "of financing a trip of Manoel's to Europe, which was what he had planned."

"What will the pearls be used for now?"

"Well," said Talisman, "my father intends the few Angrians who are left here to find some other way of earning their living than by cutting down the forest to make new plantations. The forest must be left in peace. Perhaps they can learn to make pearl ornaments. All that must be thought about."

Herodsfoot was not very interested in the future of the Angrians. He said: "Talisman, *dear* Talisman, won't you marry me? I do love you so very much."

And she answered sadly, "No, dear Francis, I cannot marry you. You know very well why I cannot. My future is here with Aratu. You must go back to your King Jamie. Perhaps we shall meet again some day, who knows? But in any case we should not suit. There are too many differences between us."

"I see none. None! You are talking nonsense."

She looked him in the eye. "What do you really know of me? A little, no more. And, whatever I am, I belong to

Aratu. Here I must stay. But an island like this, small, old, complicated, is no place for you, my friend. You must be off, back to your big, simple world." She smiled.

"But I *love* you," he said miserably. "So much! I always shall!"

She shook her head.

"Return, perhaps, in ten years, in twenty years. Aratu does not change. I shall be here, like Aunt Tala'aa. In twenty years, who knows, we may go riding to the Place of Stones and find your name still written in the dust: Algernon, Francis, Sebastian, Fortinbras, Carsluith, Baron Herodsfoot..."

"No," he muttered. "Dido rubbed it out. You knew then – that I went back?"

"Yes... I knew." She sighed. "Look, here comes my father with your little Captain Sanderson. He is looking quite surprised. He finds it hard to understand that pearls are not of much value to us."

Meanwhile Aunt Tala'aa was talking to Dido.

Aunt Tala'aa had shown interest – very considerable interest – in the story of Dido's midnight encounter with Modreda.

"She became a hyena? That is excellent! Really excellent! I am exceedingly obliged to you, my dear child, for this. I have a notion that it will, in time, be a solution to *all* the Angrian problems on Aratu."

"You mean – *all* the Angrians'll turn into hyenas? Would that be a good thing?" Dido sounded dubious.

"Oh, possibly not all hyenas – sting-monkeys, turtles, dolphins – they have a long way to go on the cycle of life, poor dears. We shall see..."

"Aunt Tala'aa, how old are you?"

"Older than you think, child. I brought up Erato, Talisman's mother. And plenty of others. As well as Yorka. Dido – I should indeed be happy if you cared to stay here and take Yorka's place. You have in you already the makings of a Kanikke. It would be a great pleasure to teach you – to set you on the way."

Dido was terribly wrung.

"Oh, thank you, Auntie Tala'aa. That's mighty decent of you," she said earnestly. "And I reckon in lots of ways I'd *like* to stay. I'm real fond of Tylo. And Doc Tally's been better to me than my own sister Penny ever was. But – I dunno – I reckon London's the place for me. I got friends there too. And I'd best see poor Frankie Herodsfoot gets back, with all his games, to try and cheer up King Jamie. But it was right kind of you to ask me – and I won't forget it in a hurry. Nor all that's happened here."

I made rain, she thought. That's a thing to remember.

Five hours later, the *Siwara* weighed anchor again. Dido had said a sad goodbye to Tylo. She would have given him Yorka's wooden ring, but he would not accept it.

"Forest folk – we best not have *things*."

"Yorka had them."

"Yorka was tree-young. She not have them long."

But he gave Dido a feather from his memory-bird. "Keep in your pocket. You dream sometimes of the forest."

"And how you saved me from those guards."

"And how you pull me out of well."

Mr Multiple was very happy to be back on board ship again. Aratu, he thought, seemed a pleasant enough place, but a little boring. He had spent his convalescence, after the nurses allowed him out of hospital, at the house of one of Manoel's neighbours, a kind lady who never went anywhere, or did anything. It had been restful, but tedious.

"Did you have trouble finding Lord Herodsfoot?" he asked. "It took you a whole week. Did you get bit by a snake, like poor old Cap Sanderson?"

"No, not a snake. But quite a lot of things happened," Dido said vaguely. "I'll tell you sometime."

She was watching the town of Regina recede rapidly as the *Siwara* tore up the long harbour on the wings of a fine southerly wind. She could hear the throb of the drums on shore, doubtless giving the news of their departure to all the people in the forest.

It was the Forest People I liked best, thought Dido, though I met so few of them.

Herodsfoot came to lean on the rail beside Dido. He looked utterly pale and wretched. She tried to cheer him up by asking about Amboina. Did they play any interesting games there? No, he said gloomily, nothing worth getting excited about. But he had left a few things there, results of time he had spent earlier in China – a number of rare rose-plants, some greyhounds, and a quintet of horn-players. He brightened a little at the thought. He hoped that Captain Hughes would have room for them on the *Thrush*.

"I reckon he will," said Dido encouragingly. "Frankie, I'm a going to give you my Persian game-cloth, that old Brandywinde left me – it strikes me you'll have more use for it than I ever shall."

She pulled it out of her pocket and gave it to him.

At that he very nearly broke down.

"Oh, Dido! Thank you! It is a treasure! But – do you think that was all she – Talisman – thought I was good for? Playing games? I begged her to marry me – but she wouldn't—"

"It would be mighty hard," suggested Dido, "being married to a Kanikke. Someone who was only there half the time. I'm sure you'll find some person in England who suits you better."

She hoped that was true.

"Never!" declared Herodsfoot. "My heart is broken. I shall never feel the same again – But *you* will be in London, won't you, Dido? You will keep in touch? I shall like to think there is someone to whom I can talk about her . . ."

"Yus. I'll be in London," agreed Dido. "I suppose my mum and dad will still be living in Battersea." And plotting away against King Jamie, she thought, but did not say.

Herodsfoot hoisted his spectacles off his face to give them a rub, and the right-hand earpiece snapped.

He gave a loud wail of dismay.

"Oh, Dido! See what I have done! And no Yorka – no Talisman – to repair them for me. *Dido*! Do you suppose you can manage to mend them? Do you think you will be able to do something?"

Dido heaved a heavy sigh.

The lighthouse on the north tip of Aratu was sliding past them. She looked her last at Regina town, like a handful of tiny white dice at the far end of the harbour.

She said: "I'll see what I can do."